The Island of Summer Sunsets

3

The Island of Summer Sunsets

SUSAN SANDS

HARPETH ROAD
PRESS"
Nashville

HARPETH ROAD

Published by Harpeth Road Press (USA)
P.O. Box 158184
Nashville, TN 37215

Paperback 978-1-7358458-7-6
eBook 978-1-7358458-6-9

THE ISLAND OF SUMMER SUNSETS:
An utterly uplifting and heartwarming story

This is a work of fiction. Names, characters, places, and incidents
are the product of the author's imagination or were used fictitiously,
and any resemblance to actual persons, living or dead, business
establishments, events, or locales is entirely coincidental.

First printing: June, 2022

Chapter One

"Hey there, Janie-girl," Joe Murphy called from atop the wood decking that wrapped around the old marina's general store.

His gruff voice pulled Janie Brooks' attention his way as she walked up. She waved, the salty air blowing between them.

"What can I get for you this morning?" he asked, wiping his large hands on a rag as a seagull squawked overhead in search of its morning meal.

Joe, owner of the general store at the end of Fripp Island's seaside marina, towered over her. At five-foot-nothing, being towered over wasn't unusual for Janie, but Joe was a giant of a man, with a steely-gray, grizzled beard that matched what was left of his hair. He reminded her of an ocean-facing house that had stood up to the salty sea air and endured the test of time. He was... weathered.

"Hey, Joe. I need a couple of bags of ice, some minnows, and Momma's newspaper. How are the shiners today?" Janie asked, peering into the murky vat of bait minnows that lined the old clapboard wall of the building, trying to determine how active they were. Their smell was oddly comforting. It reminded her of going there as a little girl with Momma and Daddy. And then, with her late husband, Daniel. She loved visiting the marina before anybody else was up and around.

Something about the familiarity kept her thoughts on the day-to-day, not allowing her mind to move into memories that were still too painful to relive. The music of sameness filled her: the gulls, the glorious sunrise, and the smells of the island. Anything else put her into new territory, and Janie wasn't ready for anything new. Even after two years.

"Just got 'em in yesterday. Should do you for a couple of days."

Janie pointed toward the vat. "Momma wants two dozen, please."

She noticed then that something was different about Joe that day; his manner was a little more distracted than usual. He'd looked over her head toward the entrance to the marina a couple of times already.

Joe pulled out the net, scooping up approximately twenty-four, then throwing in several more for good measure. Then he filled a plastic bag with water, dumped in the tiny silvery fish, and used a tube to inject oxygen from the tank before tying off the top with a rubber band. That would keep them alive until Janie got home and put them in the minnow bucket. He handed the bag over to her.

She looked up, shielding her eyes from the brightness of the morning daylight with her hand. It was early, but the sun was making a spectacular appearance over the water. The blaze of orange contrasted against the layers of cool blue in the sky just above. Below, the darker surf was almost glassy in its stillness, as it often was this early.

"Your momma fishing off the dock today, or y'all going out in the boat?" Joe asked.

"We're going out tomorrow to hunt for driftwood on Pritchards Island's beach. We've got some special orders for candle holders that could use a few more pieces." Janie referred to her "sea treasures" business that she and Momma ran together. "She's planning to do some fishing while we're at it. Might throw a line in on the dock this afternoon."

There was a limited window for maritime travel between tiny Pritchards Island and Fripp Island. Both were nestled among the string of more than one hundred islands from South Carolina down to Georgia, and if it weren't for the stretch of ocean separating the two barrier islands, it would only be a half-mile walk between them. High tide happened twice a day, but the exact timing changed daily by roughly an hour. Tides were the gods of everything here, pulling the water from the canals that snaked through the marshes, so getting across by boat had to be carefully timed.

Joe's gaze followed Janie's. "Gonna be a good day for it tomorrow."

They stood silently for a moment, looking upward at the sky, which had now transformed into a full-blown daytime blue.

"A perfect day, according to the forecast."

Most days on Fripp Island were perfect days as far as Janie was concerned. But this day seemed to sparkle. Truth was, they lived in paradise on this tiny slice of an island many people west of Georgia and north of the Carolinas had never even heard of.

Fripp was quiet this early in spring since the lucky tourists who knew about the island invaded during the warmer months. The late March weather was warm but breezy, with a few puffy white clouds floating by. Being surrounded by nature's beauty on a protected bird and wildlife sanctuary was all Janie wanted.

Janie carried over the bag of minnows and set them on the floor of her golf cart.

"I've got some of that sweet cornbread mix from the mill your momma always asks for." Joe peered up the stairs toward the entrance of the general store.

Janie was extremely fond of Joe. He ordered specific things he knew his customers liked. "Then I'd better grab the mix too while I'm here."

Janie started to follow Joe when someone caught her eye, causing her to turn instinctively. A tall, sandy-haired man had just parked a four-seater golf cart on the crushed shell lot and was walking over.

"Hey, Joe," she muttered, just loud enough to get his attention.

"Yup?" He raised grizzled brows.

"Who's that?" She nodded as furtively as possible toward the newcomer.

He was tall, lean, and moved with a grace that caught her eye. It was apparent the man wasn't a regular resident because she'd never seen him before. Not only was he unfamiliar, but, dressed in faded jeans and a worn blue T-shirt, he was clearly a misplaced underwear/sunglasses model who'd washed up on their island out of season.

Joe lowered his polarized glasses and glanced over, his sun-damaged blue eyes having a look. "Hmm. Looks like he's here earlier than expected."

"*Who?*" she hissed, wanting to know before the guy got to them. It would be nice to have a clue what was happening around here.

Joe eyed her for a long second. "That's my nephew, Ryan. Got some interest in our new resident, do you, Janie-girl?" Joe winked at her, grinning as she flushed a dark, beet red.

Janie knew she was doing this because it was the curse of being a redhead. And one with freckles, too. Her skin told the world her deepest thoughts. Like a flashing billboard.

Janie's curiosity competed with her awkwardness over Joe's nephew's unexpected appearance. So she ignored his taunt.

"Resident? How did I not know about someone new moving in?"

Joe had mentioned his nephew a few times in the past, but they'd never met. And she *would* have remembered him.

"It happened pretty quickly. Must've slipped my mind the last time you were here."

Judging by his smirk, she knew Joe had misinterpreted her reaction as interest instead of mortification. After last year, when Joe had tried to set her up and it had failed miserably, he, of all people, should have understood where she was coming from.

The nephew came closer. Joe raised a hand in greeting toward the man as he neared them. Janie eyed her golf cart and wondered if she could make it there fast enough to avoid saying hello, but then she realized how silly that was.

Joe let out a low rumble of laughter. "Come and say hello."

Janie Brooks was no coward. Never that. And Joe was like family, so she had little choice.

"Fine. He's your family, after all." There. That would stop any ideas Joe had about possible interest in his nephew.

"C'mon then." He grasped her shoulders gently and maneuvered her forward as if she were a child, causing Janie's face to flame up like a flare gun, something that didn't happen often but had happened twice in the last five minutes. But then again, in Fripp, she was rarely caught off guard.

"So glad you made it, son."

The two men slapped each other on the back and hugged it out. The man's gaze fluttered over to her curiously and then back to his uncle.

"Uncle Joe. Great to see you." Then he addressed Janie. "Hi, I'm Ryan."

She met his eyes. Momma always said she should look people in the eyes when meeting them. Janie never forgot that. "Nice to meet you." She was thankful her words hadn't failed her.

Ryan was well into the six-foot range, same as Joe, and Janie squared her shoulders met with such height.

Joe winked at her and then turned to Ryan. "Janie lives a few houses down and will be your neighbor."

"Nice to meet you, new neighbor." He smiled, showing straight, white teeth. "My uncle has mentioned you."

What has Joe said about me? Janie recovered quickly. "I hope Joe only told you the nice things." She shot Joe a questioning look, but he pretended not to notice.

Ryan grinned at Joe as if they had some sort of insider commentary. But before she could question it, he said, "I just stopped by to ask if you had a Phillips-head screwdriver? Ours are still packed away."

"Sure, son. Come on inside. I've got to get Janie her paper and cornbread mix while I'm at it." Joe stood aside, allowing Janie to lead the way.

Ryan peered over at her once more, his gaze appraising, which made Janie wonder again what Joe had told him. She straightened the old, faded St. Simon's Island T-shirt her sister had bought her ages ago and smoothed the ratty pair of cut-off jean shorts she was wearing. Then, she snatched the newspaper off the counter and grabbed the baking mix from Joe's hands in a hasty effort to retreat.

"Great to meet you." She slipped past Ryan, holding her breath to avoid inhaling a hint of what might be Irish Spring. "Bye, Joe. Thanks. Put it on my bill, please." Janie was suddenly thankful for the monthly tab she and Momma kept with Joe so she didn't have to spend extra time paying for her goods.

Slipping on her sunglasses, Janie hopped back in the cart and hit the gas, nearly running the ice machine over before switching it to reverse. The loud beeping noise turned her skin bright red again. "Darn it."

Desperate to get out of there before anyone noticed, she peeled out, spraying white shells behind her, finally making her escape, but not before the two men had come outside and witnessed the blunder. She didn't make eye contact, and just kept on driving.

Janie imagined that, given his looks, Ryan probably got this kind of response all the time from women: the whole embarrassed, tongue-tied, and clumsy reaction she'd just displayed. But his attractiveness wasn't the only reason for her response.

When she'd come to get the bait this morning, Janie hadn't expected to meet anyone new, let alone a handsome man. Her routine around the island made life predictable and easy. Her response to Joe's nephew was confusing. Janie would be the first to admit that the man was physically appealing. But she'd gotten flustered, and she usually prided herself on having good sense.

Janie had noticed the moving van parked out front a couple of doors down on her way to the marina and had been surprised to see one there so early in the day. But since so many of the local homes were rental properties, it hadn't occurred to her that a new, full-time resident might become her neighbor. Moving vans often signaled that the rental had simply changed hands.

As she tooled home in the golf cart that hadn't ever set wheels on a course for a round of actual golf, she worked on relaxing again. Janie soaked up the morning sun, took in the salty breeze that blew through her hair, and attempted to calm her nerves. She hadn't made a spectacle of herself over a guy like that since her pre-college days when she'd fallen head over heels for Daniel. He was the first guy who'd made her stumble over her words and behave awkwardly when he was near. She'd usually been calm, cool, and collected. Her late husband hadn't seemed to care about the awkwardness; it had only made him work harder to ease her nerves. She missed him so much and still woke up some mornings expecting to roll over and feel him beside her.

Turning her attention back to the road, Janie slowed the golf cart, zeroing in on the moving van she'd passed earlier, which was parked outside the house two doors down from her. This must be Ryan's house. She noticed a bright-pink kayak and a blue one sitting on the front lawn. Then, she spotted a teenager standing on the edge of the yard with her arms crossed, glaring at her.

Why is the girl glaring at me? Janie wondered. The girl looked about sixteen, slim, with long shiny dark hair. She was a beauty, and her trim legs appeared muscular. Probably an athlete of some sort.

Janie smiled and waved, again wondering why she hadn't already heard they were getting new neighbors. Very little that happened on the island was a secret or stayed that way long. She had been planning on driving straight home, but there was no denying she was curious now, and if they were going to be neighbors, it was good to be friendly and welcoming.

The teen continued to stare as Janie stopped the golf cart. "Hi there. You moving in?" Janie asked, making conversation of the obvious.

The girl kept her arms crossed and turned slightly away to signal that she wasn't in any mood to chat.

"Nice kayak," Janie said anyway, pointing to the pink one. "I'm Janie. I live just down the street. I ran into your dad at the marina. I'm a friend of Joe's."

An eyeroll from the teen surprised Janie. Trying to make sense of it, she looked the girl up and down.

"If you need anything, come by any time. I live in the house with the mailbox that says Brooks and is decorated with seashells." Janie pointed down the street.

When she didn't get a response, Janie pulled away in the cart, letting the humid island air fill her lungs. Teen girls often didn't make sense for all kinds of reasons, so Janie let the newcomer's rudeness roll off her back.

As Janie pulled into the drive of her house, Momma looked up from weeding in the front yard of the house next door and raised a gloved hand in greeting before wiping her forehead, depositing soil across her face.

Janie grabbed the ice and bait from the golf cart and brought them over. Having Momma live next door allowed her independence while letting Janie ensure she had what she needed.

"Hey, sugar. Did Joe have some good shiners this morning?" Momma's brows furrowed, and she hesitated as she stood. A hippie, some called her. She wore her graying blond hair long but usually had it piled into some form of clip or ponytail like she did that day. She adored tie-dyed clothing and dangling shiny earrings, even when they went in the boat fishing or searching for beach treasures. Her mind remained youthful despite her aging body. Spotting the bag, she said, "Shiners look pretty good." Then, after studying Janie's face, she asked, "Everything all right?"

"I'm fine. Nearly ran over the ice machine." She partially lied, then asked, "Are *you* okay?" Janie got immediately concerned whenever anything seemed off with her mother.

"Just a little twinge in my back, darling. Nothing to worry about."

"Maybe you should ice it and take it easy," Janie suggested. "It's time you slowed down a little."

"Simmer down now, baby girl. I'm not ready for a lap blanket and a wheelchair yet." Momma's spunk was not to be confused with her defensiveness about aging.

Janie exhaled. "I know. But you've got to take care of yourself."

Momma shook her head and smiled. "I take fine care of myself, and you know it."

It was true that Momma pulled them out of the house for hours, walking on sandy beaches searching for shells, sea glass, driftwood, and anything else the ocean offered up. She shopped for organic fruits and vegetables at the fresh local markets, caught fish and crabs right off the dock, and bought shrimp directly from the boats. But that didn't stop Janie from worrying about her.

"Of course you do. I know you're healthy, but you also know I worry. I wish you would see a doctor regularly."

"Honey, I get it, I do. But you've got to do some yoga or meditating or praying. Because standing over me like I'm about to die is driving me batty."

Janie lowered her eyes because Momma was right. That was precisely what she did. Janie worried her precious mother would die too, just like Dan.

"I'm sorry, Momma."

It wasn't easy for Janie to take a step back; she was the youngest of the three Brooks girls and the closest to their momma. Jaclyn and Joy checked in when they could, but they both had independent lives. Jaclyn was married, lived in Charleston, and ran a high-end home interior business. Joy was in Savannah, and she owned a home accessories shop. Both ordered Janie and Momma's beach wares for their companies, and even though both sisters were within two hours' driving distance, neither came back regularly to the island. They called every week, but it was Janie who saw their momma each day and tried not to worry over every new ache and pain. But it was difficult.

Momma crossed the grass between them, the fragrance of gardenias wafting toward Janie, and put a strong arm across her daughter's shoulder. "Baby, I know what I need to do in my life. Don't you think it's time you figured out what you want for *yours*?" It was a common but fair question, often repeated for the last year or so.

Janie blinked at her but had no response. There was a void where future goals and dreams should be. She lived day-to-day the same routine, and the comfort and beauty of it never got old. But in truth, that day, she felt out of sorts and uneasy, and it was all because of that earlier encounter with Joe's nephew. It had caught her off guard. But Janie wouldn't let anyone upend the peaceful world she'd built for herself, even if that meant disregarding Ryan. She'd be polite and a good neighbor, and, eventually, he'd be like everyone else—part of the sameness around here—and Janie could carry on with her life as normal.

She *would* disregard him... just as soon as she got the scoop about what had brought him to the island. She had to face it; it wasn't every day somebody new came here and changed the ecosystem.

"Hey, Momma." How to approach this without setting off her mother's Spidey senses to high alert? "Joe said we had new residents moving onto the island."

"Oh. Joe must be talking about his nephew, Ryan Kennedy," her mother said, taking off her gardening gloves. "I noticed the moving van. Did you run into them at the marina?"

Momma was a little too perky sounding. It was clear she'd known all about it; it seemed everyone had known but Janie.

Janie kept a poker face as she filled in her mother on the morning meeting, trying to play down the incident with the golf cart.

Momma raised her brows. "Joe says he's a nice-looking fellow."

Janie tried not to look away. "Oh, I didn't notice…."

"Hmm. You come home red-faced, and you nearly ran over the ice machine, huh?" The raised brows lowered. Momma knew her so well.

"Fine. He looked like an underwear model. But he wasn't in his underwear. I'm just assuming." Momma bearing down on her was like a giant dose of truth serum.

"I'm thrilled you noticed. That's the first time I've heard you mention a man's looks since Daniel passed."

Janie frowned. "I *notice* men. I just haven't been interested in anyone. So, what's the story on our new neighbors?" She motioned toward the moving van parked in the drive up the street, moving the subject away from her life and back to Ryan's.

"Ryan's wife left him, I believe, and he's moved here with their teenage daughter, Sibley. So, he comes to us with more than a little baggage, and hopefully not too much trouble." Momma widened her eyes as if to say, *if you know what I mean.* "I'm not at liberty to say more because that would be gossiping."

"We wouldn't want to be accused of that, would we?" Janie slid Momma a humorous skunk eye. She wouldn't precisely call Momma a gossip; she just happened to know *everything* that happened with the folks on the island. It was just a shame she had failed to mention Ryan Kennedy's arrival before Janie had bumped into him that morning. Janie was already on the back foot with her new neighbor.

Ryan rubbed the pinch in his shoulder, his whole body aching from unloading all the boxes that day. His eyes burned from dust and dirt, and his mouth was dry. As he made his way into the kitchen, where nearly everything was still boxed up and sitting on the countertops, Ryan sighed at the amount of work ahead. He thought about Leslie, his former wife, still living her life in the home they'd built together. His home. Sibley's home. Leslie hadn't asked him for even partial custody of their daughter, which had surprised him, but it seemed she was too busy with her new boyfriend in Ryan's old house.

He'd been the one to move out because living on the island had sounded like a good idea, what with its slower pace, and it had seemed like a perfect place to get Sibley away from a toxic environment. Frankly, he didn't want to squabble over their domestic situation. While he couldn't believe the way his wife had cut off their daughter, sending her adrift, Ryan was more than happy to have Sibley with him, and he was determined to make a great new life for the both of them after everything that had happened.

Leslie had had an affair with Sibley's tennis coach, Todd, lighting the fuse for their comfortable family to explode, shattering Sibley's life in every direction. Ryan's too, but he was dealing with it, though he was mainly focused on establishing a home away from the fallout for Sibley. Living out here would have its inconveniences, being farther away from work, school, and Sibley's friendship group, who all lived in Beaufort. Still, the house had been available when he'd needed it, and Ryan had wanted to move away as quickly as possible.

It wasn't as simple as pulling up stakes, though; if only it were that easy. No, Ryan was learning just how tricky it was parenting a damaged child. Sibley's reluctance to be helpful with a good attitude was wearing. In the past he'd have grounded her, but after what she'd been through, he couldn't bear to do it. Plus, the therapist Sibley saw in Beaufort suggested they use other coping methods to help Sibley adjust to her new situation caused by the impending divorce. The counselor had said she suffered from abandonment issues, anxiety, and depression. Ryan hoped that the new change of scenery would help, but with its endless marshes, spotty wi-fi, and non-existent social life, this island might prove more of a challenge than either of them had expected. This life would be so different from what they'd known in Beaufort, and it would take them both some getting used to, but in time perhaps it could begin to help them heal—that's what Ryan was hoping.

Ryan loved the friendliness and the relaxed atmosphere of the island already—and he appreciated the silence. Uncle Joe was a permanent fixture here, and Ryan would relish the support of being around family. He couldn't continue to do this alone, even though that's what he'd been doing since Leslie's betrayal.

When Ryan was a kid, Uncle Joe had regularly picked him up from his house in Columbia in his dilapidated green truck and brought Ryan back to the island to spend time fishing. Joe had taught him how to catch, clean, and cook fish and shown him little gems of the natural world around the island. Ryan had lived for those visits. Having grown up in the city with divorced parents and without his dad nearby, he'd craved a father figure—someone who got him—and Uncle Joe had been there for him.

Fripp had seemed so magical to Ryan: the dunes that looked like something off a desert island; the tidal marshes that he imagined were full of all kinds of creatures; and the wooden footbridges that made you feel as if you were on a pirate ship, walking the plank. Even the names of the local places evoked adventure and excitement to a young Ryan: Sea Dragon Lane, Spyglass Lane, and, best of all, Skull Creek.

Ryan understood what Sibley was going through right now—his parents also having divorced when he was a child—and he hated it, which is why he hoped that Fripp would eventually work its magic on his daughter as it had on him.

Grabbing a beer out of the fridge, he settled into one of the kitchen chairs he'd brought in and let out a long sigh of exhaustion, peering out through the window at the lapping water.

Ryan hadn't spent nearly as much time here on Fripp the past several years as he had as a youngster. He'd married Leslie, set up his orthodontic office, they'd had a child, and he'd worked morning until night for years to get his practice established. But he and Uncle Joe had remained close during that time, with Joe meeting him regularly for lunch or dinner in Beaufort, or stopping by their home on the weekend. Being back on the island, living here, was something Ryan hadn't expected, but there were far worse places to end up.

"Dad?" Sibley's voice cut into his thoughts. She stood in a long T-shirt, her hair in a ponytail, her face scrubbed clean, looking ready for bed.

He smiled, unable to hide his affection for his only daughter. "Hey, honey."

"Did Mom call?"

Her words hit him like a punch to the gut. Of course she hadn't called. All Leslie seemed to care about lately was her new boyfriend. Ryan couldn't understand how a mother could cut her daughter out of her life, but it seemed there was a lot he had failed to understand about his wife.

Ryan picked up his cell phone from the table next to his chair and rechecked it. He wanted to delay telling her as long as possible. "No. Sorry. Maybe she had a busy day. She knew it was moving day, so likely she didn't want to interrupt us." That was total BS, but he wanted Sibley to keep a positive attitude. Showing her his pain and anger wouldn't help either of them.

His words didn't have the desired effect, however. A gleam of pure anger quickly replaced the pain that flashed in Sibley's lovely eyes.

"Right. I'm going to bed."

"Sibley—" Ryan tried to catch her before she ran off. He stood to stop her, but she raced up the stairs, locking her bedroom's door behind her. He followed her up and put his weary head on the door, closing his eyes as he heard her throw herself on the bed and dissolve into a sobbing mess. When this happened, it was all Ryan could do not to call Leslie and give her a piece of his mind. It killed him to see Sibley like that.

Running a hand through his hair, Ryan walked down the hallway, turned off the lights, and lay down on his bed, his tight muscles reacting to the softness of the mattress. He couldn't help but wonder where they went from here.

Chapter Two

Janie was up early, as usual, and the summer morning heat wrapped around her as she walked the short path between her house and Momma's. Before they headed out to Pritchards Island for driftwood, she wanted to let Momma know she'd be checking on the swallow-tailed kites. The kites built their nests in the trees on the island, and Janie spent several hours each week ensuring the continuity of these endangered shorebirds.

She stuck her head inside Momma's kitchen door. "I'm going over to the habitat. I'll be back in a few minutes."

"Sounds good." Momma was finishing up breakfast in her sunroom.

Janie climbed into the golf cart parked outside her garage. It was difficult to see the birds when they were high up in the trees, so she brought her field glasses to be sure the nests were still intact. It was something she and Daniel had done every day when he was still with her. Now, Janie had made it her mission to care for the nests, especially this time of year when there were newborn hatchlings inside. It was her mission to see them become nestlings and eventually, fledglings if she got lucky.

An undisturbed, almost-acre of land sat on the south end of the island and had been a sanctuary for the swallow-tailed kites in the area for many years. The birds were on the endangered species list and she and Daniel had gained permission from the South Carolina Wildlife Commission and the current landowner to watch the nests.

Daniel's love of all the living things on the island had inspired Janie to continue his work after his death. There were sea turtle nests, the kites' habitat, and the fiddler crabs among so many others that he'd cared for. Janie had learned the different creatures' habits and how to determine when something needed doing to help the many species thrive.

Once at the site, she set the parking brake on the golf cart to ensure it didn't roll on the uneven ground and climbed out, grabbing her binoculars and backpack where she kept her field kit. The loblolly pines grew tall, and there weren't any other houses in view. The land was lush due to their conservation efforts over the past several years. Early on, she and Daniel had discovered that this was the best spot for viewing the stunning island sunsets.

In addition to checking on the birds and watching sunsets, Janie came here to recenter herself. Through all the difficult moments of the last couple of years, she found solace here. It allowed her the space and quiet to escape. It had become *her* sanctuary since Daniel's passing. And even on this occasion, she could feel his presence.

She sat down in the sand at the edge of the woods and hugged her knees, the rising sun painting the sky with splashes of color—pinks and oranges exploding into the sky above her. With every breath, Janie felt the calm settle upon her. Not many places on the island had a private, untainted sliver of beach. This one was special in so many ways. And she was so glad she was lucky enough to get to visit whenever she wanted.

She pulled her focus away from the spectacular sky and lifted her binoculars to get a look at the nests. There were three of them spread over a cluster of five trees. The last drone footage taken by the wildlife commission had shown three eggs in one nest and two in each of the others. She estimated they would hatch in the next week or so. Seeing the chicks emerge never got old, and she and Daniel had spent many quiet hours there anticipating that first glimpse of the new hatchlings.

Janie took a couple of photos of what she could see from the ground. She'd also brought her kit to take soil samples to gather information about the birds' diet and health. Everything around them had to support the habitat for the birds to thrive. Water, soil, food, and weather conditions all played a part.

Once Janie had finished, she packed up her kit and made her way home, down the narrow, sandy route, relishing the quiet of the island at this early hour.

Janie stood on the dock that jutted out from her backyard and put her hands on her hips to assess the direction of the wind as she got the boat ready to go out. She closed her tired eyes and tipped her face up toward the sunshine, letting it soak into her bones while Momma was still in her kitchen preparing sandwiches for the cooler. She took in a long breath of briny air and tried to clear her head.

The dreams had come last night, so Janie hadn't slept well. They were recurring dreams, especially the one where Daniel called for help from out in the water, and she couldn't quite reach him by boat or kayak, and she'd have to watch him go under the water and not resurface. They weren't exactly like what had happened on that fateful day, as her mind added and subtracted details, but they were close enough for the dreams—or nightmares, to be more exact—to resurrect the panic and the anguished helplessness she'd experienced at the time.

Despite her lack of deep sleep, Janie couldn't fault the day. The breeze was cool across the water as the sun broke through the remaining haze and clouds as she kept watch for her mother and their cooler of snacks coming her way. The sound of paddling and splashing fought for her attention and when she looked to the water it was Joe's grandniece she saw approaching in her bright-pink kayak.

"Oh, hi," Janie called to her, waving as Sibley advanced toward the dock, hoping she was in better spirits than the last time they met.

She was close enough that Janie could make out her sports tank, athletic shorts, and the water sandals on her feet. Her life vest was in the kayak but not on her body, making Janie pause. At least she knew how to dress for the canals. Going without foot protection around there was very foolish. So was not wearing a life vest. Hopefully, Sibley would put it on if she planned to leave the canal and go out into open water. The stretch of the canal ran for several miles from the tidal marshes out to Skull Inlet, where it met the Atlantic Ocean, and if you didn't know the waters, it could be dangerous, especially in a kayak.

Sibley surprised Janie when she waved back, the kayak making contact against the dock. Janie's reflexive response was to hop out of the boat, grab the kayak's rope, and then secure it tightly to the metal cleat attached to the dock. Sibley didn't say anything as she climbed up the dock's ladder from the tiny boat. Janie lent a hand, helping her up onto solid footing.

"I got caught in the current," Sibley finally said.

"Ah, yes. That can happen," Janie agreed.

Sibley folded her arms and looked around as if merely standing there with Janie was difficult.

"Y'all getting things settled in the house?" Janie asked.

A shadow crossed Sibley's face but disappeared as quickly as it had materialized. "It's a mess, but my dad keeps calling it a 'work in progress.'"

"Ah." Janie'd heard a little about what was happening in the young girl's life and could only imagine how stressful the moving process might be in addition to everything else.

Sibley's gaze fluttered over to her as Janie continued loading things into the boat. "Are y'all going out in the boat?"

"Yes, we're headed over to Prichards Island to pick up driftwood. My momma lives beside me over there," Janie told her, pointing to Momma's backyard. "Her name's Georgia. We make things from driftwood, seashells, sea glass, and pretty much anything else we find on the beaches around here."

Janie noticed a spark of interest light Sibley's eyes. "What kind of things do you make?"

"Items to decorate homes with. Candleholders, lamps, mirrors. All kinds of things."

Sibley glanced at Janie's backyard. "Your yard is nice."

Her compliment made Janie smile as she fondly remembered Daniel's exact vision of how it would eventually shape up. He'd be so proud to see it now since the plants and trees had matured. The grass was green and soft, with flowers and shrubs bordering the edges. Janie's back-porch steps led down to a patio that held heavy wicker furniture with colorful cushions and umbrellas. Momma's was almost a carbon copy. There was a cobblestone path leading to the dock that was flanked by seashells of every variety. Three ancient oaks shaded the yards and houses. It was the perfect spot for viewing the island's flawless sunsets.

Sibley shifted uncomfortably before saying, "I'm sorry for being rude yesterday when you stopped by." She wasn't quite looking Janie in the eye.

Janie was taken aback but hid that surprise by smiling. "Oh, honey, don't give it another thought. Moving is tough in the best of circumstances."

Sibley smiled shyly then, clearly relieved that Janie had accepted her apology. "Well, I'd better get back. My dad is going to be mad that I left him to deal with the kitchen alone."

Janie grinned at her, then pointed to the far side of the channel. "If you paddle over that way, you'll make it back home without too much hard work. And you're welcome here anytime. It's just Momma and me. We're always going out on the boat and hunting for treasures; you can join us if you ever get bored. Not much going on around here."

"No kidding." Sibley rolled her eyes, but it didn't seem to be directed at Janie.

Janie could empathize with how it might be for a teen here in a new place, off-season, with no friends, and nothing to do but paddle around alone in her kayak. Janie couldn't wait to leave when she'd gone off to college in Columbia, but after she'd been away a few years and then met Daniel, Janie realized she was an island girl through and through.

Momma arrived carrying a small container with their lunch just as Sibley paddled away. "Was that Joe's grandniece?"

"It was."

"Too bad I missed her."

Janie nodded, slightly distracted by worry about the girl. She had wanted to advise Sibley strongly against going out alone in her canoe, to tell her of the handful of hidden dangers, including fast-moving currents and unexpected rising tides. Still, after Sibley had made the effort to apologize, Janie hadn't wanted to overstep, though she still watched her anxiously.

Janie's over-worrying had come on after Dan's accident. She found herself fretting over things and people, even those she barely knew. It was a low-level anxiety that hummed inside her head until she resolved it with a phone call or a check-in. Momma could hardly leave the house to go into town without Janie calling to see if she'd made it to her destination okay.

Janie tried not to let fear and worry get the best of her. But she likely wouldn't let it go until she knew Sibley had made it back home safe and sound. The way she'd lost Daniel colored so many of her thoughts and actions. He'd drowned in a rip current during a thunderstorm only feet away from Janie while they'd tried to save a little girl who'd fallen overboard from a kayak.

"You're gnawing on something. What is it?" Momma asked, shading her eyes against the morning sun, even beneath the behemoth hat she wore.

Best to spit it out, or Momma would wear her down. "Sibley's life vest was in the kayak, but she wasn't wearing it. I know we're only a few docks away, but I'm worried about her getting back safely."

Momma knew about Janie's fears. Momma gave her that look, suggesting gently that she might be overreacting. "Tide is going out. If she goes in the water, she'll float right by us, and the water isn't over her head between here and there."

Janie shrugged. "You're right; I know it. I'm not sure why I think she's my concern."

"Honey, she'll be fine. Let's run by and check on her on the way out, but we'd better get cracking, or we'll miss the tide."

"We should have time if we head out now," Janie said. "You ready?"

Momma untied the line nearest to her, and Janie did the same. They jumped in the boat and Janie started the engine, pulling away from the dock, making a quick, tight U-turn. They idled a couple of docks down until they approached the new neighbors' house, where Janie spotted Sibley's kayak. It was floating empty, but tied to the cleat of their dock.

"See? She's safe," Momma said.

Janie's relief was momentary. "But does she know how to get through the tide? I barely explained it to her, and I want to be sure she doesn't go back out in it later by herself."

Momma checked her watch. "Go on up and lay eyes on her. We've still got a half hour until high tide." At high tide, the direction of the water reversed and began heading out of the creek pretty rapidly.

Janie turned the boat on a dime, threw it in reverse so as not to overshoot the dock, and Momma looped the rope on the Kennedys' dock cleat to tie up, their years of experience doing this together evident as they worked like a well-oiled machine.

"I'll be right back," Janie called over her shoulder and sprinted up the dock toward the back of the house. When she got up to their rear patio, the back doors were open to the air and that lovely breeze.

"Sibley!" Janie called out.

"Can I help you?"

Ryan appeared unexpectedly, stepping out from inside, a little closer than was comfortable. Not that he was inordinately close. But for Janie, twenty feet away might have been better. He was dressed similarly to the day before, this time in a T-shirt featuring a logo from the Medical College of Georgia in white letters.

Janie managed to control her surprise at his sudden appearance. "Hello. Sibley stopped by earlier in her kayak, and I wanted to make sure she understands the tides before she goes out again." This was as close to another man as she'd been since Daniel had died, besides Joe, and it made her fidgety.

He frowned. "Sibley knows not to go out in the water alone. Ever. She must have gone when I ran errands."

By now, Janie's face was indeed that awful shade of red. "I'm sorry if I caused her a problem or upset you. I was just checking on her."

Ryan locked eyes with Janie, stopping her in her tracks.

"Thank you."

Just then, the boat horn sounded. "I've gotta go. Momma's waiting for me," Janie said.

"All right. I'll see y'all around. I'm looking forward to meeting your mom soon."

Janie turned around and headed back to the boat, which was far enough downhill from where she spoke to Ryan that Momma couldn't see what was happening. When Janie reached it, she untied the rope and hopped in.

"I can see by your complexion that you weren't speaking to only Sibley," Momma observed once Janie had maneuvered the boat through the now shallow winding canal that led to open water. "Did you run into her daddy?"

Janie was focused on keeping the boat away from low water, so she waited until they were between Fripp and Pritchards islands to answer. "I spoke to Ryan, and he didn't know about Sibley going out."

"Ah. So, you got her in trouble?" Momma's voice was kind because she understood Janie's good intentions.

Janie sighed. "I know. Sibley probably needs someone to trust, and I don't want to break that before I've even earned it." Janie pictured the teen girl with the big, green eyes. She had such an aura of sadness around her that it squeezed Janie's heart.

"Maybe we should break the ice and invite them to dinner," Momma suggested as the wind coming off the water blew through her hair. Momma smiled and stared toward Prichards Island as it approached.

"I don't think it's necessary." Janie brushed away the memory of Ryan's frown from earlier.

Momma eyed her with that knowing look. "You can't push everyone away forever, Janie."

"I also don't need to let just anyone in." There it was: her fear of attachment and loss.

Momma stared out at the horizon, and Janie was glad that she'd let it go.

Janie guided the boat toward the sandy beach, where they would dock for several hours. There was not a single person in sight, which was no surprise. Although daytime visitors arriving by kayak or boat enjoyed taking in the sight of the island's beaches and wildlife they didn't tend to stop long as Pritchards was uninhabited. It had no electricity or running water, at least not anymore. It was tiny, consisting of a dilapidated pier, rows of palm trees, and several rusting, non-functional tractors that couldn't be removed by sea or by land once they'd died in place. There was a single structure that stood tattered but majestic against the elements of the sea and tide: an abandoned University of South Carolina marine biology research lab. The windows were all broken or gone completely, and the stairs leading to the upper floors from the beach had fallen to ruin years before. The university still owned the island, continued its local ecosystem research, and protected the unusually high population of loggerhead sea turtle nests, but they hadn't used the lab for years, tending instead to boat in and out between their observations.

Janie loved the beauty and tranquility of the island, and it also had a seemingly endless supply of driftwood. A boneyard, it was called by the locals. Large and small pieces had broken from trees, overcome by the elements, and then bleached by the sun. Some were near petrified and perfect for every kind of home accessory they made in their workshop. There were also tons of stunning shells and sea glass.

"Hey, Janie, can you help me get this guy back to the water?" Momma pointed to a giant horseshoe crab on the sand in front of her. "Looks like he got stranded when the tide went out."

"Sure." Janie grabbed her cell phone and the large rolling bucket they used to transport the items they found on the beach before securing the boat and climbing out.

The large stingray-shaped shell was almost two feet in diameter, and it had a tail that stuck out about ten inches. Janie knew all about them. Using horseshoe crabs' blood for human vaccinations had been one of Dan's many projects. Seeing one now, Janie thought of him—how he'd look at her after he'd come home from working on the beach, his face pink from the sun; the feel of his hands on hers when they sat on the old porch swing outside after dinner. His goofy smile when he said something funny...

Shake it off, Janie.

They skillfully grabbed the edges of the shell and gently moved the crab to the foam of the waves until it began to swim out into deeper water.

"He was still wet, so hopefully he'll be fine," Momma said.

Janie constantly worked to protect the animals' breeding grounds; primarily the birds, but she and Daniel both had a soft spot for the land and marine animals. Fripp was a rich landscape where raccoons, deer, dolphins, and barracuda thrived. It was the little moments like these that tugged at her heart because she missed sharing them with him.

Pushing away the sad thoughts, Janie looked at the bright-blue sky and felt the thrill of anticipation run through her, excited for what they might find.

"Dad, you don't have to freak out." Sibley stood, hands on her hips. "I know how to swim."

She was acting out because she was sixteen. But, unlike other sixteen-year-olds, Sibley was suffering from her mother's abandonment and a lot of unexpected change.

"It's not about being a strong swimmer," Ryan said. "It's about the currents and tides and sharks, for God's sake—and every other thing that might be under that water that you can't see." With everything else happening in his life, she had to stay safe. She was, and always had been, his number-one priority.

"I can make good choices." She said this with the confidence only a teen could. One who didn't understand the risks and consequences of believing she was invincible.

Ryan took a deep breath; he didn't want to push any further, but he needed to protect his daughter. Fatherhood, he had learned, was a delicate balancing act, and he wasn't sure he always got it right, but he would keep trying. "I'll make you a deal. You follow my boating rules, and I'll take you to get your license."

She frowned, clearly confused. "What? I've done all my road hours, and I can legally get it in two weeks."

"I have to feel you're responsible enough to have it, and you can prove that by making better choices with the kayak."

Sibley's brows shot up, and her mouth hung open. She appeared shocked that he'd called her out.

"That's the plan, and I'm sticking to it." Ryan was resolute. He'd learned that backing down after making that kind of statement made her see him as weak. Sometimes parenting was like girding for battle against an army of hidden booby traps. Saying one wrong word could set them off.

She crossed her arms, withdrawing into herself.

Ryan's heart sank. He wanted to make her smile, to tell her he'd take her to get her license, that he'd do anything for her. But he had to be a good father, and keeping her safe was his top priority.

"May I go now?" she asked, her voice distant.

"I'll tell you what. Why don't you take the golf cart and head to Uncle Joe's for some supplies?" He had to find some common ground for them. Being the heavy all the time wouldn't do either of them much good.

She brightened at that, sending a wave of relief through him. Sibley's smile had been genuine, and he'd seen that sparkle in her eyes. It had been so long...

"You know all the safety rules about driving the cart. Make sure you take your permit." He pulled the keys from his pocket and tossed them to her.

While she ran off to get her purse and shoes, Ryan dialed Joe to let him know to watch for her.

Chapter Three

"You ready to put the bread in yet?" Momma asked as she maneuvered around the small kitchen dining table to where Janie kept the tablecloths and dinner napkins inside the antique sideboard.

After spending most of the week working on their accessories, Janie was now helping her mother put the finishing touches on the dinner they were having for their new neighbors. Janie had to admit that she was looking forward to seeing the Kennedys again. Even Ryan Kennedy, who somehow managed to make her blush scarlet each time they met.

Every day that week she'd passed the house and there'd been no sign of anyone home. Ryan worked in Beaufort as an orthodontist, and Sibley attended Beaufort High—Janie's own alma mater—but that was all Janie knew, so she had been pleased when her mother had gone ahead and planned this dinner with them. Momma would have known Janie would feel awkward going over there and asking them herself, especially considering how she'd left things with Sibley and Ryan the last time she'd spoken to them. Hopefully they'd all be able to start fresh tonight.

"Let's wait until they get here,' Janie said to Momma. 'We'll do drinks and then put the bread in."

The blend of spicy aromas in the kitchen from the sweet stone crabs, smoked sausages, and onions made Janie's stomach growl in anticipation. Instead of preparing the whole crab, Janie clipped off one claw from each crab in the trap, then released them, leaving them able to use their other claw to defend themselves while the missing claw grew back. Stone crabs were a renewable resource around there, and she only wished everyone else harvested them as she did.

Since they were having guests for dinner, Janie had decided to wear a dress, something she enjoyed but rarely had the occasion to do. It was a floral sundress that hit just above her knees and tied around her neck. When she'd seen it in the boutique window in Beaufort a couple of years back, she'd bought it in a moment of pure weakness. She knew Daniel would love it. It was just so *pretty.* Janie had bought it the week before his accident, and this was actually the first time she'd worn it.

"Darlin', they're here," Momma called from the living room.

Janie stocked up on all kinds of drinks to be sure they were covered and had even made a pitcher of iced tea. It had been a real coon's age since they'd entertained anybody but Joe or any of Momma's bridge ladies here.

Janie smoothed her hair, feeling the curls spring to life under her fingers.

"Y'all come on in. So glad you could join us tonight," she heard Momma say as she spoke to their guests at the front door.

Janie pulled out a dish filled with baked Vidalia onion casserole from the oven, filling the air with the rich scent of the onions, along with butter, garlic, and the spice of jalapenos. Just as she set the dish down on the countertop, she looked up, her gaze colliding with Ryan's across the kitchen island.

"Hi there," she said. It was odd having a man in her kitchen, she had to admit. Janie felt the urge to laugh nervously. Instead, she busied her hands with straightening the napkin holder.

"Thanks for having us over." He smiled at Janie.

She nearly had to take a step back because he was just that handsome.

Sibley entered the kitchen, and Janie pulled the oven mitt from her hand. "Hi, Sibley. It's great to see you."

"You too. Something smells good."

There seemed to be no ill-feeling toward Janie or between father and daughter, so that was an excellent start to the evening.

"We've got beer, sparkling water, lemonade, iced tea, and sodas." Momma spoke as she shut the oven, where she'd just put the bread in.

They'd left the double doors leading out to the screened back porch open, inviting their guests to spill outside and enjoy the evening outdoors. The sunset over the water was inarguably one of the very best things about living on the island. The layers of orange, purples, and yellow were ever-changing. The canal snaked its way to where it met the ocean, and their yard backed up to the creek, so their perspective was perfect. It only got better at the end of the canal at the tip of the island, where the sun set behind Pritchards Island. That stretch of beach was Janie's second-favorite place to watch the sun set.

Ryan held a beer in his hand as he stepped onto the porch and got a look at the exterior yard area. "Wow, this is amazing."

Janie flushed with pride. "Yes. My husband, Daniel, had a real talent for landscaping." Daniel had been such a part of everything, and she couldn't help but give him credit. "I mean, we all worked together on his design plans. We're still adding plants and hardscape here and there. But it's finally coming together."

Ryan appeared interested and hadn't done more than raise his eyebrows slightly when she'd mentioned Daniel.

"Is our backyard going to look like this?" Sibley asked Ryan.

"It could, I guess. Once we get the house started, we can do a landscape plan."

"Joe said you planned to build here on the island?" Momma asked.

Ryan nodded. "I'm working with an architect in Beaufort on a house plan."

Janie digested this new information. "Where are you building?" she asked, frowning just a little, thinking about the available lots on the island.

Ryan grinned at her and took a swig of his beer. "I've got a realtor helping me find a good spot that overlooks the water. We might have to do a teardown if one becomes available. We'll be renting here until I find a property."

"There aren't many buildable lots for new construction." Janie realized his construction project wasn't her business, but the island and its creatures were definitely of great concern to her. Not everyone appreciated or took care of the environment, and she hoped that Ryan wasn't like that. There was so much to enjoy and see on Fripp, but the islanders had a responsibility.

"Well, we're glad to have you as neighbors. Welcome." Momma held up her glass in a toast, and everyone followed suit. "Now, let's get the food out here to the table. Crab claws are best eaten outdoors."

The outdoor dining table was set with a red-and-white checked vinyl tablecloth, and they all grabbed the dishes and utensils from the kitchen and made a parade to the table before sitting down. Flames flickered in one of the low, driftwood candle holders that stretched along the center of the table. Sibley lowered herself next to Janie and offered her a small smile. It was a glimmer of relief that the young girl seemed less angsty this evening, and Ryan seemed to be more relaxed because of it. He was leaning back in his chair, an arm draped behind his daughter.

Janie worked to let go of the subject of Ryan's new home and the repercussions of new construction to the local wildlife habitats. Momma and Ryan talked about one of the plants she'd recently bought as they passed around the corn, potatoes, and crab claws. There was a cool breeze despite the humidity. Their conversation and laughter filled the air, along with the tapping of hammers to excavate the crabmeat from the claws.

"So, Ryan, you're an orthodontist?" Momma asked.

"Yes," he replied, dipping a piece of crab into the little bowl of melted butter and popping it into his mouth.

Momma's eyebrows raised in interest. "Oh, how nice. Where's your office located?"

"It's on Sea Island Parkway near the Publix in Beaufort."

"I've seen it. You've got the big green sign, right?" Janie asked, leaning in and joining the conversation.

"That's me." He grinned as if pleased they'd noticed his office. It was clear that, besides Sibley, his business was a source of pride. "It's a great practice," he said, cracking another crab. "I've been there since I graduated dental school, so I was glad that moving here wouldn't change the commute a whole lot."

"Where did you go to school?" Janie asked, curious about his background.

"I attended the Medical College of Georgia in Augusta. They offered me scholarships, so it made the most sense. My parents were divorced, and I didn't have help with tuition." He didn't sound resentful, only realistic.

Janie experienced a sudden rush of empathy for Ryan as a bright young man struggling to pay for dental school. She'd gone to college in-state, so the expenses of her undergrad education weren't as outrageous as they would've been someplace else. She'd been aware of her family's financial limitations. Janie had worked hard and gotten scholarships as well, so the expenses weren't as burdensome.

After dinner and cleanup, Momma took Sibley into the garage to show her their workshop. Janie was happy to see Sibley respond to the invitation, her mother chatting away to the young girl. But it left Ryan and Janie to finish clearing the dishes, putting her on edge. She'd spent most of the dinner chewing on the idea of his building a new home on the island. The island was small, and keeping the undisturbed areas natural was a constant challenge.

Ryan rolled up his sleeves to just below the elbows, revealing his muscular forearms, causing Janie to tear her gaze away and focus on the dirty silverware.

"Everything okay?" he asked as he rinsed plates.

Heat crawled up her neck and into her face. "Yes," she said, swimming out of her thoughts. "Everything's fine... Thanks for helping with the dishes."

"No problem. Dinner was fantastic. It's been a long time since I've had a low country boil like that. My mom wasn't much of a cook, and my ex-wife detests seafood."

"That's unfortunate." Janie wasn't sure how else to respond as they moved from the kitchen back to the screened-in porch, where the cicadas, field crickets, and tree frogs were cranking up for the evening's symphony.

"It's not a problem anymore, I guess," he continued. "Sibley and I can eat all the seafood we want now that we're on our own. I guess that's one good thing about all of this."

He appeared to shrug it off, and Janie didn't question him further. There were things she didn't want to discuss at length either.

Chapter Four

Ryan had already begun to crave the slower pace of the island after a long day of seeing patients and putting out the fires of running a small business. He had become a big fan of sitting and watching the sky at sunset from his deck. He only wished Sibley could find something that would give her peace at the end of the day.

Lately, she'd become even less communicative with him. The longer the silence between her and her mom, the quieter she became with Ryan. It was time for him to confront Leslie. Just because she had a boyfriend to distract her didn't mean she could stop talking to Sibley. She might not want to deal with him, but he believed she would do what was best for her daughter.

Sibley had team tennis practice after school that day, and he wasn't due to pick her up for another hour. Just before he crossed the bridge that led to the island, he made a sharp turn and headed toward the home they'd shared near the sound, on the off chance he could catch his soon-to-be-ex-wife at home. Up to this point, he'd avoided any confrontation with Leslie except through his lawyer. Still, he was allowed to knock on her door and ask her to have an adult conversation about their daughter. He didn't give a rip if Coach Todd was there or not.

Leslie's gray Volvo SUV was in the drive when he pulled up. He paused outside, mustering up the energy go in. The house still looked the same. Well, the grass needed mowing—something he'd done every Sunday, weather allowing. The white two-story Greek-revival house with the large front porch had been their dream home. He had imagined it always being their family home, their escape and retreat, the place they made happy memories to last a lifetime…

Frustration washed over him. How could Leslie have done this to them? To Sibley? He got out of the car with renewed determination and rang the doorbell. He heard Leslie's footsteps on the hardwood floor as she approached.

"Ryan? What are you doing here? Is Sibley with you?" Leslie leaned out just a little and peered toward his truck. She wore jeans, a white cotton blouse tucked in, and a silver-buckled black leather belt at her waist.

"No, Sibley's at tennis practice. But you wouldn't know that, would you? Since you haven't bothered to ask her, and you haven't called in almost a week." He shoved his hands into his pockets, unable to stop the wave of frustration from erupting.

Leslie's face flushed, and her voice held an edge as she stood in the doorway. "I just asked for a little time. All those years you worked nonstop, I handled *everything*. You didn't take the time to know her schedule then, did you?"

"I worked to support you and your lifestyle; in case you've forgotten." Ryan indicated the house and yard with a gesture of his hand. "But I'm not here to discuss our marriage. I'm here to discuss the damage you're doing to Sibley."

Tears welled up in Leslie's eyes. "I—just can't."

"Can't what? Speak to your own daughter? I don't understand, Leslie. And neither does she."

Ryan tried to control his anger and frustration. Before the affair, Leslie had been a good mom. She'd worked hard to create a stable and loving home for all of them, especially Sibley, so it was mind boggling to Ryan how much she seemed to have changed.

Before, Leslie worried about what others in her social circles thought. She'd insisted on things like Sibley always looking "presentable" to Leslie's friends by wearing the "right" clothes and keeping the "right" company. Leslie had often even bought clothes for Ryan and asked him specifically to wear them on special nights out. A little controlling? Maybe. Other people's impressions mattered to her. But then she'd "run off" with the tennis pro and, well, that was shocking in the extreme. It was as if she'd thrown caution to the wind and given up all pretense of caring about others or their opinions.

"I can't because then I would have to explain what happened. I'm not ready to do that yet, and I can barely understand it myself. This isn't easy for me either, you know." Before he could tell her how selfish her response was, she lowered her head. "I'm sorry, Ryan. I know how that must sound."

"You bet. It sounds selfish. None of this would've happened if it weren't for your actions. And, yes, I do blame you for what our daughter is going through right now. You don't see her crying every time she asks if you've called or care how I feel when I have to tell her no."

Tears ran down Leslie's face, but Ryan wasn't moved by them.

She took a deep breath. "I know it's my fault, Ryan, and I don't have any defense except that I was lonely and bored."

Leslie's affair had ruined everything, and her current behavior was no less acceptable. "Lonely and bored" usually didn't lead a partner to cheat—nor was it a satisfactory excuse.

"When you started an affair with Todd, you knew there would be consequences. Your marriage and your relationship with Sibley weren't enough to keep you from doing it, though."

Leslie's features crumpled, and she covered her face with her hands. Ryan was doing this for Sibley and couldn't allow her tears to sway him. As much as he wanted to shout at her, that wasn't working, and he needed to get through to her, for Sibley's sake.

"You're still her mother, and she needs you. Promise you'll at least speak to her a couple of times a week. I'll talk to her therapist about how to deal with it, but you have to do your part, too."

Leslie nodded, wiping tears from her face. "I'll talk to her. And I *do* want to know what's happening at school and in her life. I love my daughter, Ryan. I just don't love me so much right now."

Ryan was stuck between pity and an eyeroll. He didn't understand Leslie's actions at all. Nor had he seen the affair coming. Coach Todd had trained Sibley privately for three years, since she'd turned thirteen. Todd and Leslie had spoken frequently about Sibley's progress, but Ryan had had no clue that they were more than friendly. The fallout had been devastating, and Sibley had lost the most: a mother, a home, and a coach and mentor. Tennis was the thing Sibley had loved the most, and Leslie's actions had ruined even that.

"Make sure Sibley knows that," Ryan said. "She doesn't understand what's happening to her life right now. Everything has changed and, in her eyes, you were the one who did that. The more support you can show her, the better."

"I've let her down, and I know it. I don't expect her to trust me, but I do want to talk to her."

"Evenings after homework are best to call. She's got tennis practice Mondays and Wednesdays, and the matches are Tuesdays and Thursdays starting next week. I'm sure she'd love it if you made some of the matches." Leslie had been the one who'd handled Sibley's schedule in the past. Now, he had to inform her of Sibley's daily activities.

They didn't have a legal custody agreement yet, and their attorneys had suggested they work it out between them, if possible, while considering Sibley's needs and desires. Still, it hadn't even come to that, as Leslie had seemingly given up all responsibility for Sibley.

Leslie's face took on a pained expression. "I'll do better for her. I promise."

He stared at his wife, barely recognizing her as the woman he'd married and shared a life with. She'd been a devoted mother to Sibley and a loving wife to him, despite their arguments about his work schedule, which he'd had to alter significantly since taking over Sibley's care full time. All that mattered was doing right by Sibley. Once upon a time, Leslie had felt the same. Why had a new relationship changed her behavior so much?

Ryan had done what he came to do, so there was nothing else to say. "I'll see ya," he said before turning toward his truck. "Might want to get that grass mowed. It's a bear once it gets too long."

As he got in, Leslie was still at the doorway with tears in her eyes. He drove away, leaving the pieces of his broken life behind him.

Ryan entered the open garage where Janie was trimming a large piece of driftwood using a table saw. Her back was facing him, so he knocked on the inside wall of the garage and called out, "Hello!"

But she couldn't hear him through the headphones she had on, the loud music playing, and the buzz of her saw. Not wanting to startle her, he waited, studying her as she worked.

Her auburn hair was tied back, and she wore a pair of safety glasses to protect her eyes as she moved the large piece of driftwood across the saw's blade. She handled the power tool with the precision of a seasoned professional.

He'd so appreciated the dinner invitation from Georgia and Janie to welcome them to the island. It had been a relaxed and pleasant evening, and Sibley had appeared surprisingly comfortable with them—as comfortable as he'd seen her since everything had hit the fan in her life.

Janie hit the stop button unexpectedly and turned to catch him staring.

"O-oh, hi."

Her face became flushed, or had it already been like that?

"Hi. I didn't want to interrupt your work. I stopped by to ask a favor."

"How can I help?"

When she pulled up the protective glasses and set them on top of her head, Ryan noticed how clear and green her eyes were as they peered at him. She really was a stunning woman.

"I hate to ask you this. Joe said he would if I didn't, so I figured I'd better stop by...."

"What is it?" she asked, her eyes curious.

"I'm headed to a full-day work conference in Charleston on Saturday and wondered if you wouldn't mind letting Sibley hang out with y'all while I'm gone. Joe is good with her at the marina, but I doubt she'll want to stay there shilling bait and bread all day."

It saddened him that she couldn't just stay with her mother. The irony of asking this big favor of Janie, who he barely knew, over asking Leslie to do something as simple as taking care of her daughter wasn't lost on Ryan. But he'd not felt comfortable after his conversation with Leslie to leave Sibley with her. Leslie didn't appear to be able to handle Sibley right now—especially if Sibley decided to ask Leslie all the hard questions she'd been wrestling with. Ryan understood that whatever was going on with Leslie, they would need to tread carefully.

"Of course she can stay with us. But do you think she'll want to?"

"She loves anything artistic and creative." He motioned around the workshop. "And she enjoys the outdoors, so inside or outside, I know she'll be happy to tag along."

"I'd be happy to have her." Her eyes were honest and warm.

"I didn't want to mention it to her until you approved the idea. But I'll confirm as soon as I discuss it with her. Can I get your number so I can give you more details?"

"Oh, sure." Janie reached over to where her phone sat to the side of the workbench and picked it up.

They exchanged numbers.

"Thanks. I owe you one."

"Have a good evening." She pulled her eye gear and headphones back on and continued working.

Ryan drove back to his house with a feeling of lightness, something he'd not experienced in many months. There was something about Janie that could do that to him.

Chapter Five

When the doorbell rang promptly at seven thirty on Saturday morning, Janie nearly jumped off her barstool. She opened the front door to find Ryan standing next to Sibley, who had a pink duffle bag slung over her shoulder.

Janie was looking forward to spending time with the teenage girl, and she'd gotten everything ready for their day. Typically in the morning, Janie would've researched the local endangered animals, done a supply inventory of the workshop, and made a list for the next day. But she could do those things tomorrow; she wanted the day to be fun for Sibley.

"Good morning."

"Good morning,' Janie said and smiled.

Ryan's face was cleanly shaven, and she thought about holding her breath to avoid taking in his slight smell of pine and soap. Her efforts failed, and the comforting scent of him made her want to lean toward him and allow herself to breathe it in.

He grinned back at Janie with relief and appreciation in his gaze. "You've got my number in case you need to contact me."

Janie pointed to the phone in its spot on the countertop. "Yes. Got it."

Sibley gave Ryan a little side hug when he kissed her on the top of her head. "I'll see you this afternoon, okay?"

Sibley nodded and entered the house without looking back.

In the kitchen, Janie explained what she had lined up for them. "Our plan today is to finish up a few things in the shop and then take the boat out on the water for the rest of the day. We'll go up to Bull Point to collect shells and sea glass. How does that sound?"

"Sounds better than being bored at my house all day," Sibley replied. She took a sip of orange juice that Janie had laid out for them and then asked, "Where's Bull Point?"

"It's a tiny island about two miles out where we take the boat to shell hunt. There are huge conch shells and lots of others."

"Sounds cool. I've never found any really big shells, but I found a sand dollar once."

"We'll see plenty of sand dollars, too."

After eating the breakfast Momma had prepared for them, Momma took Sibley out to the workshop in her garage while Janie cleaned the kitchen and gathered things for the cooler.

When Janie joined them in the workshop, Momma was showing Sibley how to choose shells to create a picture frame.

"Ooh, I love this one," Sibley said, wholly involved in the task.

"We space them out evenly. Kind of like flower arranging. Then, we fill in the spaces with smaller shells, shell clusters, and sea glass." Momma placed the shells Sibley had chosen on the frame and showed her how to attach them with the glue gun.

"I feel like I'm at summer camp." Sibley said this as if summer camp held good memories. "I always chose arts and crafts instead of archery."

"I love choosing the colors and shapes I want for our projects." Janie brought over a tray with sea glass they'd carefully separated into color hues for Sibley to choose from for her frame.

"The blue is so pretty." Sibley reached out to touch the oddly shaped pieces.

Janie pulled up the stool next to where Sibley was working. She had a feeling it was going to be a good day.

As they idled out of the canal, Sibley pointed excitedly at a pair of dolphins on the starboard side, only having caught sight of them as they swam away, dipping below the surface and then arching into the air with perfect precision.

"I've never seen them so close up." Sibley's expression was pure delight. She pulled out her phone to try to capture a photo.

"Yes, and you'll likely see more today," Momma said, clearly enjoying Sibley's enthusiasm, "so be on the lookout. They're off in that direction, a lot of the time." Momma loved sharing her many years of experience on and around the island with someone who had the opportunity to see it fresh for the first time.

"Hang on." Janie opened up the throttle. The wind whipped their hair, and the salt spray from the boat slicing through the dark water landed on Janie's arms and legs. The fluffy white clouds were like cotton floating in the clear blue sky.

In about twenty-five minutes, they'd reached their shelling destination. Janie beached the boat and trimmed the motor, then Momma hopped out and pulled the shore anchor past the tide line. Sibley helped them unload the cooler as well as the handcarts for transporting their treasure. She was a fast learner and pitched in right away. Already she seemed so different from the sullen girl Janie had met that first day. Janie hoped the island was already beginning to work its magic.

"We're going to walk that way a couple of miles along the beach," Momma said, pointing to the wild and natural coastline.

But Sibley had already stopped and was bending down toward the sand. "Wow, look! I found one!" She held up a large, fully intact conch shell.

"Let's have a look to make certain there's no resident inside. If there *are* animals still inside, we just put the conch in the water and keep looking. You likely won't hurt them if you don't poke anything inside the shell," Janie explained.

Sibley looked up, wide-eyed. "Oh, wow. I've never seen a shell with something still living inside of it."

"This is a natural island, so we never know what we'll find." Which is why Janie loved living here so much. "We should go ahead and eat our sandwiches now before we get going."

"Sounds like an excellent plan." Momma laid out a large quilt to sit on while they ate. The quilt had been around since Momma and Daddy had gotten married, and it had stood the test of many sandy, damp beach outings over the years.

"It's so cool here. I mean, it's like we're the only people on the island." Sibley looked around and noticed the raw beauty of the place.

"We could be the only ones for the entire day, depending on if anyone else decides to take the trouble to plan an afternoon here." Watching Sibley's responses to things Janie'd taken for granted reminded her of what an extraordinary privilege it was to live and work there.

"I don't think I've ever been on a deserted island before," Sibley said, taking her sandwich from Momma. "It's so—different."

"We enjoy it while we can. It's not always this deserted, but there's never been a crowd here that I can remember," Momma said. "Lots of visitors to Fripp don't have access to a boat, and they don't know about this place."

Sibley took a bite of her sandwich. "What kind of jelly is this? It's good," Sibley asked.

"It's Momma's homemade strawberry-fig," Janie replied.

Momma grinned from ear to ear, clearly thrilled that Sibley liked it. "I'll send a jar home with you today."

"Thanks. Me and my dad eat a lot of toast."

After finishing their sandwiches, they headed out to find shells. Shelling here wasn't a leisurely walk on the beach. It was gritty and sweaty and required trudging around in smelly, slick mud surrounded by oyster beds that covered the very best shells.

However, it didn't stop them from discovering some gorgeous items. Janie found fanning oyster shell clusters with barnacles on them for the large bottles Momma had ordered a few days ago. Momma focused on finding the elusive lettered olive shells. Sibley seemed to have an affinity for the large, colorful conch shells, so she'd gathered a good number of those.

Sibley kept a smile on her face for most of the day, laughing as she discovered new treasures. "I've never done anything like this with my mom. I mean, we used to do things together, but she didn't like the sand very much."

"I guess we all like different things." Janie tried to sound magnanimous, giving the girl's mother a pass on "not liking sand". But how odd that seemed to Janie.

Momma's expression said the same, but this was a child who needed pure acceptance right now, so they gave it to her, and did everything they could to make the day fun and memorable.

By the time they all got hungry again, they'd discovered loads of gorgeous treasures. It was a perfect day for finding some distinctive pieces of glass and a few unique shells with bluish hues.

As they made their way back to the boat, taking turns pulling the carts, there was a skip in Sibley's step that made Janie feel as if they'd done something right in bringing her here.

Chapter Six

When Ryan arrived at Janie's, Sibley's laugh carried on the wind from out back. It was a sound he'd missed these past few months. Instead of ringing the bell, he walked around the side of the house.

Janie and Sibley looked up when he came across the yard.

"Wow, look at all this," he exclaimed, pointing to where they'd spread out their finds. There were huge conch shells, sand dollars, lots of oyster shells stuck together, and a pile of colored glass.

"Yes, it was a great day for hunting treasure," Janie agreed and then looked to Sibley to confirm.

"Dad, you should've seen it. The island was *deserted,* and we were the only ones there for the whole afternoon. And there were so many shells. And Janie let me drive the boat when we were out in the open water." Sibley paused only to take a breath. "Oh, and I saw *dolphins*!"

Ryan was processing Sibley's excitement while trying to respond to it. "Sounds like you got some special treatment. And dolphins? That's so cool."

"Sibley has a great eye for shelling," Janie said as she pulled up an enormous conch shell that had a strange blue hue to it. She handed it to Sibley.

Ryan smiled. It was great to see Sibley like this. "She's loved shell hunting since she was a little girl."

Sibley's love of all things related to the beach began when she was barely two years old, and they'd taken their first family beach vacation. She'd spent an excessive amount of time beachcombing over the years, but, in truth, it was something Ryan mostly did with Sibley, as the beach was more like a chore for Leslie. She preferred sitting by the pool under an umbrella. Ryan felt guilty that they'd not done it for a couple of years now that he saw the joy it brought his daughter. He promised himself that he would take her out shelling now they lived on the island; they needed to spend more quality time together. At the moment, more than ever, Sibley needed to feel loved and appreciated.

"Do you want to see the shells I found?" Sibley sounded enthusiastic, which was such a nice change.

"Of course." He admired the specific shells as Sibley pointed them out.

"I need to get a bag for them." She ran over to the back patio and selected a tote bag from a pile of them.

Ryan spoke to Janie. "Thanks again for doing this."

"Of course." She seemed a little uncomfortable as she looked toward where Sibley had run across the yard. "Gosh, I need to cut this grass."

He agreed that her grass was a bit long but not overly so. "It grows so fast here with the rain we get." They were making small talk about her grass, but he got the impression Janie was a little embarrassed about it being a bit overgrown since the last time he'd been out there.

"Our mower needs a new belt, so I'll head to Beaufort on Monday and pick one up." She pointed to the small riding mower sitting under the back overhang of the porch. "Momma hates the long grass because it makes it hard to weed and work in her flower beds."

"I could get a new belt for you. I'll be in Beaufort Monday." It was the least he could do.

"That's a kind offer, but I've got a few other errands to run while I'm there."

She smiled at him, and it gave him a little jolt. She had a lot of charm but seemed so unaware of its impact.

Sibley gathered her shells, picking up each one gently and placing them in the canvas tote she'd brought over. "Can I get the sand dollars from you later?" she asked Janie. "I'm afraid they'll get broken if I put them in here."

"Of course, but we have to bleach them, or they'll smell fishy. I'll do yours at the same time I clean some of our items."

Janie walked with the two of them around to the front of the house. Sibley stopped at the patio and grabbed her backpack where she'd kept her sunscreen and personal items.

"Thanks for having me." Sibley knew her manners, and Ryan was glad he didn't have to prod her to thank Janie.

"It was fun, Sibley. Let's do it again, okay?"

Janie waved as they pulled out of the drive. Ryan was beyond grateful to her for giving Sibley such a memorable day, and he wanted to thank her somehow. After being cooped up in the conference hotel on a Saturday, he made a decision.

"I'm going to bring the mower over and mow Janie and Georgia's grass. What do you think?"

"That's a nice idea. Janie mentioned how long the grass was this morning."

Sibley's response confirmed his decision and, as they arrived back at the house, he hurried upstairs to change into an old T-shirt and gym shorts. After putting on a pair of protective glasses from his tool kit, he drove the mower the space of two driveways to Janie's home and began mowing the yard. He hoped it would be a pleasant surprise for the two women to open their doors and see the freshly cut grass out front. Of course, he would do the back as well, but likely they would hear the mower at some point before that. Until then, the front yards were his top priority.

As he made the turns, he thought about Leslie's grass and how it needed mowing. She'd never mowed in her life, and he wondered if Coach Todd would do it for her. Then again, perhaps Leslie didn't care how the yard appeared anymore. Just as she didn't seem to care about a lot of things. Ryan took a deep breath and blew it out. That wasn't constructive thinking.

The riding mower took a little under a half hour to cut both front yards. Ryan had just rounded the side of the house to start on the back when he saw Janie and Georgia. They stood at the edge of the dock rinsing off some kind of carts.

They both looked up when they heard the mower approach. Janie frowned as if she were confused.

Ryan powered down the mower and parked it nearby, then headed over to where they were working. There was a built-in bench seat and table at the dock where they'd moved the items from the day's shelling.

Sibley came over through the backyards that separated them.

Janie smiled but then asked, "What's up with the mower?"

"I thought after our conversation about the grass that it was something I could do to pay y'all back. I hope that's okay…."

Janie frowned just for a second. "We usually mow every Sunday unless it rains—when the mower is running."

Suddenly, Ryan felt like a jerk for not asking if they'd like him to mow the yard. "I hope I didn't overstep. I have this fancy mower that gets the job done quickly, so I thought—"

"That was a nice thing to do. I'm just not used to someone else doing it."

Sibley paid close attention to the adults, probably sensing minor tension. Ryan understood how sensitive she was to it.

"Do you want me to leave the back for you to do?" he asked.

Janie smiled and shook her head, and then motioned toward his lawnmower. "You've got the mower and you look ready for the job, so feel free to finish up. And thanks."

A colossal weight suddenly fell off Ryan. "I'm on it."

Sibley relaxed visibly and turned to Janie. "Do you want me to bring the life jackets up from the boat?"

"No, thanks, we'll leave them there for now."

Ryan watched the interaction between Janie and Sibley. It was kind, and there wasn't a trace of attitude when Sibley addressed Janie. She was respectful and seemed to want to please Janie. Janie spoke to Sibley with equal respect and the same way she spoke to the adults. Ryan was already happy to have Janie and Georgia as neighbors, and he sensed that it would also be good for Sibley.

Ryan climbed back on the mower and continued what he'd started in the front yards. At first, he was puzzled by Janie's reaction to his decision to mow the grass, but it was somewhat high-handed of him now that he thought about it. He had just wanted to repay Janie and Georgia for their kindness with Sibley, but he realized he would have to be careful not to overstep the mark.

The sight of Ryan mowing her yard caused a flip in Janie's stomach that caught her off guard. Mowing was something Daniel had always done. Ryan and Daniel looked nothing alike, but it still gave her a pang. In her mind's eye, she could see her husband atop the lawnmower on any regular day. Ryan was kind to take care of the chore for her and Momma. She'd so enjoyed having Sibley with them for the day and understood how much Ryan appreciated it, so being gracious about him doing such a nice thing for them shouldn't be a big deal. Ryan brought new things into her life, she told herself. Not anything bad. Just new.

The evening was cooling off, and they'd finished most of the after-boating chores. Janie let her mind wander to dinner. She and Momma shared most meals, and since Sibley and Ryan were still here, it was likely they hadn't eaten yet either.

Momma asked Janie the question before she could ask Momma. "What should we do for dinner?"

"Maybe we could get cleaned up and go to the Boathouse since it's getting late." Janie thought of it as she said it. The Bonito Boathouse was one of two restaurants on the island, and they had a killer view upstairs and boasted the best fried shrimp around, and that was saying something.

"Hmm. Sounds good. Should we invite our neighbors to join us?" Momma said this as a suggestion.

"We can ask." Janie experienced a moment of uncertainty about inviting Ryan and Sibley out to dinner with them. It was moving a little farther out on a limb for her, which she seemed to be doing a lot lately.

"Ask what?" Sibley suddenly appeared beside her.

"If the two of you want to join us for dinner at the Boathouse. It's by the marina." Janie smiled at Sibley, not knowing how much she'd heard of their conversation.

"That would be great! Let me check with my dad." Sibley ran off toward where Ryan was climbing off the mower and wiping his face with a towel. It wasn't super hot this time of day, but the heat of a lawnmower's engine almost always made it a sweaty job.

They watched as Sibley asked her dad. She pointed to Janie and then toward the street. Ryan looked over toward where Momma and Janie stood, still at the base of the dock but on the grass. He raised a hand toward them. Then he and Sibley moved in their direction.

Janie would have had to be blind not to notice what an attractive man Ryan was. Athletic build, great legs, and he clearly worked out.

"Sibley tells me you've invited us to dinner at the Boathouse. Can you give me a few minutes to shower and change?"

"I think showers all around might be a good idea before any of us go out in public. We'll meet you at the Boathouse in, say, an hour?" Janie suggested.

"I'll give Joe a call and see if he's eaten yet. He might want to join us." Momma had a soft spot for Joe, though she wouldn't admit it. They'd been friends for years, and Momma and Joe's late wife, Mary, had been besties when Janie was a child.

"Sounds good. See you there."

Sibley skipped through the backyard that separated theirs to get back home. Nobody minded around here, and nobody was there currently. Joe had shared that the owners weren't full-time residents and rented out the house during peak season.

"Oh, and thanks again for mowing our grass. It looks great," Janie said.

"Anytime." Ryan turned and walked over to where the mower sat, raised the mowing blade, and rode it home.

The cool breeze lifted strands of Janie's hair as she sat on the covered deck at the Boathouse, a favorite island restaurant that overlooked the marina. They were all dressed casually in shorts, as everywhere on the island was casual, waiting for the host to show them to their table.

"Thanks for calling, Georgia. This is nice," Joe said to Momma. "We haven't done this in quite a while."

"Glad you could make it. It's good to see you someplace outside of the store."

"Y'all have a nice day?" Joe asked Sibley.

"Yes. It was so much fun. I worked on a picture frame, we saw dolphins, found the *best* shells, and then checked the crab traps on the way home."

"Sounds like you got the full treatment from these two." He indicated Janie and Georgia.

"It was a great day," Janie confirmed. And it had been, for all of them.

"We loved having you with us, Sibley." Momma made sure to follow up with that just before Janie could.

So, she agreed. "Yes, we did."

Ryan hadn't said much during the wait on the deck, and Janie wondered about it.

"Is everything okay?" she asked him as they walked together to their table after the host announced it was ready.

"Yes. Everything's fine."

He smiled at her then, but Janie still got the impression from his quiet manner and stiff shoulders that he had something on his mind.

"How's your tennis season going?" Joe asked Sibley as they made their way to a table beside the window, through which they could see the sun was beginning to set.

She shrugged. "Fine."

"Just fine?" Joe asked. "You used to love it."

"It's not as fun as it used to be when I lived in Beaufort," Sibley replied, her voice melancholy. "You know, when Mom went to my matches and picked me up from practice."

Janie got a punch in her gut on Sibley's behalf and had a strong urge to put an arm around the girl and assure her it would get better. At least Janie hoped it would. Joe had filled Momma in a little about what had gone on with Sibley's mother, so of course Momma had shared that information with Janie to help her understand the teen a little better. Janie glanced over at Ryan, and his frown told her he was uncomfortable with the subject.

"Mom will come around, honey. Remember, we agreed to give her a little time," he said.

"When do you play matches?" Momma asked Sibley, distracting her from the awkward conversation.

Sibley unwrapped her silverware and fiddled with her fork. "After school on Tuesdays and Thursdays. Sometimes we're at our home courts, and sometimes we have to travel to away matches." Sibley gave Momma a shy smile.

Momma always knew the right thing to say.

The waiter brought them menus then, and it was a welcome distraction. They ordered a round of lemonade.

"So, what's good?" Ryan asked as he looked the menu over.

"The fried shrimp here are fantastic," Janie said. "And their salads are good, too."

"The clam strips aren't bad," Joe suggested. "Except for my waistline." They all shared a laugh.

"I love clams. We have this place where they're so good near our house in Beaufort," Sibley said and then looked over at Ryan, a bleak look in her eyes.

It was clear Sibley was struggling with missing her old life, and Janie's heart went out to her. Being a teenager wasn't the easiest thing at the best of times, but the upheaval of moving somewhere new and adjusting to a different way of life, especially with her parents' divorce, was a lot for Sibley.

Ryan frowned at her comment, but he quickly slipped on a neutral expression to hide it. "Why don't we try the clams here and see how they measure up? We can get clams in Beaufort one evening next week after tennis."

They ordered their food then, and Joe and Momma kept the conversation flowing, managing to steer clear of any further awkwardness, for which Janie was grateful. They all dug in when their meals arrived, and the earlier tension dissolved. Sibley's melancholy seemed to ease then. The conversation settled on the scenery as the server cleared their empty plates.

"You can see for miles from here." Ryan pointed toward the enormous picture windows surrounding the restaurant's upper floor on three sides. The sun was at eye level and putting on a show of oranges, the light playing in the clouds against a darkening blue sky.

The waiter stopped by to check on their table. "Can I get y'all anything else?"

The sunset had Janie feeling like a cocktail to end her meal. This evening had turned a bit cloudy, the sun peeking in between the clouds, showing a red-orange fireball as it moved and changed by the minute.

"Could I get a South Island?" Ryan obviously had the same idea, as he ordered the local brew from the menu.

Janie nearly laughed out loud at their similar mindset but, instead, she simply smiled and put in her order. "I'd like a Hang Eleven, please," she said with a glance toward Ryan.

After they'd finished their drinks and paid the bill, the small group made their way outside. As Sibley, Momma and Joe went ahead, chatting about Sibley's sand dollars, Ryan pulled Janie to the side.

"So, I'm thinking about buying a boat, but I don't want to get Sibley's hopes up in case it doesn't work out right away. Where do you suggest I start? Is there someone nearby you'd recommend?"

Janie considered his question. "We bought our boat from Low-country Marine out on Sea Island Parkway, and the owner cuts a fair price. What kind of boat are you looking for?"

"I'm not sure yet. So far, it's been an idea I've had rolling around in my mind. It's a big purchase."

"Huge. Well, let me know how I can help with your search." Janie remembered the excitement of shopping with Daniel for their first boat. The memory was a nice one and didn't seem quite as painful at this moment, which surprised her a little.

"Thanks. I might want to pick your brain again about this in the next few weeks if that's all right."

Janie was touched that he trusted her opinion. "Anytime. You know where to find me."

Chapter Seven

Janie made it to Beaufort by ten on Monday morning when the lawnmower repair shop opened. She picked up the mower belt and did a little shopping at the garden store next door. She was at the gas station filling up when she spotted Ryan at the gas pump next to her. He saw her at about the same time.

"Oh, hey. Did you get your mower belt?" he called over to her.

She waved a hello and answered, "Yes. I was lucky they had some in stock because I had to order one last time."

"How often does the belt snap?" he asked.

"Too often. I should probably give in and buy a new mower, but I just haven't."

"Sounds like you do need a new one." He topped off his tank and replaced the gas cap, then asked, "Hey, do you want to grab some lunch? I've got an hour before I have to get back to the office."

It was only eleven thirty, but she'd eaten early, so lunch sounded good. "Sure."

She'd accepted his invitation without a thought, but the second she'd agreed, Janie experienced a tiny feeling of guilt. Not because she was doing anything wrong; it just felt like a big first. Okay, it was only a bite to eat with her neighbor, nothing more than that, but it was the first time she had been for a meal where it was just her with another man who wasn't Daniel. She knew Daniel would want her to be happy and live her life. But knowing it and doing it sometimes felt at odds.

Ryan walked over to her. "Do you have a favorite lunch spot here in Beaufort?" he asked.

"I hardly ever go out to lunch anymore, so I'll let you decide."

He wrinkled his brow as if he were scrolling through options in his head. "How about the Country Café on Carteret Street?"

"Yes, I know the place. I'll meet you there."

Janie drove to the café, her heart pattering a little in anticipation of lunching in public with Ryan.

Once she pulled up and parked, he joined her on the sidewalk almost immediately and opened the door to the café, stepping back for her to precede him inside.

The historical building had towering ceilings and enormous windows, letting in wide beams of light. A three-sided counter sat in the middle, where white-aproned staff prepared orders. The hostess greeted them and showed them to a booth at the back of the restaurant. As they followed the young woman, Janie passed the section off to the side that sold kitchen wares. Gorgeous tea towels, seagrass baskets, and aprons, among other items, were displayed on old furniture and racks against the wall. There were also dishes of every kind and paintings for sale. It was a lovely place, and Janie always spent a little time browsing when they came here.

The hostess left when they were both seated, promising their server would arrive shortly.

"This is nice. I'm glad you could join me. I rarely leave the office for lunch these days. It's good to get out again," Ryan said.

"Again?" Janie was curious what that meant.

"Since my wife, Leslie, and I split. I used to go home at lunchtime since I lived only a few minutes from the office. Now, I mostly just bring a sandwich or something from home."

"Oh. I'm sorry, I didn't mean to pry." Janie could feel her face flush in embarrassment. Who was she to open up his can of worms?

"No worries. It's been an adjustment, but I'm trudging forward." He smiled at her then as reassurance.

Janie's heart squeezed. She could see the instant surge of... something... in his eyes when he'd said it, but he made a good recovery. Janie couldn't tell for sure what emotions were there, but she thought she'd seen hurt and anger.

Ryan picked up his menu. "So, what's your favorite thing to order here?"

It was clear he didn't want to talk any more about his marriage breakdown, and Janie was happy to move on to smoother territory, too.

"I would have to say the eggs benedict. They serve it over grit cakes." She and Momma ate here occasionally, and both were huge fans of the eggs benedict.

Ryan peered down at his menu. "I'm not sure where to start. The BLT looks good and maybe those house-made fries."

They ordered, and then Janie remembered the donuts. "I've got to tell you that the homemade glazed donuts here are to die for," she said. "Momma has a recipe where she uses them to make a breakfast casserole."

"That sounds like dessert to me, but we'll add some to our order next time our waiter comes by." Which Ryan did a couple of minutes later when he spotted her, motioning her over.

While waiting for the food to arrive, they talked about trivial things, for which Janie was grateful. Talking about personal lives often meant her having to explain Daniel, which was never an easy or welcome conversation. Discussing mowers and the weather was much easier and passed the time until their waiter came back.

"It all looks amazing."

"Do you want to try my eggs?" Janie offered.

"Oh, sure. Thanks." Ryan accepted a sliver of the creamy offering from her plate.

She reached over and plucked a fry from the edge of his. "These are the *best*."

He laughed at her mischievous action. "Ah, I get it now. You offer me food so you can eat my fries. Ulterior motives, huh?"

She raised his hand. "Guilty."

As they were bantering over lunch, Janie noticed Mr. Gardener, their neighbor from across the street. He raised a hand in greeting and headed toward their table. Janie suddenly felt mortified at being caught laughing with another man.

"Hey there, Janie."

Putting on a bright smile, she greeted the man. "Hi, Mr. Gardener. This is Ryan Kennedy, our new neighbor, two doors down." Janie had known the older man since she'd been in her teens and he'd moved in with his wife. They weren't super close, but they were neighborly.

"Great to meet you," said Ryan.

The two men shook hands and exchanged a few words of small talk. All the while, Janie transitioned from embarrassment to a sudden urge to bolt out the door of the lovely restaurant and run home as fast as possible.

Mr. Gardener moved away from their table, leaving Janie and Ryan alone again.

"He seemed nice." Ryan seemed unaware of her discomfort.

"Yeah, he's lived across the street for a long time."

Janie worked to regain her composure. Sitting there, having lunch with a handsome man who wasn't her husband was a giant leap forward from where she'd been only a few weeks ago. But it wasn't coming easily.

Janie was in the kitchen when Momma appeared through the side door. "Were you able to get the belt for the mower?"

"Thankfully they had one in stock." Janie squatted down, swapping out older potatoes for new ones in the bin at the bottom of the pantry. "I ran into Ryan at the gas station and he invited me to lunch."

Momma's eyebrows raised. "How nice of him. Where did y'all go?"

Janie had moved to put away the eggs and milk in the fridge. "The Country Café. I had the eggs benedict, and Ryan had the BLT. And I snagged a few of his fries." Janie filled Momma in on the details, including that they'd bumped into Mr. Gardener.

"Sounds like a nice lunch." Momma's gaze was speculative, and Janie had an idea of what she was thinking.

"It was just lunch, Momma. But yes, it was nice."

Momma held up a hand as if to defend her unspoken words. "Honey, I'm just glad you agreed to go. That, in itself, is a big step."

Janie sighed. "I think a lot about Daniel and our years together." It may only have been a friendly lunch with a male neighbor, but Momma was right. For Janie it was a big step, even though she knew Daniel would have wanted her to move forward with her life. Still, two years on, that was easier said than done.

"And you always will. I've missed your daddy every day since he passed."

"But you didn't find someone else and remarry."

"You were only seven when your dad died. I was busy with you girls still. But, looking back, I kind of wish I had put more effort into myself as well." Momma closed her eyes as if remembering. "That wouldn't have been the worst thing, would it? Finding someone to share my life with? It's been a long time since I've had that."

Janie smiled gently; she would never begrudge her mother's happiness. "Maybe there's still time."

"Oh, honey, not for me. I'm too set in my ways to share my house and my days with a man now. But it's not too late for you. You've got a lifetime of new experiences headed your way if you'd just allow yourself to open up to them."

"I'm trying, I am." She could feel the shift already, and she couldn't deny it felt a little frightening, but Janie knew there was so much more to experience in her life, and she'd start with getting to know the couple of people who'd just been added to it.

Chapter Eight

"So, what's your plan for the day?" Momma asked from her driveway as Janie made her way out to her golf cart. A cool breeze blew in, and a family of deer scampered across the yard. It was a beautiful sight to start the day.

"I'm off to get soil samples where the kites are nesting to make sure they aren't in any danger before the hatchlings start to fly."

Momma wiped her forehead with the back of her garden glove. "Do you need help?"

Janie set her sampling kit on the seat beside her. "No, I don't think so. Thanks, though. The habitat team is sending up a drone in the next few days to get a bird's-eye view of the nests."

"I know they appreciate all you do to protect the birds on the island."

"We're just lucky the kites have chosen Fripp for nesting." She got into the car and started the engine. "See you later!"

Momma threw up a hand and went back to her gardening as Janie drove away.

Janie felt a little thrill of anticipation every time she approached the kite habitat. A sense of purpose and familiarity. Sharing this island and caring for the birds made her days feel more worthwhile. She couldn't imagine not sampling soil, testing for enough rainfall and nutrients near the nests, or worrying if the next big storm would bring ruin to it all.

When Janie arrived, she noticed several large footprints on the soft ground. It looked like a couple sets of them, from what she could see—big boot prints. So far, they'd managed to protect this land. The last thing she needed was to have people who knew nothing about wildlife start invading the area.

Instead of driving herself crazy about it, she focused on her work. She took her soil samples and photos. She'd mention it to the habitat team when she saw them. Perhaps the prints were theirs, and they'd already sent up their drone.

By the time Ryan and Sibley pulled into the driveway that evening, they'd already had two disagreements on the ride home. Ryan's entire day had been challenging. Two of his assistants had called in sick that morning; he'd been booked solid and even had to ask for his front desk worker to give them a hand, which left the desk open and the phone ringing with no one to answer it. He'd not even had time for lunch, and his stomach rumbled as he drove.

"I don't see why I can't go with my friends to a concert," Sibley moaned, continuing their latest argument.

"I'm not comfortable with you going to Charleston without an adult, Sibley," Ryan said, getting out of the car.

Sibley shuffled up beside him as he got the mail and went up to the door. "Why does everybody else get to go but me?"

"Who is *everybody*?" he asked as he slipped his key in the door and let them in.

She rattled off a group of about four names, only two of whom he recognized.

"Who are Jess and Amy?"

"They're a couple of older girls at my school. They can drive us."

He set the handful of sales fliers and bills onto the kitchen counter, flipping through them quickly. "I don't know these girls and, if they're older, I'm not sure you should be hanging out with them."

She shot him a hard eye-roll. "This wouldn't have happened if we hadn't moved. It's like I'm an outcast now. I'm lucky even to get invited anywhere."

Ryan turned his attention to his daughter. "What do you mean you feel like an outcast?"

"My friends do things without me all the time now."

A wave of guilt flattened Ryan for taking Sibley away from her social life. He understood how important having friends and feeling included was for her right now. "I'm sorry you're feeling left out of things."

Sibley sighed. "I like the island, but I feel like I'm constantly missing out on all the fun stuff going on in town. It might be better if I could stay with Mom on some weekends, you know?"

Ryan could hear the vulnerability in her voice, and it pulled at his heartstrings. Even after visiting Leslie the other day, she still hadn't tried to get in touch with Sibley. Ryan wasn't sure what more he could do, but he would keep trying for Sibley's sake.

"Yes, I can see how that would help things with your friends. Mom's going through a rough time right now, but I'll speak with her about you staying there sometime soon."

"Getting my license would solve most of my problems, you know. Then we wouldn't have to ask Mom every time I wanted to do something. I can tell she's not herself lately," Sibley said sadly.

Ryan knew she was trying to put a brave face on things, but he wished Leslie would reach out to her. And as much as he wanted to prolong the inevitable, it was probably time for Sibley to get her license.

"Okay, let's make a deal," he said, relenting. "We'll get your license next week, but the concert is still a no."

He could see the inner struggle of whether to fight for the concert or get the much-anticipated driver's license play out in her expressions.

"Fine," she eventually said. "But once I get my license, you'll need to let me drive by myself to Beaufort."

"Baby steps. We'll discuss it when the time comes."

"You promise to take me to get my license next week?" she asked through a pout.

"I promise."

At least somewhat satisfied with his answer, Sibley went upstairs to her room and left Ryan in the kitchen. He was glad to be home, and all he wanted right now was to eat something, sit out back, and watch the sun set on this day.

After converging once more for a quick dinner of tomato soup and grilled cheese sandwiches, he and Sibley went to their separate corners of the house. She had a ton of homework, and Ryan breathed a sigh of relief as he sat on the back deck and sipped a beer, rolling his head on his shoulders to relax, and closing his eyes.

"Hi there." Janie's voice cut through his moment of Zen.

Ryan opened his eyes to see her standing in front of him. Despite his wanting to be left alone, Janie, with her flaming hair pulled back in a ponytail, was a welcome sight. Her cheerful smile permeated the weight of his stressful day. Whenever he saw her, it was as if the colors around him were brighter.

Janie pointed in the general direction of her yard. "I was out on our dock and saw you sitting here. Mind some company?"

"Glad you stopped by. Would you like a beer?" Ryan offered.

"I would love one. Thanks."

"Awesome." He pulled one of the deck chairs closer to her. "Have a seat and give me just a sec." He unfolded himself from the old chair and headed into the house.

As he ducked inside from the humid evening into the air conditioning, Ryan's exhaustion seeped away. There was something about Janie's spirit that energized and relaxed him all at once. He could tell she was a bit of an introvert, but when she smiled at him, he got a little kick in the gut.

The house was quiet, except for Sibley's music playing behind her closed door upstairs. Ryan grabbed a cold beer from the fridge for Janie. He headed back outside and slid the glass door shut as he handed her the open beer.

"Thanks." She took the bottle and raised it. "Long day at work today?"

Ryan stretched, but his muscles were more relaxed than they had been when he'd first come outside. "Very long. I'm glad to be home. It's nice to see you."

Sharing a beer while the sun played in the sky was comfortable, but he felt an underlying excitement when she was near. He wanted to know her better.

"So, do you know anything about installing lawnmower belts?" she asked. "I've been fighting with it, and it's winning."

"Sure. I can help." He'd been mowing grass since he was fourteen and knew his way around basic repair.

"Tomorrow evening, maybe?" she suggested, raising her eyebrows in question. "Or whenever works best for you."

"Sibley's got a tennis match tomorrow after school, so I should be back here by six. I'll call you after that."

"I would love to watch her play sometime."

"Tomorrow's a home match, so it might be a good one to see." He was thrilled to have her interested in seeing one of Sibley's matches. "I'm sure Sibley would love that."

"I'll plan on it. What time?"

"Four o'clock at Beaufort High," he confirmed.

She nodded. "I'll see you there."

Ryan had to admit that the more Janie came around, the more he wanted to spend time with her. They sat together in comfortable silence as the tide rose.

Ryan later worried a little about the optics of Janie attending Sibley's tennis match. Leslie hadn't bothered to show up at any of them since the season started, which he knew troubled Sibley. He'd invited Janie when she'd shown an interest before thinking it through. Hopefully, there wouldn't be any gossip within the tennis circle of both parents and players about it. Of course, he could be overthinking this. After all, they were neighbors, and Janie had become a friend to Sibley. He could ignore a little gossip. He knew Sibley would love to see Janie in the stands rooting for her.

Chapter Nine

"Good morning, ladies." Joe greeted Momma and Janie from his seat in the shade outside the marina as they drove up in the golf cart. "You're here early this morning."

Momma grabbed the bait bucket from the back of the golf cart and climbed the steps ahead of Janie. "I need a hundred crickets to do some fishing on this fine morning and chicken necks for the crab traps."

"I can definitely take care of that," Joe said with a smile, hoisting himself out of the chair and taking the bucket from Momma. "Got your paper, too. If you want, you can go inside and get it, so you're out of the heat."

"Always remembering my newspaper," Momma said with a smile. "What would I do without you?"

"Y'all are my favorite customers." Joe winked at Janie, the bucket swinging by his side as he headed over to fill it with bait. "Janie-girl, you're looking rather pretty today. New dress?"

"Thanks, Joe," she said, squaring her shoulders, delighting in the compliment. Janie smoothed out her simple cotton tank dress. "It had hit me this morning that I don't dress up anymore, so I figured I should fix that." It was definitely time to bring out some of the things she hadn't worn in a couple of years and she had to admit it felt nice.

Momma stayed outside and made small talk as Joe moved under the shaded lean-to area that housed thousands of crickets, all chirping their song in a large wooden box with a fine mesh across the sides and front. The cricket box smelled terrible, so Janie stood a short distance away. She could handle the odor of shiners and even worms, but the cricket smell was one of her least favorite. It didn't seem to bother either Momma or Joe, though, as they stood shoulder to shoulder peering inside while Joe gathered Momma's bait in a small tube. It would hold roughly one hundred bait bugs.

Janie breathed in the ocean breeze mixed with the usual boat exhaust and gasoline smell associated with the marina. Some things were timeless, like mornings with her momma, going about the routine things they'd done together for so many years. It was comforting to Janie.

"Let's go on inside and grab your paper and whatever else you folks need this morning," Joe said, hunching a little when he walked. Once inside, while Janie perused the shelves of the store, Joe asked, "Y'all see my nephew and grandniece much?"

Momma saved Janie from answering the question. "We see them a bit. Busy people, aren't they?"

When Joe referred to Ryan, Janie had a rush of nerves, especially as she remembered the night before's shared time on the deck. It had just been a drink between friends—they'd hardly talked much—but it was easy and comfortable with Ryan, Janie realized.

"Ready to go, darlin'?" Momma brought Janie out of her musings.

"Sure. After I pay for this." Janie held up a packet of Oreo cookies.

Momma eyed her knowingly. When Janie bought Oreos, there was always something on her mind.

Once they were on their way home, Momma said, "I noticed the cookie purchase. Everything okay?"

"Just a little nervous about the tennis match this afternoon." She'd had a hard time falling asleep last night as she wondered if inviting herself had been a good idea.

"Don't second-guess yourself, darling. What's the worst thing that could happen?"

Janie didn't answer that question. The worst thing had already happened to Janie, so her fears weren't legitimate. It was just a slight case of nerves, she reminded herself.

They returned home and spent a good part of the day working on a tall floor lamp using a unique and significant piece of driftwood for the base. It was a big piece and it took the two of them to stabilize the base while they drilled holes to run the wire through from the floor to the top. The balanced piece of wood stood on its own without a pole, which was a rare find, and they were both pleased with how it was coming on.

"You'd better get showered if you want to make the match on time," Momma reminded Janie.

Janie'd gotten involved with the lamp and, as usual, time had flown. She had loved arts and crafts ever since she was little, building all kinds of things with Momma as a child, and she still had that same sense of wonder and enthusiasm every time she created something new. Her work always managed to soothe her, and her earlier anxieties faded away. Janie had to admit she was looking forward to watching Sibley play. Although if she didn't get a move on, she would be late.

"Oh, you're right. I'll clean this up later." She motioned to the messy workspace with its bits of soldering metal and wire she'd used for the lamp.

Janie rushed inside to get ready, eager to get to Beaufort High to support Sibley.

As Janie made her way to the tennis courts, she walked the familiar paths she'd taken as a youngster. The school still looked like it had when Janie had been a student there, though she noticed the courts had been resurfaced and painted a bright blue with white lines against a green background, instead of the old green on burnt red when Janie had played on them. She approached the low metal bleachers and found Ryan sitting alone. "Hey there." She took the seat next to him.

Ryan turned toward her and greeted Janie with a broad smile, as if her appearance brightened his day. "Thanks for coming."

His reaction put Janie at her ease. She had wondered if he would mind her being here, but he seemed genuinely pleased to see her.

Sibley appeared in her uniform and smiled at Janie. "Oh, hi. I didn't know you were going to be here."

"Your dad said this home match might be a good time to watch. I played line two doubles when I went to school here. Not a superstar, but I still love the sport."

"That's so awesome."

The home team coach called to his players, pulling Sibley's attention in that direction.

"Gotta go. Team meeting."

The home team took over with warmup as the visitors left the courts. Janie couldn't help but admire Sibley's beautiful strokes as she rallied with the other singles player. She was incredibly athletic. Her strokes were near perfect as she hit the ball harder than Janie ever had.

"Wow, she's really talented," Janie exclaimed.

Ryan smiled at that. "She's worked hard to develop her game. Wait until you see her serve."

They sat together in near silence watching his girl, and Janie could see the pride in his expression.

Sibley's opponent entered the court and put down her bag while Sibley spun the racket to determine who should serve first. As the match got underway, Janie became fully invested, watching every serve, every point, every game with a mixture of nerves and excitement, while Ryan sat riveted beside her. They didn't speak, instead following every shot and rally with their eyes. Sibley was fierce and confident, and she seemed to be in her zone while playing.

The match was close, with Sibley winning in a third-set tie-break to Janie's delight.

"That was impressive. I'm so happy I got to watch her play," Janie said, her heart still pattering from the excitement of the match.

"That was a little too close for comfort," Ryan said, the earlier intensity she'd seen in the rise of his shoulders subsiding.

After receiving kudos from her coach and fellow players, Sibley approached happily, her face flushed.

Ryan squeezed her shoulder with evident pride. "Great job, honey."

"Awesome match, Sibley. I picked a good one to watch," Janie said.

"Thanks for coming. I'm so excited that we won our first two singles matches!" Sibley was jubilant, and Janie was thrilled to see her in her element.

The small crowd around them on the bleachers cheered on Sibley's teammates as the matches continued.

"Do you need to stay and watch the rest of your teammates play?" Ryan asked.

Sibley shook her head. "No, I asked my coach if I could leave after my match."

The three of them made their way from the courts, with Sibley still on cloud nine, speaking rapid-fire about the match.

When they reached the parking lot where Janie's car sat, Ryan asked, "You still want help with the mower today?"

"If it's not a bother," she replied, not wanting to step in on Sibley's celebrations.

"No bother at all. I'll be over in a little while."

"I appreciate it."

"Sibley, did you want to ask about your project?" Ryan asked.

"Oh, yes!" Sibley shuffled over to Janie. "I have a project to do for my art class, and I wondered if you could help me with it. You and Miss Georgia are so creative."

Janie felt touched by the girl's compliments. "Of course, I'll help in any way. I can't wait to hear about it. Come on over when we get back so you can show me what you have in mind."

Sibley smiled. "Thanks so much."

"See you both soon." As she drove home, Janie basked in a tiny glow of satisfaction at Sibley's asking her for help.

By the time Sibley came over by herself later that evening, Ryan had been and gone, and Janie had a mower that was working again. Sibley pulled out a sketch from her backpack and showed it to Momma.

"It's a necklace made out of a shell and some beads on a leather cord. The design sketch is part of my grade, and then creating the piece is the other part."

Janie took the page from Sibley and studied it, noticing how artistic and detailed it was. Sibley had rendered a tiny clamshell with a bead on each side. They could knot the cord on the end and crimp a tiny metal clasp as a fastener. It was simple but, with the right shell, would be worthy of any local jewelry store. Janie was impressed.

"Oh, this is lovely."

"Thanks. I thought I would use saltwater pearls for the beads," Sibley suggested, looking at Janie as if for approval.

"What a nice idea. You could add another saltwater pearl for the clasp if you wanted," Momma said.

"Have you chosen your shell?" Janie asked.

"Not yet, but I can find one on the beach."

"No need." Momma ran over and grabbed a few of the jars they used to hold all the shells. "Honey, we've got buckets. Every time we go out, we pick up a few special shells. You're welcome to go through them and find the perfect one for this piece."

Sibley's eyes lit up. "Oh, wow. That's great."

"Whenever you want to come, I'll make sure to open up the doors and turn on the fans. Just text me." The temps were rising in the afternoons lately, so the more ventilation, the better.

"Thanks so much for letting me do this. I need to sketch it to scale tonight, with as much detail as possible. Can I look through the shell bucket now so I can add it to my sketch?"

"Knock yourself out." Momma grabbed a couple of the large plastic bins from under a shelf. "Here they are. You can choose whatever strikes you and take a few different ones in case you aren't sure which might work best."

"Y'all have the best stuff in here." Sibley walked over and ran her finger along the large lamp on the workbench. "Wow, that's pretty cool."

It was cool. Or it would be once they'd finished with it and added a nice shade. It had been a consignment order from her sister Jaclyn's accessories shop for a client.

"Thanks. We're almost done with it," Janie said.

Janie smiled to herself. It was nice to have Sibley visit. She pushed down the pang of longing for a child of her own to love and teach. She and Daniel had planned to try to start a family around the time he'd passed away. Still, she felt lucky to be able to share her time with young people like Sibley Kennedy. Sometimes life just didn't turn out the way you had hoped.

Chapter Ten

The fish were biting. Janie was glad that she and Momma had gone out on the water as soon as the tide would allow. The trout all but jumped in the boat with them. They were good-sized and very few were under the legal weight limit, which meant they were keepers.

Momma fought with her rod, leaning back. "Wow, this one's a fighter."

She reeled in the line and Janie grabbed the net, scooped up the flopping fish, and dropped it in the boat's live well.

They were so busy rebaiting their lines and hauling in the fish that the tide had gotten low. Before heading home, they quickly checked and rebaited the crab traps, which had been empty earlier. Janie had to carefully maneuver the boat through the canal, hoping to avoid the shallowest spots where they might get stuck in the mud.

It was past five o'clock when they finally unloaded and hosed off the boat. Using the winch to lift the hull out of the water, Janie throttled it onto the rollers to dry-dock it. Not leaving the boat down in the water helped preserve the fiberglass bottom.

Janie rolled the cooler filled with all the fish they'd caught up to the top of the dock. As she opened the cooler, preparing to start the cleaning process on the outdoor wooden surface near the hose bib, Janie noticed Sibley walking through their backyard.

"Wow, y'all caught a lot of fish today," the girl said.

Janie was hot and sweaty and likely smelled as bad as the actual fish. "Yes, it was a good day on the water."

"Is it okay if I work on my necklace in your shop?" Sibley asked.

Momma had just finished hosing off the life jackets and was laying them out to dry. "I'll take you while Janie cleans the fish. Is that okay?"

Sibley glanced over at Janie. After a slight hesitation, she said instead, "Okay, great," and followed Momma.

"The jewelry tools are in a small yellow box on the back shelf," Janie called out to their retreating backs. She then noticed Ryan was heading her way through the yard.

"What a mess of fish," he said when he reached the end of the dock, peering inside the cooler at Janie's feet. "That's a big job. Do you need some help?" He stepped toward her and wiped something off her forehead. "You had a little something…"

Janie wished she'd had the chance to shower and change her clothes before seeing him. "Um… thanks. You're welcome to clean some of these and take them home with you if you'd like."

"How can I refuse? I'll go get my fillet knife." Ryan grinned at her. "Be right back."

When he jogged off, she couldn't deny the happiness that bubbled up inside her.

On Ryan's return, he pulled the knife from its sheath. After a lifetime on the island, Janie knew a quality blade when she saw one. She raised her brows at the masterful craftsmanship of it.

"Wow. Very nice."

"Joe gave it to me when I turned fifteen. He was insistent that I learn to properly fillet my catch. But the quality of the knife says nothing about my skill, so no judgments." He smiled at her.

"I'm thrilled to have help with this embarrassment of riches, so I promise not to judge."

They worked together, teasing each other about the other's fish-cleaning technique. And Janie had to admit, he was very good at it. His strong hands worked deftly on the task. She almost cut herself because she was distracted watching him.

"You're falling behind," he joked as he reached down and grabbed another trout from the cooler.

"I hate cleaning fish, so thanks for helping and keeping me company." Janie tried hard not to think about how she must look—and smell—with her hair falling out of its tie and the stench of a day's fishing clinging to her.

"It's not where I saw myself this evening, but I can't wait to grill these up." Ryan indicated the mounting pile of fillets.

"It's a great fish for grilling. Even better right out of the water."

It took another solid hour before they got the job done. They had fifty or so fillets between them, and Janie handed Ryan five or six bags with three-to-four pieces in each.

"Are you sure you want me to take all these?" he asked as he looked down at the packages in his hands.

Janie rinsed the cleaning surface, cooler, and surrounding area. "Absolutely. If you run out, please ask for more. We had a huge haul today, and there are already plenty in the freezer. Thanks again for helping me get this done so quickly. I would've had to finish in the dark otherwise." As it was, the sky was still bright and sunny.

"How about I grill them, and we can share them for dinner over at my place?" Ryan suggested.

"Um, okay. That sounds awesome." She stacked another bag of fillets on top of the ones he held. "These are for us."

He laughed. "Give me an hour."

"We'll bring salad and potatoes when we come."

"Great. See you in a bit." Ryan turned and carefully made his way toward his house, juggling the bags of fish.

Relieved that the job was done, Janie replaced the remaining filled bags into the now-clean cooler so she could roll them across the yard and straight into the garage where the outdoor freezer sat. Ryan had made a mundane task fun.

"Hi, Janie," Sibley said as Janie headed into the garage. She and Momma appeared hard at work on something at the workbench.

Momma moved to where Janie was transferring their catch into the freezer. "Well, you cleaned the fish fast."

"Ryan came over and helped me. I promised to share." Janie pulled out a bag of ice and slid it into the utility sink.

"I'm almost finished with the necklace." Sibley was sitting on a stool beside the work area. "It's coming out great."

"Fantastic. I'm sorry I couldn't help you today, but your dad is going to grill some of the fish for us at your house."

"Ooh. He makes the best grilled fish with lemon and butter."

"Sounds heavenly." Janie turned to Momma. "I told him we'd bring over a salad and some potatoes."

"Okay, how about you shower off while I go inside and get it started."

Sibley stood and zipped up her backpack. "I'm finished for now until the glue dries, so I'll head home and get cleaned up. I'm still sweaty from tennis practice."

As Sibley headed back home, Janie stood for a moment. The anticipation of going to Ryan's place for dinner gave her a thrill. Every time she saw him, her heart sped up just a little… or maybe a lot. Either way, she was looking forward to spending another evening with him.

Janie showered quickly and dressed in another one of her closet-recycles she'd recently pulled from the back. It was a gauzy navy-and-white sleeveless tank—a definite step up from her fishing duds but still fairly casual paired with white cotton shorts. It felt good to have a reason to look nice.

So many of the people Janie knew on the island had been a part of her life for many years, and she was comfortable in her daily interactions with them, never feeling that she needed to dress up. This was definitely a change to her regular evening routine. Once again, the new neighbors factored into her and Momma's actions, and Janie had to admit that having them there added a cheerful air to her day. It had forced her out of her comfort zone lately, and Janie was pretty okay with that. She was much more okay with it than she had imagined she would be.

Ryan stood at the grill on the deck and brushed the fish with garlic butter, sprinkled on dill, and squeezed fresh lemon on both sides.

"Looks delicious."

He turned to find Janie admiring his work. Having her there added a tinge of excitement for Ryan—something he'd not experienced in quite a while.

"Should I put these inside?" She held up a bowl and an insulated zippered bag.

"Sure. You can use the oven if you need to keep something warm." Ryan pointed toward the back door that led into the kitchen. "Grab yourself a beer if you want one."

"Can I get you anything while I'm inside?" she asked, her skin glowing in the evening humidity.

He raised a glass bottle from the surface beside the grill. "I'm good. Thanks."

Ryan turned and watched as Janie made her way through the grass to the back deck. She moved with natural grace and was so different from Leslie. Janie seemed more connected to nature and less fussy about her clothing and appearance. She appeared comfortable in her skin, except when she blushed, which was a breath of sweet, island air.

Leslie had always been an attractive woman, but over time she seemed more concerned about how things looked from others' perspectives. Maybe it was insecurity, or she wanted her life to be different. She'd certainly made it different the moment he'd found out about her affair with Sibley's coach. Before he could dwell on that thought any longer, Janie returned, holding a local brew Ryan had recently discovered.

"This is good. I haven't tried it before." Her tanned limbs were perfection in her shorts and sleeveless top.

"It's new to me, too. I'm a fan," he said, adjusting the flame now that the grill was up to full heat. "It's from a local brewery on the way to Charleston."

Janie's attention moved to the bright-blue sky above her, and she pointed. "Look, a kite."

His eyes followed her finger to where a large bird flew above the treetops. "Wow, such a pretty bird. A kite, huh?" He watched the large black-and-white bird with its forked tail.

"Yes, it's called a swallow-tailed kite," she said, her eyes not breaking contact with the bird since spotting it.

Georgia made her way toward them through the backyard.

Ryan waved her over. "I'm glad you could make it."

"Oh, honey, me too. It's nice not to have to do all the work once in a while."

"Thank y'all for doing the sides. Makes my job easier too," Ryan said. "You ladies have a seat. The fish is almost ready."

Janie and Georgia lowered themselves into a couple of chairs near the grill at the bottom of the deck.

Sibley came bounding out from the back door.

"Got all your homework done?" Ryan asked her.

"Yes. *Finally*." She gave a dramatic eye roll, and they all laughed.

Ryan had noticed that she'd been on her phone a lot more lately, both texting and talking, so he wondered how much of her time she spent upstairs actually doing homework. As long as her grades were good, he wouldn't complain.

"Fish is ready." He carefully picked up the grilling pans, using a potholder on each side. "I figured we could eat at the table on the deck, if that suits everyone."

"Sounds great. I'll go in and get the salad and potatoes," Janie offered.

Sibley jumped up. "I'll give you a hand."

Ryan brought the two grilling baskets to the table and set them down on the trivets in the center.

Janie and Sibley came back with the dishes Georgia had prepared. The potatoes were simple, with a hint of sea salt and garlic, and a salad rounded out the meal with garden tomatoes and cucumbers. Once all the food was on the table, they dug in.

"Dad, this is the best fish you've ever cooked." Sibley closed her eyes and gave a delighted little moan.

Her compliment warmed Ryan's heart. Moving here to the island, Ryan had noticed some promising changes in Sibley's outlook. She was far less emotional lately and easier to reason with, and she had begun to accept that things here were different but not so bad, and that it was a trade-off from living in town. There was no doubt in his mind that Janie and Georgia had helped Sibley immeasurably, and he was grateful to them both for taking the time to spend with his daughter, helping her to settle in and appreciate island life.

Ryan occasionally noticed how she breathed in the air here and looked out over the water, drinking in the sight of the sunset, and how she appeared more peaceful. Nothing was solved, but she was less reactive and more accepting. Sibley had always been a kindhearted, loving child, and he was beginning to see that young woman again, and that meant everything to Ryan.

Chapter Eleven

Janie jumped when the thunder cracked less than a second after the flash of lightning. Intense storms were forecasted this afternoon, so she and Momma worked out in the shop for as long as possible until the thunder began, one rumble after another. Lightning flashed through the small windows that lined the top of the garage door.

"Might be time to head inside," Janie suggested.

Momma eyed the dark-gray sky through the open garage door. "Those clouds are rolling, and you know what that can bring."

"Tornadoes," Janie replied.

Janie quickly capped the adhesive and tidied up the workspace where they'd been fashioning a mosaic of sea glass for a client of her sister Joy. Once they got everything secured, they dashed inside, keeping one eye on the storm in case they needed to find shelter in the basement.

Janie settled in, facing the troubled sea with a hot cup of tea, and a blanket on her legs to try to calm her nerves, as a streak of lightning lit the sky. The following boom was so loud it shook the house.

"That was a close one," Momma said.

The island's tornado sirens went off then, causing Janie to grab her tea and move into the house's interior with Momma. Janie pulled up the weather app on her phone. The radar showed a cluster of colorful storms heading their way.

"It's not looking good at all."

Tornadoes scared her for obvious reasons and also because they could unseat the kites' nests in the tall trees on the other side of the island. They'd been lucky enough that the birds had come back after the last big hurricane, but it was always a worry that they wouldn't do so again.

Janie thought too of the day during an unexpected storm, a lot like this one, when she'd lost Daniel. They'd been out on the water in the boat and cut it too close leaving Prichards Island. Since then, Janie truly comprehended how dangerous the weather could be and how suddenly things could change.

"I'm worried about the hatchlings." Janie felt an immediate urge to go out there and make sure they were okay.

"There's nothing we can do until this weather passes." Momma eyed her as if to say, *don't even think about it.* It was a throwback to when Janie was younger and more foolish. She'd ignored her mother's warnings then and gone out in the middle of a storm to check on the birds when Daniel was away. The birds had weathered the storm, but a falling tree had nearly landed on Janie.

Janie knew her momma was right, and she'd just have to ride out this storm, hoping the birds' nests went untroubled.

When the storm finally moved away and the radar was clear, Janie grabbed her binoculars, a light rain jacket, and tennis shoes, and headed outside. As she was about to pass Ryan's house, she noticed he was out picking up tree limbs. The giant pin oak in his front yard must've caught some wind.

Janie stopped and called to him. "You need any help?"

He shook his head and threw a few small branches in a pile by the base of the tree, then walked over to where she sat in her golf cart on the edge of his driveway. "Where are you off to?"

"I'm going to have a look around the island. The storm was pretty intense, and I like to know that everything is okay. It's kind of a thing with me." She didn't expand on *why* it was such a thing with her.

"Do you want some company? I'm happy to help."

"Sure." Janie was a little surprised at his offer, but it would be nice to have an extra set of hands and eyes, just in case.

"Let me stick my head inside and let Sibley know where I'll be." He jogged over to his front door and leaned in. A minute later, he was back. "Okay, all set."

Janie wasn't ready to share the bird habitat with Ryan or anyone, so she decided to delay heading over there until she'd done her usual rounds of the island. It shouldn't take too long, and her sense of urgency to check on the nests could wait just a little while.

"I guess with as many afternoon storms as we have here, you make the rounds pretty often," Ryan said.

His shoulder occasionally brushed hers as they bumped along, and she could feel the warmth of it.

"They keep me hopping, for sure."

He looked around as if soaking in the sights. "This island is wilder and more natural, as opposed to some of the other country club vacation islands."

She was thrilled that he'd realized how lucky they were to live on Fripp. "Yes. What we have here is special."

They made steady progress, waving at those outdoors and lending a hand to a few folks by helping them pick up limbs and debris. Janie stopped at the house of Mrs. Eldredge, an elderly lady who was slowly making her way around her yard, collecting small sticks. Janie noticed there were a few larger branches that had fallen as well.

"Oh, hi, Janie. I wondered when I might see you. So, is this Joe's nephew, Ryan?"

There weren't any secrets on Fripp, so it didn't surprise Janie that Mrs. Eldredge knew Ryan's name.

"Yes, this is Ryan. Ryan, this is Mrs. Eldredge. She makes the best key lime pie on the island."

Ryan waved and grinned. "Hello. It's nice to meet you."

"Aren't you a handsome devil, just like your uncle back in the day."

"Thank you." Ryan grinned graciously. Then he got to work, dragging a large limb to the edge of the yard, where the local trash pickup would clear it.

Janie went to grab one of the larger ones, but it was heavier than she'd first thought.

"Here, let me help." Ryan gripped the limb on the other side and helped her drag it to the small pile they were creating.

"You two are so kind. I'll have to make you a pie." Mrs. Eldredge winked at them both.

"Sounds incredible, ma'am."

They moved on through the narrow streets. Thankfully, the storm hadn't caused too much damage. Mostly just fallen branches. The deer were coming out again and appeared to be okay.

"Thank you for coming with me."

Without even thinking, Janie put her hand on Ryan's arm, and his gaze zeroed in on it. Her breath caught when she noticed the hint of a smile.

After she'd dropped off Ryan, Janie headed back out to check on the kites' nests. It was her sacred spot—well, hers and Daniel's.

As soon as she arrived, Janie pulled out her binoculars. She peered through them to check the tall, skinny trees and noticed immediately that one in the small grouping of loblolly pines was leaning against the others.

"*Oh, no,*" Janie whispered. If she wasn't mistaken, there was a nest at the top of that tree, but Janie couldn't get a good look at it from the roadside.

She worked to calm her hammering heart and prepare herself for what she might find as she crashed through the brush without regard to the puddles of water and mud. The second she got close enough, it was evident to Janie that the leaning trunk was the second-tallest one, and it had a nest still clinging to the treetop. It appeared not to have toppled sideways... yet.

Janie was overwhelmed with emotion but fought her reaction to think clearly. The bark was sheared off the leaning tree, so she first looked around her feet carefully to see if any of the hatchlings had fallen, but, fortunately, she couldn't see any. Then, Janie pulled out her binoculars and focused them on where the lightning had struck. The nest sat precariously on the very tip of one of the branches.

The hatchlings were only twelve days old. Janie pictured their little bald bodies, mouths wide open, waiting for incoming food from their momma's beak. Janie fought the tears that came instantly. They were so helpless.

She would need to contact the wildlife commission to see if they could get a drone up there to assess the nest's risk. And, in the meantime, she could only pray they didn't have another big storm.

Ryan couldn't get Janie off his mind. Her dedication to the people on the island had impressed him. It was the same way she'd handled his daughter these past few weeks. Lending support to a young girl she'd just met.

The more Ryan learned about Janie and her big heart, the more he was drawn to her and hoped to know her better. Every time he caught sight of her, even in passing—that quick flash of red hair never failed to draw his attention.

"Hi, Dad," Sibley said, rubbing her eyes. Her face was scrubbed clean for the night, and her hair was pulled back in a ponytail. "I'm going to bed." She yawned.

"Did you talk to Mom?" he asked. Ryan had pretty much left their communication between the two of them, and Leslie had seemed to step up when Ryan sent her another message letting her know that Sibley could do with some contact.

Ryan spotted the relief in Sibley's eyes as she answered. "Yes. She says she's going to try to make my next home match. Mom's gotten a job. Did you know that?"

Leslie hadn't worked since Sibley was born. Before that, she'd been the office manager at a local doctor's surgery. Their separation had come with a temporary property settlement. Ryan had agreed to continue to pay most of the bills, and he also sent a monthly amount to cover other household expenses, so the news came as a surprise. "I hadn't heard that. Where's she working?"

"At a boutique downtown. She's the manager." Sibley sounded slightly proud of her mother's new status, and Ryan hoped that mother and daughter were beginning to build bridges.

"Good for her." He tried to remain neutral when discussing Leslie, but the tension was still palpable. So, he changed the subject to something else. "How do you feel about getting your license after school next Wednesday?"

Her face lit up. "Yes! Do you have an appointment? Because we'll need one."

"I didn't realize that. You'll likely have to miss tennis practice to get there before closing time."

"I'll talk to Coach tomorrow about it. Thanks, Daddy."

She leaned down and kissed his cheek, her clean, powdery scent taking him back to the early days when he'd throw her up on his shoulders. She'd cover his eyes to hold on, giggling.

He watched her bound back up the stairs, an extra spring in her step. Seeing Sibley more relaxed and less angry was good for his soul. Her happiness meant everything to him.

Chapter Twelve

A missed call from Leslie illuminated Ryan's phone, knotting his stomach. She'd left him a voice message to call her back when he got the chance. Since he had a half hour until it was time to pick up Sibley from the school, he worked on finishing his patients' charts for the day before dialing Leslie's number.

She answered on the first ring. "Hi, Ryan. Thanks for getting back to me."

"No problem. What's wrong?" They didn't call each other just to chat these days, so he figured there must be a problem.

"I was wondering if you'd be able to stop by and check out the sink in the kitchen? It's dripping, and I can't get a plumber out until tomorrow."

Ryan wasn't sure how to respond. Instead of remarking about not being a handyman, he said instead, "I'm nearly certain it can wait for a plumber."

"The drip is under the sink and it's puddling in the cabinet. I knew you could fix it in a second like you did the bathroom faucet a few years ago. I can't get it to stop."

He exhaled loudly into the phone. "You know I'm picking up Sibley soon, right?"

"It's fine to bring her with you. It would be nice to see her."

His daughter was finally showing signs of life after their split, and returning to her old house, reminding her of life as it was before she and Ryan had moved out might not be in her best interest.

Conflicted, Ryan said, "Leslie, I'm going to need to speak with Sibley before I can agree to that."

There was a brief hesitation on her end. "Okay. Let me know once you talk to her."

"I'm assuming you've got something under the sink to catch the drip? And make sure to wipe up the water so the wood doesn't absorb the wetness and warp. Also, you might want to turn off the water underneath the sink, just in case."

"Got it. I've dried underneath and put a Tupperware container under the leak in the meantime."

"Okay, I'll call you back shortly." When he disconnected the call, he shook his head, wishing he could avoid going back into his old life, especially with Sibley.

He pulled into their regular meeting place in the school parking lot. A sweaty Sibley approached the car with her Beaufort High School tote bag and pink backpack dangling from her shoulder. Seeing her was the best part of his day, no matter how long a day it was.

"Hey there, honey." Ryan grinned at her.

"Hey." Her shoulders sagged a little from her exhaustion. "What's for dinner? I'm starving." He tried to feed her as soon as possible after her workouts.

"I haven't made a plan yet. Any good ideas?"

She slid into the seat and closed the car door. "Can we get clams at the waterfront?"

"Okay, but your mom called about the kitchen sink leaking. How would you feel about stopping by so I can have a look at it? It should only take a couple of minutes." Ryan was curious about Sibley's reaction, so he watched her closely, protective of his daughter's fragile emotions.

"Um, I mean, I guess that would be okay. I haven't been there in so long... Do you think my room is still the same?"

Sibley's question hung between them.

Ryan hoped so; he really did. "I assume it's the same."

After Ryan found out about the affair, things had been tense in the house leading up to the move. It had taken a couple of weeks to find a rental on the island, so they'd had to wait to move out. Sibley had brought her personal items with them, but most of her furniture and décor had stayed at the house with Leslie. Ryan had wanted to leave a comfortable space for Sibley at her mom's if she visited. Much of what he'd moved had been spare bedroom furniture, a few lamps and accessory pieces, and his office furniture. Leslie was a big fan of redecorating every few years, so there had also been quite a bit of furniture in the storage area over the garage. He'd gone through that and found most of what they'd needed to outfit the rental house.

"Okay. Can we get clams after?" Sibley asked.

"You bet."

They drove the ten minutes from the school to the house. It was like second nature to take this route, although he felt different driving it since the move.

Ryan pulled up and looked over at Sibley. "You okay?"

She nodded, but there was a tiny line of concern between her brows as if she were nervous about coming back. Ryan understood that feeling, but he didn't plan on hanging around; he would go in, get the job done, and they'd be on their way.

They climbed out of the truck, and Ryan and Sibley approached the front steps. Before they could ring the doorbell, Leslie opened the door. Instead of her usual well-groomed self, she appeared haggard and wore a pair of old sweats, her hair thrown up in a ponytail. Ryan tried to hide his surprise. Leslie had *always* showered and dressed carefully for the day as long as he'd known her.

"Sibley. I've missed you so much, honey." Leslie greeted her daughter with emotion, her arms outstretched. "Can I give you a hug?"

Sibley hadn't missed her mother's dishevelment—Ryan could see the question in her eyes.

But she said, "I've missed you, too, Mom." Then she stepped into her mother's arms.

Leslie was the first to pull back. She placed her hands on Sibley's shoulders and stared at her daughter for another few seconds, a yearning in her expression.

Then Leslie turned her gaze to Ryan. "Thanks for coming. You've always been so handy with things like this." There was something in her eyes that he couldn't quite read.

"I'll just go have a look," he said, eager to get this over and done. It wasn't easy for him, either, coming back to the home they'd shared as a family.

Leslie moved aside to allow them to enter.

"I'm going to my room." Sibley didn't waste time getting to what was important to her.

"Sure. I'm storing a few things in there while I redo my office." Leslie turned to Ryan. "You know I've gotten a job, right?"

"Yes, Sibley told me. Congratulations." Ryan was glad she'd gotten a job because it gave her something on which to focus.

Sibley took off toward her room, and Leslie followed Ryan into the kitchen.

"Is everything okay?" she asked as he reached down to open the cabinets under the sink.

Ryan contemplated what she'd meant with her question. "Things are fine. The office is busy as usual, and we're settling in on the island."

"Todd and I broke up." She dropped that like a bomb between them while Ryan's head was inside the cabinet. "He wasn't who I believed he was."

Ryan let out an incredulous laugh and looked up from where he was lying under the sink. But the anguish on her face softened him. "I'm sorry you were misled," he said. How the tables had turned.

Leslie dropped down to the floor beside him, so they were nearly at eye level. "I'm so sorry for what I put you and Sibley through. I'm so ashamed." She covered her face with her hands.

Ryan ducked out from under the sink. "Leslie, I don't know what to say to that. I'm making a home for Sibley out on the island. She's been incredibly hurt by all this, and my focus is on her."

"You were always such a good daddy to her." Leslie stared at him with tears brimming in her eyes.

"She's my whole life now." That was the truth.

"What about me? Do I still fit anywhere in your life?"

Ryan just stared at her, entirely without words to respond. "What in the hell is that supposed to mean, Leslie?" he eventually asked.

"I just…" Her lip wobbled, and then she looked at him with the fondness that she had in the early days of their relationship. "Sometimes I think—"

"The garbage disposal is leaking," he said, cutting her off. How dare she put him in this position. "Keep the water turned off, and don't use it until the plumber can get here tomorrow. You might need a new one."

"Dad, look what I found. I thought I'd lost him." Sibley entered the kitchen, tearing through the moment.

He stood up and looked to see that Sibley held a stuffed monkey. The one he'd given her after a trip to the zoo when she was about ten. "Wow, Mr. Smiley. I haven't seen him in a long time," he said, producing a smile for Sibley's benefit.

"I found him in a box in my room."

"Yes, I found him in the attic." Leslie smiled sadly at her daughter, her eyes showing regret.

But Ryan wasn't about to let Leslie manipulate his daughter, even if she didn't have bad intentions. Only selfish ones.

"Well, that's it," he said, wiping his hands on his jeans. "Sibley is starving, so we need to go." He ushered Sibley out the door, reconsidering his decision to come back.

Chapter Thirteen

Janie returned to the habitat, hoping and praying that the nest was still hanging on. She'd already contacted the head of conservation with the shoreline group where Daniel had worked for help. She'd loaded up several flat pieces of thick foam packaging from two pairs of fragile glass lamps, old towels, and a thick comforter that had seen better days to help with their mission to create a soft landing place for the nest, should the worst happen and it, or any of the babies, fall.

Even though Momma had offered her help, Janie didn't want her to risk tripping on the uneven ground since it was still slippery in places from the excessive rain of the past week. So it was taking her several trips to move the items to where the nest still tilted precariously. It didn't appear to have moved since her last visit, which was a relief.

Janie noted as best she could the likely landing spots, should the nest fall. The sharp Palmetto was her main concern, so she laid the thick foam on the spiky bushes that surrounded the tree, then she spread the towels and the comforter around any possible landing areas. Janie was sweating buckets by the time she'd finished. The humidity was extremely high, and it was getting hotter by the day.

Once she'd padded the area, Janie took more photos to show Bob at the university. The drone photographer was scheduled to come out tomorrow afternoon, so that would give an accurate bird's-eye view of the babies in the nest. Even with a telephoto lens, the hatchlings weren't visible; she just hoped they were all safe. The birds were like family, and Janie would do anything to protect them.

"I don't know, man. Let me see what arrangements I can make for Sibley. I haven't left her overnight in a long time," Ryan said to his old college buddy, Mark. He had called Ryan, just as he was leaving the practice, with an invitation for an overnight trip to go fishing on Mark's new cruiser in Hilton Head. Ryan's interest was piqued at the idea of a fishing trip, but he had to think of Sibley. "I'll let you know tonight."

Ryan had continued to search for the right boat for him over the past few weeks but hadn't made a purchase yet, and just thinking about being on the water again made him wish he had. After Ryan hung up, he immediately felt guilty for considering leaving Sibley overnight. But maybe he could make it work. Still, he hesitated to ask Leslie since they'd not done anything like this since he and Sibley had moved out.

When Ryan picked up Sibley, he switched to the passenger's side so she could drive. She'd had her learner's permit over a year, but he realized she hadn't done a lot of driving recently. She seemed to have lost a little of her initial excitement about getting behind the wheel since they'd moved.

Sibley grinned when he handed her the keys. "I'm driving home?"

"It's time you got used to the route—especially in traffic. You've mostly driven without any, and I know you can do it." Ryan smiled his encouragement.

"Thanks, Daddy." Then she asked, "Did you get my driver's license appointment?"

He nodded. "I scheduled it for Wednesday. Does that work?" Ryan asked.

"That works for me. I talked to Coach Walker, and he said to let him know when it was. Of course, he didn't want me to be away on a match day, but he said I could miss practice this once."

She adjusted her seat and mirrors as he'd taught her. She'd had driver's ed training, too, so Ryan felt pretty confident this was a good idea. Well, almost confident. He tried not to seem anxious when she drove, but she'd caught him gripping the passenger door from time to time. He sent up a silent prayer as she put the truck in reverse.

"Slow down a little as you approach the bridge, okay?"

She rolled her eyes. "I know."

The journey passed without incident, and Ryan found himself relaxing as they headed toward Fripp.

He waited until she'd safely parked in their driveway to mention the fishing trip. "Hey, honey, how would you feel if I went fishing this weekend? I'd be gone one night."

Sibley's head swiveled his way at his unexpected question. "Where would I go?"

"I could try your mom, if you're ready, or I guess we could ask Janie." Janie's name came so easily to him. She was one of the few people with whom Ryan felt utterly confident in leaving Sibley.

"I don't want to go back to Mom's house yet, Daddy." Sibley slumped her shoulders. "I felt awkward when we stopped by to fix the sink. And she has so much stuff in my room, you know? It's like she's turned it into storage instead of keeping it for me. Can I ask to stay with Janie?"

He tried to suppress a heavy sigh at his disappointment in Leslie's choices. "Okay. I'll speak with her about it this evening."

"I think Janie likes hanging out with me. I wonder if she's lonely all by herself," Sibley said, sounding especially wise for her years.

Ryan thought about her words for a second. "I don't know if she's lonely, but I do know she likes spending time with you." Janie always seemed so filled with purpose that it hadn't occurred to him that she might be lonely. Uncle Joe said she'd lost her husband in a tragic accident a couple of years ago, so it made sense that she could be lonely. He, too, was lonely sometimes. Sibley was excellent company, but it was a different kind of seclusion when one's spouse was gone for good.

He opened his door and got out, and Sibley did the same, grabbed her backpack, and then came around the back of the truck and handed him his keys.

"Thanks. Great job on the driving."

"Do you think I'm ready for my license?" She slid a glance at him. Sibley had been so insistent on getting her driver's license it hadn't occurred to him that she might be a little nervous about it.

"I do."

"Thanks, Daddy." She threw her arms around him and hugged him before she raced toward the front door.

Ryan felt overjoyed by Sibley's affection, and he finally felt as if he was making slow but steady progress with her. The past months had been incredibly rocky, and it warmed his heart that they were getting back some of the closeness they'd lost.

Janie and Momma were still working in the shop when Ryan poked his head inside. He wore his work scrubs and sported a deliciously handsome five o'clock shadow. Sibley stood just behind him.

"Hi there," said Ryan.

"Oh, hi," Janie said.

Ryan leaned against the jamb of the door, appearing relaxed, and made a bit of small talk about Sibley's tennis match until Momma showed Sibley some new sea glass she'd gotten.

"Sibley and I have a favor to ask," he said once it was the two of them. "Well, mostly me. I'm considering going on an overnight fishing trip with a buddy of mine. I wondered if Sibley might be able to spend the day and then stay overnight with you Saturday?"

A little thrill ran through Janie at the thought of chitchat and laughter filling her normally quiet house. "Of course she can."

"Oh, I've got plans Saturday, dear," Momma said, catching the conversation, "so you and Sibley are on your own." Momma leaned across to them. "Joe and I are going to bingo and then dinner."

Janie's brows shot up. "That's the first I've heard of this. You don't usually go out in the evenings. When did you make plans with Joe?" Of course she didn't mind and loved spending time with Sibley, but she couldn't remember the last time her mother had gone out.

"He mentioned it when I got my paper yesterday at the marina," Momma said, as if it wasn't a big deal.

Janie still thought it odd that they were going out at night *together*. But she turned her attention from Momma back to Ryan. "Okay. Well, I would love to spend some time with Sibley this weekend. Where are you going fishing?"

"Hilton Head. We're going offshore, so it's going to be a full day."

Janie didn't miss the thread of excitement in his voice at the idea of a day of fishing. She experienced a similar feeling when it was a fishing day.

"Take as much time as you want. We'll keep ourselves occupied. We'll go into town for a girls' day." The more Janie talked to Ryan about it, the more excited she became about treating Sibley to a fun day out.

Momma headed over to Sibley at the back of the workshop so they could finish finding a few pieces for the mirror she was working on.

"That sounds like exactly what she needs," Ryan said. "She's been feeling somewhat displaced from her friends since we moved. I mean, she sees her friends at school, but they go and do things without her beyond daytime hours now. Once we get home, it's hard to get back out."

Janie's heart broke for the young girl who'd been ripped away from her life as she'd known it. And for Ryan, whose worry for his child was palpable.

He seemed to shake himself out of his melancholy. "Well, we'd better get back. Sibley will be thrilled to spend the day with you."

"I'm excited to have her."

He called his daughter back over and the two of them headed out.

"See you later," Ryan called.

After they'd left, Janie noticed Momma eyeing her closely. "Why are you looking at me like that?"

"I'm picking up on some vibes between you and Ryan."

"Oh, please," she said, her skin heating right up. "I'm just happy to have Sibley over. It's nice that Ryan trusts me to take care of her." Janie's gaze slid over to her mother. "And it's nice that Sibley *wants* to come over."

"Mmm-hmm. You can deny it if you want, but I've also noticed some recent upgrades in your wardrobe lately. And a little mascara being worn here and there. Don't get me wrong, I'm thrilled to see it, and I think you should be doing it, too. It's a huge step, having an interest in someone."

Janie sighed. "I doubt he's ready to date again. And dating scares me to death."

"It's a risk, honey. It's always a risk."

"Looks like you're making some changes, too. Going out with Joe? To bingo and dinner? That's new." Janie couldn't help but give Momma a little of her own medicine.

Momma winked at her. "There's still life in this old gal."

Chapter Fourteen

Janie left the house just before sunrise Saturday morning to check on the nest. She rarely went out when it was still dark, instead spending her early mornings doing conservation research and getting ready for her day, but since Sibley was coming over soon, Janie needed peace of mind that things were okay with the hatchlings.

After the relief of finding that the nest was still perched high in the tree, Janie settled on her favorite seat of driftwood on the tiny beach to watch the sun complete its rapid climb, bathing the shore with a bright-orange glow. The wonder of a new day filled her, and she was excited to be spending time with Sibley. Sibley still saw the world through fresh eyes, making Janie wonder what kind of a relationship she might have had with a daughter of her own.

Janie had desperately wanted children, which was one of the most heartbreaking things about losing Daniel so soon. They'd spent time together, imagining what their children might be like—planning for it. For now, she was happy to spend time with Sibley.

Janie grabbed her backpack and headed to the golf cart, a small spring in her step.

Janie's heartbeat quickened as she passed Ryan's house on the way back to hers. She expected them soon. Instead of going back inside, she watered the plants on the front porch, hoping her tomatoes would ripen soon since Momma's already had.

Janie glanced up from her vantage point on the porch when Ryan's truck approached, and went to meet them in the driveway.

"Don't forget to text me if you leave the house, okay?" Ryan said to Sibley.

Sibley gave an exasperated sigh. "Go and have a good time fishing, please." She shooed him with her hand, making Janie smile.

"Don't worry, I'll take great care of her," Janie called, making her way to the truck as she tried to reassure Ryan.

"I might not have service while I'm out in the open water, so don't panic if you don't hear from me. I'll check in as soon as I can."

"Daddy, I'm fine. It's not like I'll be doing anything dangerous." She pulled her bag from the backseat of the truck.

"We'll be fine. Lots of fun things to do while you're gone. Girl things, so you wouldn't be welcome anyway," Janie joked with him.

"All right. Have fun."

Ryan gave Sibley a quick hug, and then she got out. She and Janie waved as Ryan backed out of the drive and headed down the road.

"Let's go inside and I'll show you your room." Janie led the way to the front door.

When they got into the house, Sibley looked around, noticing things. "I love all this artwork. Where do you find this kind of stuff?" Sibley pointed to a large, flat fish sculpture assembled from layered scrap pieces in different colors.

"Everywhere. There are tons of small galleries and roadside shops and markets that feature local art."

"I like all the folk art. We learned a lot about it in my art class this semester."

Janie glanced fondly around her living room, its shelves filled with all sorts of whimsical and colorful items and paintings.

"Your room is through here." Janie moved down the short hallway and opened the door to the bedroom where Sibley would sleep. The walls were a deep sea-green with more one-of-a-kind artwork on the walls. The queen bed sported a blend of basic pale-yellow linens with large and small eclectic pillows she'd collected through the years.

"Wow! How cool. Look at all this stuff." Sibley dropped her bag on the bed and moved around the room.

"There's a story behind every piece. I've got so many memories tied to these things." Janie swept a hand around the room. "You see that?" Janie pointed to a yellow carved wooden bird sitting on the antique dresser. "It's from the South Carolina state fair when I was fifteen. I won it from a booth playing a water-gun game. The owner carved every kind of animal by hand and used them as prizes."

"It's like the story of your life with things that remind you of the years past," Sibley said as she continued to touch small items on the dresser.

"I guess it is. It looks like clutter to anyone else, but it's all special to me."

"I love it. All of it."

Janie walked over to the doorway. "I'll let you get settled in. I'll be in the kitchen if you need me."

Sibley unzipped her bag. "Oh, I forgot to wash my tennis uniform. Do you mind if I wash it?"

"It's no problem. I'll throw it in for you."

Sibley handed the uniform to Janie in a wad. "Thank you."

Janie backed through the doorway, to give Sibley a few minutes to acclimate to her new surroundings, and headed to the laundry room. It had been two years since she'd shared the house with anyone, and already it felt different having someone else here, but different in a good way.

"So, what do you want to do first?" Janie asked Sibley as they crossed the bridge headed into Beaufort. The sky was crystal blue and the water shimmered like a mirror's reflection.

"Could we get our nails done first?" Sibley glanced at her hands.

"Absolutely. Do you have a favorite nail place you like to go?" Janie couldn't remember the last time she'd had her nails done and figured Sibley might have a preference since she did not.

"Juju's Nail Salon is downtown, next to the Bait House restaurant where we're going to for lunch." Sibley pointed left as they came off the river bridge into downtown Beaufort.

Janie put her blinker on and quickly got in the left-turn lane for Bay Street. The buildings were mainly historic and two-storied, a charming old downtown strip of restaurants, galleries, and boutiques that fulfilled both the tourists and locals. The left side of the street sat a hundred feet or so from Port Royal Sound. The view from the battery, with its shimmering water and cloudless bright-blue sky as far as one could see, was spectacular, especially on such a lovely day.

"Juju's is just up here on the left," Sibley said, tapping her window.

"Have you lived in Beaufort your whole life?" Janie asked as she scanned for a parking spot nearby.

"I *did*."

There was a slight edge to her voice as she said it, and Janie decided not to press her. It was meant to be a fun girls' day for Sibley, and Janie didn't want to ruin that already. She backed into a parallel spot a half block from the nail salon and fed the meter for two hours. They got out and headed to the shop, its front window presenting a bright, stylish space inside. The bells attached to the door of the nail salon jingled as they entered.

"How can we help you? Manicure? Pedicure?" asked an older woman wearing an apron with her hair scraped back in a bun as they entered.

"Both?" Janie answered for the two of them as she raised her brows in question to Sibley.

Sibley gave a thumbs up.

They made their color choices—Sibley's a bit bolder than Janie's neutral—and then were directed toward two oversized massage chairs, where they settled in while the techs got to work on their feet and hands.

Janie closed her eyes as the massage chair worked its magic. "This is nice. It's been so long since I've sat still like this." She looked over at Sibley, who appeared to be equally enjoying the pampering.

"For me, too." Sibley grinned. "Great idea, Janie."

"So, tell me what's new with you," Janie said after a few minutes.

Sibley looked to her left and then right, and hesitated before saying, "I've got a boyfriend." Her tone was conspiratorial, just above a whisper, as if she were concerned someone else might hear.

That wasn't what Janie had expected her to say. "Wow. Really?"

"His name is Conner, and he's a really tall senior," Sibley replied, her expression dreamy.

"A senior?" Janie experienced a fissure of concern since Sibley was only a sophomore.

"Yes, he's going to USC in the fall though." She deflated a little when she said it.

"That's tough, I know. But Columbia isn't too far from here." Janie was in uncharted territory with this conversation. "I actually used to live in Columbia."

"Did you go to USC in Columbia?" Sibley asked.

"I sure did. It was a great experience."

"I'm starting to look at colleges that aren't too far away. I don't think my dad could handle me being more than a couple of hours from him."

"Your dad tells me you've got a great academic record, so that should help you go wherever you want."

Sibley shrugged. "I guess so. It still feels so far away sometimes."

"It'll be here before you know it. Don't rush it. Do you know what you'd like to study yet?"

"I like animals, so maybe a vet? I'm not sure."

Her response warmed Janie's heart. "I do quite a bit of work as a shorebird conservationist."

That seemed to spark Sibley's interest. "What sort of things do you do?"

"We make sure birds and other animals are protected from too much hunting, and we try to preserve their habitats as much as possible, especially the endangered species. There are lots of conservation groups and opportunities to volunteer nearby."

"Hmm. I knew people worked to save endangered animals, but I've never checked into it as a career."

"USC has a few great programs." Janie paused. She didn't want to get into tricky territory with Sibley, but she felt she should delve a little deeper, if only for Ryan's sake, since Sibley had confided in Janie about Conner. "Speaking of USC, does your dad know about Conner?"

Sibley shook her head vigorously. "I have no idea how he would react."

Janie suspected he wouldn't find it easy, at least to begin with, but she knew he just wanted the best for Sibley. "But keeping a secret from your dad doesn't seem like a good idea to me. And he might actually be happy to know."

Sibley met her eyes. "Don't tell him, please. I'll tell him soon, but not yet."

"Uh, okay, but for the record, I think you should tell him soon," Janie said.

Panic rose in Sibley's eyes, her chest rising and falling quickly. "Please don't tell him, Janie." Desperation tinged her voice.

"I won't, but promise me you'll let him know. I'm not comfortable keeping secrets."

They sat quietly while the nail techs continued their work, and Janie hoped that she hadn't upset Sibley. She didn't want to push the girl away, but it was important to Janie that she was honest with Sibley, and she was only looking out for her.

Afterward, Janie and Sibley carefully slid their feet into their sandals and walked next door to the restaurant for a quick lunch before visiting the candy store, a gallery, and a couple of boutiques. The conversation turned to lighter matters, and any earlier tension dissolved as the two of them chatted about food and clothes.

It was just after three o'clock when they returned home, and Janie suggested they go out in the boat and check the crab traps. To her delight, Sibley was excited to go.

"I hoped we could go out in the boat today. I had so much fun the last time."

Janie had checked the tide charts, and they would have adequate time to get out and back into the canal in a couple of hours. High tide was late that day, thankfully. The breeze was warm and the day humid, and Janie was in her element.

Janie used the winch to carefully lower the boat into the canal as Sibley stood nearby, holding the life vests and a bottle of sunscreen. Sibley climbed aboard, and they headed out. Janie maneuvered through the narrow waterway toward the open water. Once they'd gotten clear of any low spots, she let Sibley steer the boat.

"My dad says one day we'll get a boat now that we live on the island."

Janie understood that Ryan wanted to surprise Sibley with the boat purchase once it was done, so she held back discussing Ryan's plan. Instead, she said, "That sounds awesome. You'll love having one."

"I can't wait." Sibley's words were a pure delight, and her dark hair flowed in the wind. She'd clearly been bitten hard by the island bug, which thrilled Janie.

They spent another hour checking and rebaiting traps and wound up with quite a few stone crab legs as well as a dozen whole blue crabs. Blue crabs were usually more hit or miss, but that day they got lucky.

"Are you going to cook these?" Sibley asked, motioning toward the crabs as they crawled over one another to get out of the cooler.

Janie shut the lid so none could escape. "Absolutely. I'm going to show you how to cook them, too. Maybe tomorrow around five?" Janie asked. She'd enjoyed her time with Sibley and was more than happy to hang out again.

Sibley gave a little bounce. "Awesome! I'll check with my dad. Crabs are my favorite next to clams. And they were so good last time."

They began to bring in their haul to put it on ice. When Janie tried to transfer the first crab from the boat's cooler, it slipped from the grasp of her tongs and onto the kitchen floor, where the pesky side-runner then tried to make his getaway. As they watched him clacking across the floor, Sibley and Janie began to shriek, both of them doubling over in hysterics. Whenever they'd get close enough to catch it, the crab raised itself in a defensive posture and snapped its claws at them, sending them into fits of laughter.

After many hilarious attempts and lots of crab calamity, Sibley finally cornered the outlaw crab with a pair of long-handled tongs. "Gotcha, big guy."

"We've earned our supper with that one." Janie was out of breath from laughing so hard by the time they'd slammed the cooler shut.

After a night of bingeing on movies featuring vampires, and eating popcorn, they'd finally gone to bed around one a.m., which was incredibly late for Janie. She found it a struggle to get out of bed the following day and get breakfast started. She'd heard Joe's truck just before midnight and hoped he and Momma had had a lovely evening.

Sibley entered the kitchen looking no worse for wear for their late night.

"Hi there. How did you sleep?" Janie asked from the kitchen table, where she was enjoying her steaming cup of coffee, the deliciously sweet scent of vanilla from the new blend she'd purchased rising from her mug.

"Great. I was so tired. I don't remember anything from the minute I got in bed and closed my eyes."

Janie mixed up some homemade pancake batter while Sibley sliced strawberries on a small cutting board at the bar.

"It's been a while since I've made Momma's buttermilk batter from scratch," Janie said, pouring the batter into a hot pan. "It looks a little soupy…." She grabbed the spatula as Sibley set down the knife and looked over her shoulder.

"It's awfully thin," she said with a giggle.

"It's like riding a bike. You just have to get back on." Janie slid the spatula underneath to flip it, the whole thing falling apart.

They laughed together at the first pancake being a bit of a flop.

"This is what I call the *test* pancake. The first one never comes out as good as the others," Janie said as she threw it in the sink with a plop.

Once she'd made several more, their color and thickness just right, Janie divided them between two plates, with Sibley's freshly cut strawberries on the side.

Sibley stabbed a bite of pancake and ate it. "Mmm. I love this syrup. What kind is it?" she asked.

"It's called ribbon cane syrup. My grandad was the only one who used it that I know of, and every time I have it, it reminds me of him. It's not for everyone, but I love it and the memories it always brings back when I smell and taste it."

Sibley nodded. "My mom's mom and dad live in Savannah. They've got a big old house that looks like the one in *Gone with the Wind.*"

"Love that movie and that house."

Sibley continued. "Grandma Pearl makes cathead biscuits, and she mixes maple syrup and butter together for dipping. It's something I've only had at her house, so when I eat biscuits, it reminds me of them."

"Cathead biscuits are the *best*, but I've never tried to make them. Momma usually makes the biscuits around here, and she's convinced she doesn't need to go to all the fuss of cathead biscuits. Too fancy, she says."

"Grandma Pearl is fancy. She wears big hats and does a lot of social stuff, like Junior League and the garden club. It's what she loves to talk about when we see her." Sibley smiled as she spoke of her grandmother.

"I can just imagine Momma at a garden club meeting—wearing a string of pearls and a fancy hat." The very idea of her hippie-esque mother trying to impress anyone tickled her.

Sibley laughed, too. "Grandma Pearl wears a hairnet and sleeps on a satin pillowcase. My mom says that's why she has such great hair still."

Janie laughed at the thought. "I'll have to tell Momma about that, and maybe she can learn something from your Grandma Pearl."

"Daddy says Grandma Pearl 'puts on the dog.' I think it means she's showy."

"I'd say that's exactly what it means."

"Daddy didn't grow up like Mom. He didn't live in a big house or anything. His parents were divorced, and he lived with his mom, mostly. He doesn't talk about his childhood much like my mom does," Sibley explained.

Janie knew that Ryan's mother and Joe were siblings, but Joe hadn't said anything much beyond that, and neither had Ryan. So, Janie stayed clear of anything that might be gossip. "We didn't do 'fancy' at our house either."

"Grandma Pearl bought my dad a set of satin sheets as a Christmas gift one time, and Daddy swore he had to wear a shirt to bed to keep from slipping onto the floor while he slept. He didn't want to hurt her feelings, so he slept on them the entire time she was visiting."

Janie pictured Ryan sleeping on fancy satin sheets, a smile playing at her lips. But something about picturing him sleeping also caused a swell of fondness in her chest. His tousled hair, that shadow of the day's beard…. "Your dad's a nice guy."

"Yeah, he really is." Sibley sounded proud of her dad, and it warmed Janie's heart.

Chapter Fifteen

Ryan arrived in time to see Janie and Sibley sitting outside in the rocking chairs on Janie's front porch. Janie was showing Sibley something on the bottom of an object that, when he squinted, looked like a tomato. They were both cracking up—at what, he had no idea, but it didn't matter. His heart caught in his chest at the unguarded laughter between them. He couldn't remember the last time he'd seen Sibley laughing like that. Leslie had rarely taken the time to entertain Sibley or teach her new things in recent times. Leslie had a sense of humor, but she hadn't been playful with Sibley since she'd entered her tween years.

"Oh, hey, Daddy." Sibley waved to him as he approached the front porch.

"Well, hello. Did y'all have a nice time?" he asked, genuinely wanting to hear all about it.

"We had a great time. Check out my nails." Sibley showed him her electric-blue fingernails.

"Great color." He pulled her in for a hug.

"Oh, and we caught lots of crabs. You should've seen them trying to get away."

Janie cast him an interested glance, her bright-green eyes speculative, as if she knew a secret. "I hope you had a great time fishing. Did y'all catch many?"

"We did catch quite a few reds and several black drums. I figured it was only fair to leave them with my buddy since we went in his boat." He turned back to Sibley. "You want to get your things so we can head home?"

"I'll be right back," Sibley said.

When Sibley went inside, Ryan turned to Janie. "It looks like y'all had a great time. I can't thank you enough."

"Of course. And we did have a great time. You should've seen what went on in this kitchen after we got back from our boat excursion yesterday," Janie said as she filled him in on their escapade chasing the crabs.

There was such an easy way about Janie, even when she was telling dramatic crab stories. She was funny and unguarded, but Ryan worried his attraction to her was becoming slightly problematic. Part of him wanted to stay there and laugh and talk with her for hours, but while he'd been away, he'd wondered if Sibley getting so close to Janie was such a good idea. Sibley was so vulnerable right then, and she craved motherly attention. Leslie had kept her word and begun to call Sibley, but he could tell there was still a distance, a stiffness, between mother and daughter.

Ryan hadn't known Janie long enough to guess if they could move forward with their flirtation. His unexpected response to her every time they were together had kind of crept up on him. Looking ahead, it could be a real blow to Sibley if things didn't work out. And protecting his child was number one on his list. *Not* a flirtation with his charming neighbor, no matter how much he'd love to pursue that. And he wasn't ready for a new relationship, honestly. He was still dragging around too much baggage from his ongoing divorce, and nobody else needed to get tied up in that emotional mess. But yet, he had to admit Janie kind of pushed the right buttons for him.

Sibley came out carrying her bag.

"I think it's time for the two of us to get cleaned up, so we'll get out of your way," Ryan said to Janie. 'Thank you for this weekend.'

"It was my pleasure," Janie said. She turned to Sibley. "Thanks for getting me out for some fun."

"Oh, are we still going to cook crabs at five?" Sibley asked.

"Yes we are, if it's okay with your dad." Janie looked toward Ryan expectantly.

"Sounds good to me. Let us know if we can bring anything."

Sibley stepped forward and hugged Janie, which surprised Ryan, and clearly surprised Janie, based on her expression.

"Thanks, Janie. I had a great time," Sibley said. Then she stepped back and added, "I made my bed."

Ryan got a rush of pride. Sibley was growing up.

Sibley grinned from ear to ear.

"Thanks for doing that," Janie said. "We'll have to get together again soon, and I'll let you know if we go out on the boat. Maybe your dad would like to join us."

Ryan gazed over at Janie. "I'd love to."

Janie hoped Ryan had mistaken the scarlet climbing up from her neck as her having gotten some sun when she and Sibley were out on the boat. Every time she got near Ryan, she flushed. He'd never mentioned it, but it was so obvious, there was no way he hadn't spotted it before now.

Janie realized that she hadn't yet checked in with Momma with all the fun she'd had. She was about to do so when a faint ping alerted her to a message on her phone. It was from the drone photographer. It read:

Hi, Janie. I took some short videos and lots of photos of all the nests. I'm wondering, though, how many hatchlings were supposed to be in the at-risk nest? I only see two, but there were three eggs when I was out here last. I thought you might want to check to see if one is missing.

The text jumpstarted Janie into panic mode. It was getting late, but she grabbed her binoculars and camera, and headed out straight for the nests.

As Janie drove her golf cart, she hoped the nest was still hanging on. The hatchlings had a couple more weeks before they would be able to wander around on their own, even longer before they learned to fly.

The first thing she noticed when she arrived at the habitat was a rezoning notice stapled to the utility pole at the edge of the property. *Rezoning?*

"What the heck?" she whispered as she read the poster. Rezoning for what? There was a hearing date—two weeks from Monday—at the Beaufort courthouse. An icy dread took hold in her belly. Nothing about this could be good.

Who would know about this? She could try to contact Bob from USC, but he likely wouldn't know anything. This was outside his immediate sphere. They'd left the care of the nests to Janie, pretty much. So, it was up to Janie to find out what was happening with the habitat.

Stopping about twenty feet from the nests, she locked her gaze on the ground, careful not to accidentally step on a baby, should one have fallen out.

At first, she didn't see it, but then she heard a little screech. Janie's heart pounded, and hope blossomed because the bird was alive, but panic chased the hope as she finally spotted it. Its tiny little bald body sat on top of the foam packaging. Relief flooded in, but only for a second. The hatchling was in distress, flipping and flopping as if it was trying to figure out what had happened.

Janie then heard a loud screech overhead. The mother bird flew lower than usual, circling and yelling to Janie in a universal mother's language.

Janie gently leaned down and picked up the tiny naked thing, its overly large eyes glazed in panic. "Come here, buddy. I'm going to help you."

Janie was well-versed in how to manage the situation. The guidelines were clear: hatchlings were to be rescued immediately because they couldn't move around on their own power. They also couldn't locate food, and they were vulnerable to being eaten by other birds and animals.

Janie pulled out her T-shirt and laid the tiny creature several inches from the hem and cocooned his body by pulling up the shirt from the bottom. Janie then looked overhead where the mother bird was perched, staring worriedly at what was happening below.

Janie made eye contact with her. "I'll take good care of him, I promise."

She wrestled her phone into her camera's case and hung it around her neck, along with the binoculars, so she would have both hands to manage the baby in her T-shirt and steer the golf cart. Her mind went into overdrive with planning what to do. Worms. She needed worms.

Joe had worms.

Relief flooded through her when he answered.

"Hey there, Janie, what's up?"

"I'm so sorry to bother you, but I've had a hatchling fall from his nest. Can I come by and get some bait worms to feed him?"

"I'll meet you at the marina right away."

Janie drove one-handed toward the marina, the tiny, helpless bird squirming inside the hem of her T-shirt while she steadied it with her other hand. As soon as she parked, Joe materialized.

"Let's see who you've got there."

Janie carefully exposed the tiny bird so Joe could see him. His little wings flapped madly the moment Janie unwrapped him from her shirt. "He's completely helpless, and I need to get him back to the habitat as soon as possible. After I took him away, the mother was in a state of panic."

"I'll bet so. But I know this little guy is in great hands with you to rescue him." Joe produced a container of bait worms. "Let me know if you need more, okay." Joe leaned in and spoke to the squirming creature. "Hey there, little guy."

Janie looked down, focusing on the bird in the low light of dusk. "I'm going to call my vet friend in Beaufort when I get home. I don't know if he's injured or just scared and struggling to get away."

"Let's find a box for him, why don't we?" Joe suggested and pointed to the marina store. "I've got some small ones inside. Give me a minute." He bounded up the weathered exterior stairs leading to the entrance of the store surprisingly fast for his age and size.

Janie hoped the baby would calm down once he got more comfortable.

Joe returned with a small cardboard box filled with a shredded towel he'd ripped up. "This should work until you get him home."

"Thanks. The mother should take him back if we can either get the nest down or figure out a way to put him back in it."

"She'll take him back even though you've touched him?" Joe sounded surprised.

"She should if we can replace him inside the nest or nearby." But time was of the essence, and the sooner they could get him back with his mother, the better.

"Keeping my fingers crossed for you."

As Janie drove slowly home with her charge, she spoke softly to him. "I think I'll call you Bert." Even though there was no real way of knowing if Bert was a male or female kite at this stage, it made her feel better to name the tiny creature. Janie took a deep breath, relieved that the hatchling appeared calmer inside the box.

The salty breeze blew through her hair, and Janie was relieved now that she had a plan. There was an entire team of like-minded bird specialists whose mission was to protect and help when needed. Bert would be all right.

Chapter Sixteen

"Wow, look at these," Ryan said, waist-deep in garage organization with Sibley. He dipped his hand into a box of old photos of Sibley when she was a little girl, thumbing through them. They ranged from Sibley's toothless newborn days until around middle school.

"I was bald, wasn't I?" Sibley scooted over on the garage floor, taking one of the photos from her dad's fingers.

"You were the most adorable little thing I'd ever seen. I've never been more scared and excited as the night you were born." He passed over a second newborn photo where he was holding her only minutes after her birth. Ryan was amazed at how young and happy he appeared in the picture. His relief at seeing his perfect child had been overwhelming.

"You looked so proud."

"I was proud and still am, honey. You're the most important and best thing that's ever happened to me."

"Thanks, Daddy."

How had his little angel grown up so quickly? Her sixteen years had gone by so fast, and Ryan knew he only had a couple more years before she left home. He didn't even want to think about that and was determined to make the most of the time they had.

"Can you put those on the front steps? I want to bring them inside so they don't get damaged." Ryan handed the box to Sibley.

She did as he asked, then turned back to the task at hand. "So, why are we doing this right now?" Sibley grimaced, wiping sweat off her forehead. "I mean, what's the rush?"

What Sibley didn't know was that he'd already bought a boat. It was a significant purchase, but he figured his fortieth birthday was coming up, and what better way to celebrate than to spend long days out on the water. It was being delivered tomorrow, and they needed somewhere to put it.

"It just needs to be done." He tried to keep his answer vague to not arouse her suspicions.

"Is it for a car?" she asked, lighting up.

It made him chuckle but he shook his head.

Sibley pouted playfully at his response. "When do you think I can get a car?"

"Sometime after you get your license. And as soon as I'm convinced you're ready to have one."

"Seriously?" She put her hand on her hip, offering up that sassy grin of hers. "You know I'm a good driver."

"Yes, you are a good driver, and when you've had a little more practice, we'll find you a car. But my heart isn't ready for that yet. License first, please."

"Are we cleaning out to pack up for the new house then?" she asked.

"Not yet. I'm still looking for a nice lot to build on. And the architect is working on the house plans while we wait."

"I like living here for now."

Relief flooded through him. "Moving here was a scary thing for us both, you know? I'm so happy to hear that you're okay with it, for the most part."

Sibley smiled and nodded and then changed the subject. "We're supposed to go to Janie's at five," she reminded him.

"So, it looks like we're about done in here." Ryan checked his watch; it was three o'clock. He was looking forward to spending time with Janie. He refocused on Sibley. She looked hot and tired. "We've got a couple of hours until it's time to leave for Janie's house. Do you want to go out for a bit in the kayaks?"

"Yes! We haven't taken them out together since we moved in."

"Okay, grab the life vests and sunscreen, and we'll get them down." He closed the newly cleaned garage, feeling a spark of excitement at the arrival of the boat the next evening. Ryan looked forward to surprising Sibley with the purchase. After seeing her interest in being on the water that day with Janie and Georgia, he was thrilled. It was an unexpected commonality that gave them something new to do together.

Ryan met Sibley at the back of the house.

"I brought these to keep our phones dry." Sibley held up two Ziplock bags.

"Good idea."

They transferred their phones to the bags, snapped the buckles on their life vests, then moved over to where the long, heavy-duty polyethylene boats were stored. These were built to be lightweight, but that was a relative term. They weighed enough and were awkward enough that it took two people to get them down from the racks.

"Okay, can you push the higher one toward me while I pull?"

They slid Sibley's narrow pink boat to the end, and Ryan pulled it down. They repeated the action for Ryan's blue one. Sibley and Ryan then grasped T-handle grips attached to the bow on each kayak, enabling them to slide the boats through the grass in the backyard toward the dock. It was a little more challenging for Sibley, but she managed.

Lowering the boats into the water was easier than pulling them out. Ryan climbed in his boat first, then steadied Sibley's kayak while she climbed in. Getting in and out could be tricky, but both did so without a hitch. Once seated, they used the long paddles with blades on each end to maneuver their boats until they were both headed toward the mouth of the canal.

The cloud cover had thickened in the last couple of hours, but the clouds were still white and puffy and posed no threat to their outing. Ryan took a deep breath, relaxing into the gentle pace and the splashing sounds of their paddles slicing in and out of the water; paddling out with the tide flow required a calm and easy rhythm. Spending time out on the canal reminded Ryan of an earlier time when he and Uncle Joe used to fish off a tiny local pier at the front of the island. He'd sneak out there as a kid, sometimes just to look out over the water and find peace. Ryan wondered if the pier was still intact. Maybe he would take Sibley out there and have a look one day soon.

"Can we paddle out to Prichards Island?" Sibley asked, signaling just across the inlet where the small island could be easily seen from the mouth of the canal.

Ryan considered her suggestion. There was a sliver of rough water about fifty yards wide between their position and the island that required some focus to get across.

"Sure. We've got time to get out there and back," he said.

"Look! Dolphins!" Sibley pointed to a pair that had emerged to arch perfectly over the surface of the water to the right of their kayaks.

"Oh, wow. I see them."

"They're so pretty." Sibley grabbed her cell phone, snapping photos.

"We're coming up on the rough water," Ryan warned her. "Look at those whitecaps. It's gonna get choppier than usual, so stay close, and if it gets to be too much, we'll turn back."

Sibley put away her phone, grasping the paddle firmly with both hands. She was a strong, athletic girl and perfectly capable of getting through a short stretch of challenging waves. Still, Ryan stayed behind her and watched like a hawk as she maneuvered the bobbing canoe through the choppy water.

After a few minutes of navigating, the water calmed for a boat length or two before they beached onto the shoreline at Prichards Island. They climbed out and pulled the kayaks high up on the sand so the tide couldn't drag them off and leave them stranded.

"Let's check out the tide pools," Sibley suggested.

Ryan could see that Sibley was in her element out here and that living on Fripp was having a positive effect on her.

Sibley gently picked up a sand dollar as they bent down to look for shells and creatures in the shallow, warm low spots. "This reminds me of shell hunting with Janie and Miss Georgia. That was such a fun day. I never knew how the creatures who live inside the shells could get stranded at low tide when the water goes out."

Ryan had noticed quite a lot of recent "Janie" references. Janie said or Janie did... It made him wonder if Sibley was leaning on Janie a little too much and if Janie was okay with it. Though, he had to admit, it was nice that the two of them got on so well when he also enjoyed Janie's company so much.

"Oh, and Janie gave me a couple of ideas about things to study in college while we were at lunch on Saturday."

"Oh? What do you think you might want to study?" He kept his tone neutral. Sibley hadn't shown much interest in a field of study yet, which was fine since she had at least another year before she needed to figure that out.

"I told Janie I might be interested in veterinary medicine, but she also suggested a major in biology with a focus on wildlife conservation if I have an interest in wild animals."

Ryan was a little surprised at hearing that Janie and Sibley had discussed her education. Any time Ryan tried to have that conversation, Sibley hadn't wanted to discuss it. But, again, thanks to Janie, they were talking—really talking about her future and her interests.

"I think you'd be great at both of those things. You could always get a biology degree and decide later if you want to do vet school."

Sibley seemed to absorb his words as she picked up another shell, but she didn't respond. Ryan felt, though, that she had finally begun to open up to him, and things between them were getting back on track. It was a good feeling.

"What do we have here?" Lynn Norris, the veterinarian Janie knew in Beaufort, asked as she peered into the box that Janie held in her hands.

Lynn's waiting room was empty, given that it was off hours, and Janie could hear the sounds of animal movement in the metal crates coming from the back room. Lynn was kind enough to take in strays and work to find them homes.

Janie pulled back the flaps of the box, revealing the tiny patient. The hatchling had dug its way under the towel strips and had calmed somewhat.

"I've got a baby bird that needs tending to," Janie replied, already relieved to be in Lynn's presence. She was a trusted friend—Janie and Daniel had worked with her to take care of the island's shorebirds and sea turtles over the years. "He still isn't eating," she told Lynn.

"Hmm." Lynn reached in and delicately assessed the animal. "I'd like to keep him under an incubator light for a few days since his feathers haven't come in yet."

"I hate to leave him, but I know you're the expert, and his chances are better with you looking after him."

"You know I'll do everything I can," Lynn said.

A high-pitched bark came from the back room.

"Okay, I'll keep an eye on the nests to be sure they stay stable," said Janie.

"If another one falls, bring it over."

"Thanks for seeing me on a Sunday."

"Of course." Lynn placed Bert on a stainless-steel table and situated the small light at the proper distance.

As the two of them moved around, Janie could hear whining from the cages in the back room.

"What's wrong with that little one?" she asked, peeking beyond to see some sort of spaniel-hound mix shaking and peering up at her with sad eyes.

"Nothing's actually wrong with her. She was abandoned, so she's scared. You don't have any interest in fostering a puppy, do you?" Lynn asked. "Somebody dropped her off last night, and she's a real beauty."

A puppy? "Oh, I don't know…" But when Janie caught sight of the little sweetheart again, her heart skipped and her resistance slid away. "I wasn't in the market for a dog, but I could take her for a few days to help out. After all, I owe you big time."

"That would be fantastic. She seems to need a lot of attention, and puppies this age are hard to keep caged."

They moved into a large room where there were several kennels with recovering animals, mostly dogs and cats. Some had IVs.

"I haven't named her yet," Lynn said.

Janie bent down to a kennel on her left. The dog was shaking and whimpering.

"Oh… you poor baby."

The little brown pup had huge, sad eyes and a silky black, brown, and white piebald coat. She appeared to have shortish legs, maybe part basset hound, but the eyes were pure spaniel, and their soft sadness made Janie determined to help.

Chapter Seventeen

Ryan and Sibley cut through the empty backyard next door with brownies in hand, just before five. Neither expected to find Janie running around the yard with a small puppy.

"Oh my gosh, she's so cute." Sibley immediately ran over to join in the fun.

Janie dove toward the pup, her arms wide, missing it and stumbling after it as it barked in a series of high-pitched squeaks. "Come back here, you," Janie said with a hint of exasperation in her voice while she attempted a few more times to catch the brown-and-black speckled animal as it whizzed by her. When Janie noticed Sibley join the fray, she said, "Try and grab her if you can."

"Where did you get her?" Sibley yelled over the shrill barking, swiping gently at the dog as it raced past. "She's the *best*."

"My vet friend needed someone to foster her for a few days." Janie finally plopped down on the grass, breathing hard. "She's giving me fits."

"Looks like she's having a blast doing it." Ryan laughed at the puppy's antics.

Sibley squatted, then sat down a few feet from Janie. "Maybe she'll come if we don't chase her," she suggested.

The puppy ran up to where Ryan stood, and he bent down and scooped her up with one hand while he tried to protect the plate of brownies in his other hand.

"Wow, who's the puppy whisperer?" Janie got up from where she'd sat on the ground and marched through the thick, soft Saint Augustine grass in her bare feet. She plucked the wiggly little animal from his hands. "Whatcha got there?" she asked, pointing to the plate in Ryan's hand.

"These are my special brownies." He couldn't help but bait her.

Janie eyeballed him. "How special?"

He laughed, getting her meaning. "Special from a box with extra chocolate chips and chopped pecans." He remembered eating brownies with pecans at Uncle Joe's as a kid.

"They sound perfect to me. Sibley, can you grab this little demon for a minute?" Janie held the puppy toward Sibley. "I've got to get back to the burner."

Sibley ran over and gently took her. "What's her name?" she asked as she followed Janie to where the cooking pot sat atop a gas flame on the concrete patio underneath the deck.

"If I name her, I'll have to keep her." Janie joked with Sibley as she stirred the water in the large stainless pot with a long wooden paddle. "And I'm not sure I'm ready for that."

"You *have* to keep her. How could you give her back? I mean, look at this face." Sibley held up the doe-eyed pup.

"I can't even keep up with her, and it's only been a few hours."

Despite Janie's tough words, Ryan didn't see this puppy leaving her custody, seeing as she kept casting loving glances over at the little ankle-biter.

"So, I promised to teach you how to cook these crabs, didn't I?" Janie asked Sibley as she lifted the lid and stirred the pot that hadn't yet come to a full boil.

"Yes, you did." Sibley appeared eager to learn something more from Janie.

"Here, I'll take the pup and let the two of you discuss this crab cooking." Ryan held the dog like a football, tucked into his chest, and juggled the plate of brownies. "I'll go put these inside."

"Thanks, Ryan." Janie turned to Sibley. "I've filled the pot with water up to around three-quarters from the top, and then I added the liquid crab boil and salt. But be careful not to inhale the steam, or the spices will make you cough…" Janie continued to show Sibley the process as Ryan made his way across the backyard toward the house.

As soon as Ryan stepped inside, he encountered Georgia wearing a brightly flowered apron and stirring something at the stove. "Oh, hey there," he said.

She started at his voice. "Lordy-be, I didn't hear you come in, Ryan. Looks like you've met our messy little houseguest." Her words contradicted the gushy look she bestowed on the puppy, who was squirming in Ryan's arms.

"It's okay to put her down if you want. We've got gates put up, so she can't leave this area," she said, "and her toys are over there." Georgia pointed to a small dog bed with several chewing toys scattered nearby.

"She's such a cute little thing," Ryan said as he lowered the pup to the floor.

"She's very naughty, but I expect she'll grow out of most of it."

Ryan nodded. "Most likely so." He set the brownies down on the kitchen island. "Can I help you with anything?"

"It would be wonderful if you could take the cooler with the crabs to Janie. The pot'll boil soon, and they'll need to go in." She indicated a large red-and-white ice chest sitting on the white tile floor. "Also, I've cut up some lemons, onions, and sausage. And there's some corn on the cob. You can take that down too when you're done, if you don't mind."

Before Ryan could pick up the cooler, he felt a tug on his pants leg. "Oh, no you don't, you little rascal." He squatted down and disengaged the razor-sharp teeth from his hem. Then, he threw a soft toy to distract the pup. She skidded and then rolled across the floor as she tried to stop. "You're a funny girl," Ryan said, trying again to pick up the cooler. But the little gal wasn't going to let him off that easy. She grabbed his pants once more.

Laughing, Georgia walked over and lifted the animal, who was wiggling excitedly from the new game with Ryan. "Gotcha."

"Thanks. That could've gone on for hours."

"You'd never know the little rascal hasn't been here her whole life, as comfortable as she is."

Ryan hefted the cooler and took it outside.

Ryan came out of the house toting Janie's cooler filled with crabs. She immediately noticed how his muscles filled out his bright-blue golf shirt as he flexed with the weight of the heavy cooler, and she worked to keep from looking at them.

Janie opened the cooler's lid carefully, the crabs' misbehavior still fresh in her mind from the day before, which also reminded her of the puppy inside. There was no denying the little girl was full of mischief, but she was just the most adorable thing.

"Do you mind grabbing the sausage and corn from the kitchen?" She turned to Ryan when she realized it was missing.

"Absolutely. Be right back." Ryan headed toward the house.

Janie turned to Sibley after Ryan had gone. "So, do you get your license this week?"

Her eyes sparkled with excitement. "Yes. I take my road test Wednesday after school."

"I remember being nervous for the road test, but then it was so quick and no big deal. How do you feel about it?"

"I know how to drive pretty well, so I should do okay." Despite her words, it was clear Sibley was a little worried about it. "They say the main thing is to stay under the speed limit and signal before changing lanes. Oh, and the parallel parking is a little tricky in Dad's truck."

"Yes, parallel parking takes practice," Janie agreed.

Ryan reappeared, holding two pans overflowing with corn, potatoes, onions, and two-inch links of smoked sausage.

"So, what's our next step?" Sibley asked, now clearly distracted by the food in front of them, as she peeked under the foil.

"We start by putting in the potatoes first because they take a little longer to cook." Janie added them as she explained. "Once the water comes back to a full boil for a few minutes, we can add the other things. Crabs go in last."

Sibley clapped her hands together in excitement. "I'm getting hungry just looking at all of it."

Janie smiled at her. "Don't worry, it'll be ready soon. Could you get some newspaper from inside for me? Momma will show you where it is," Janie said.

Sibley took off at a run, reappearing soon after with her arms filled with newspaper. "Mmm, it smells good."

Janie pointed to the table. "You can spread it out here. It protects the table and keeps the excess moisture from dripping onto the ground."

"Should I go get some picking tools and hammers for us?" Sibley then asked, obviously remembering the last time she'd eaten a crab meal here.

"Yes, please. They're sitting in a box on the bar." Janie pointed toward her back door. "Once we get the hot burner up off the ground, we can let the puppy out. Well, after we finish eating. I don't want her getting a taste for crab shells."

Sibley turned, her face lighting up from the idea of playing with the pup again. "Be right back." She took off to complete the errand.

"She's such a great girl," Janie said to Ryan.

Ryan gave an affectionate shrug. "I think she is." Then he said, "Sibley tells me the two of you have been discussing college."

"Yes, she told me how much she loves animals and that she's considering vet school."

He nodded. "She'd been reluctant to talk to me about her plans for college until spending the night here. We discussed it some today."

"Oh?" Janie asked.

Ryan continued. "I was surprised she spoke about it. You seem to have unlocked something within her. That's progress." His eyes were warm as he spoke.

"Sibley is a pleasure. Always happy to help." Ryan's compliment, combined with his intense stare, caused Janie to fan herself with a paper plate. Was it her, or had it gotten several degrees hotter during this conversation? Fortunately, she was hot and already red in the face so he wouldn't notice her blush this time.

"You okay?" he asked, clearly noticing her unease.

"Of course. This boiling pot is putting off some serious heat." It was, so *that* wasn't a lie.

Not long after, when all the ingredients had been added to the pot, and Janie's face was only red from standing near the flame, rather than from feeling self-conscious, she lifted the lid and saw that the normally dark-gray-and-blue crabs had turned bright orange. "Oh, looks like we're almost ready." She set the lid down beside her and turned off the burner to let the crabs soak in the hot water for a few more minutes. She was so distracted by her response to Ryan she didn't realize the potholder had slipped when she reached to lift the lid back onto the boiling pot. "Ouch!"

Seeing what she'd done, Ryan grabbed her hand and placed it on the glass of ice water Janie had sitting nearby. "Hold it there for a few minutes, and we'll have a look at it."

"Thanks." She did as he said, hoping her mortification didn't show.

Ryan picked up the potholder, ready to take over from Janie while she cooled her fingers. A couple of minutes later he asked, "Are we ready to take out the basket?"

"Yes, it's all ready now. You can lift the basket and let it drain for a few seconds into the pot. Then feel free to spread everything out directly across the table."

Ryan gripped the handle of the boiling basket wearing the potholder. As he lifted it, the contents of the pot were revealed, and the savory aroma surrounded them like a cloud. They all coughed a few times from inhaling the steaming combination of spices. Ryan placed the hot pot on the covered table.

"We could grab a beer if you want," Janie suggested to Ryan.

"You read my mind. How's the hand?"

"Better. The cold glass was quick thinking." She was still a little embarrassed at her misstep.

"Of course. I'm just glad you didn't burn yourself badly," he said. "Should I go get those beers now?"

"They're in the outdoor fridge in the garage. Here, I'll show you." Her comfort level with Ryan had gotten so that their sharing meals and beers was becoming natural. They walked shoulder to shoulder through to the refrigerator in the garage. "I've got a couple of choices." She showed him her small stash of craft beers. It wasn't every day that she had one, but Janie enjoyed keeping them on hand when she was in the mood.

Ryan chose one after Janie got hers. Their hands brushed during the close exchange, which caused Janie to blush again. He smelled nice, like sage and bergamot, and they were close enough that she could feel the heat from his body envelop her.

"Thanks for showing me your stash."

Janie picked up on Ryan's interested gaze. "Anytime."

The moment was over and they moved from the darkened garage back into the daylight, confusion filling Janie. How had these bursts of attraction happened with Ryan so easily? She and Daniel had been the very best of friends and lovers, and they'd shared a bond of closeness she couldn't imagine having with anyone else in her lifetime. But Janie reminded herself that moving forward was a good thing. Daniel was gone, and she wasn't. The whole idea made sense, except to her heart.

The four of them gathered around the table once Ryan had helped Janie secure the cooking area and make it puppy-friendly. Janie and Ryan sat across from each other, and Janie caught Ryan's gaze occasionally. Was he thinking about their close encounter in the garage? Janie definitely was, but maybe not in the same way. She was trying to figure it out.

"This is so good. I think I like the blue crabs more than the stone crabs," Sibley said. "But they are harder to eat." She was struggling to figure it out.

"Maybe we should have a quick lesson on how to clean crabs. Once you know how to handle them, it's much simpler." Janie showed Sibley how to manipulate the crabs and use the crackers and picker tools to do the job better. "Oh, and don't forget to remove these. They aren't edible." She pulled off an extraneous part.

"I was doing it the hard way, for sure." Sibley found success with Janie's method. "This is so much easier. Thanks."

"Of course." It thrilled Janie just a little to teach Sibley a life skill. Well, a life skill for living on the island. "Glad I could help."

"I've been doing it wrong my whole life, and nobody ever taught me step-by-step how to do this either." Ryan's expression was warm, and he appeared surprised at learning something new.

Janie grinned. "Momma showed us as soon as we were big enough to use the tools."

"You weren't much out of a high chair the first time. You insisted on doing it yourself—as always." Momma laughed at the memory. "Between you and your two sisters, y'all made a huge mess, so we always ate crabs outside."

"Oh, I didn't know you had sisters," Sibley said, sounding surprised.

"Yes, Jaclyn and Joy. They are both older than me. But they don't live too far away."

Once more, Janie was struck by how easy it was with Ryan and Sibley and how nice it was to share her evening with them and Momma. The first few months after Daniel's death had been incredibly difficult, but Momma had gradually coaxed Janie into a routine, and she'd felt comfortable enough in recent times, just her and Momma. However,

Ryan and Sibley's arrival in her life had shown her what she had been missing out on—friendship, companionship, and fun—and Janie was beginning to feel as if she were moving forward again.

When they finished eating, Ryan asked, "How can we help with cleanup?"

"Oh, thanks. Just leave everything on the table beside the tools and leftover corn and sausage," Janie directed. "I'll roll the shells up in the newspaper."

Sibley pitched in by grabbing the leftover corn, sausage, and onions, and Ryan and Momma picked up the utensils. They left the Solo cups on the table as trash, but they saved the beer bottles for the recycling bin.

Janie motioned to Sibley and then toward the house. "Can you go and free our little friend? She probably needs to go outside."

"Sure." Sibley was gone in a second.

"She does love animals." Ryan stared after Sibley.

"I do, too, but I'm not sure I'm ready for a full-time puppy." Janie said it as much to herself as to Ryan.

"Maybe fostering her will help with that decision."

Janie wasn't sure; the longer the little dog was here, the harder Janie would find it to give her back, but she owed Lynn a favor, so she would look after the puppy for as long as was needed.

Sibley brought out the puppy. Immediately, they engaged in a game of chase, much like before, and Sibley's delighted chuckles and the puppy's equally joyful barking filled the air.

"Looks like the sunset is gonna be a stunner." Ryan pointed to the sky, where the sun was just beginning its descent amidst a hundred different shades.

That gave Janie an idea. "Have you ever watched the sun set over the water from the beach at the end of the island?"

Ryan shook his head. "Joe suggested it to us, but I haven't taken the time to go over there yet."

"We could go now," she suggested, suddenly inspired by their moments together that evening. "It looks like Sibley is in puppy heaven."

He gave a small laugh. "Yes, it seems so. Sunset at the point sounds like a great idea."

His eyes were kind when he said this, and Janie got that tingling she often did around Ryan. It wasn't an unfamiliar sensation, given that she'd experienced it in the past and understood what it meant. And that scared her just a little.

Chapter Eighteen

Janie drove the golf cart along the narrow, pitted paved road to the very tip of the island, just over a mile from the house. Sand lightly coated the route after being blown and tracked in from the constant beach traffic.

Once she parked the cart, Ryan grabbed the quilt Janie had brought with them from the back.

"The best way to get the full effect is to sit close to the water," Janie said, leading them down the beach. It felt odd repeating the same motions she and Daniel had but with another man. Knowing that Ryan was a good guy and that Daniel likely would have seen Ryan as a friend lessened the guilt a little. Janie recognized her progress as she faced her feelings for the first time. Before she'd met Ryan, it would've been inconceivable.

"This is amazing. I can't believe I haven't been here before now," Ryan said.

Janie inhaled as his hand brushed against hers as they were getting settled on the quilt.

The expanse of sky here was unimpeded but for a distant row of palm trees on the Pritchard side of the inlet, which framed the view perfectly. A few clouds hung low and contributed to the scene, adding something for the light to play with as it made its descent, the sky's colors changing every minute or two. The background became solid orange for a time, before the tones changed to purples and pinks as a few clouds rolled into the mix.

Janie and Ryan stared ahead, taking in the spectacular sky, unspeaking. Then, without warning, Ryan reached over and tentatively curled his warm fingers around Janie's. She gasped silently in surprise, but it felt so right in the moment. She responded by lightly squeezing back. They continued to sit like that, still not speaking, until dusk shrouded them. Janie was afraid to move, afraid to break the spell.

Eventually, it was time to return home. When she turned toward Ryan, he was already looking at her intently. Janie didn't break his gaze. He leaned in, and a quick, breathless anticipation that he might kiss her washed over her.

Then, he pulled back suddenly, clearing his throat. "I guess we should head home, huh?" he said, his voice a little gruff.

"Um, yeah. I guess we should," Janie said.

Their moment had abruptly ended, and Janie was left to catch her breath, confused by his change in behavior.

Ryan stood and held out a hand to pull Janie up from where she still sat. She got the same warm sensation as before when she'd touched his hand, but she avoided his eyes, worried about what she might or might not see in his expression. She mumbled a thanks and turned away from the water, then headed toward the parked golf cart.

They rode back together in silence, the lights cutting through the darkness of the night now. It seemed as if they'd been gone for so long, but it was less than an hour.

They found Sibley and the puppy cuddled on a chaise on the back patio.

"Y'all look comfy there," Ryan said when he saw them.

"I've decided to call her Lulu." Sibley stroked the nose of her charge. "She just seems like a Lulu, don't you think? I mean, we've got to call her something besides *the puppy*, right?" Sibley looked up at Ryan and then Janie hopefully.

"Lulu sounds perfect. But we're still not sure how long she'll be with us," Janie said. She sensed both her and Ryan were trying to keep their focus on Sibley rather than their moment back at the beach.

"I know. I just thought she needed a name," Sibley said, pulling Janie's attention back to her and the dog. The girl reached down and snuggled the puppy with longing in her eyes.

"Honey, you know we can't have a puppy right now," Ryan said gently. "We're not home enough, and puppies need lots of time and attention."

"I know. I wasn't asking to keep her. I would be sad if she were alone in the house all day."

Relief visibly flooded Ryan, his shoulders relaxing.

"She'll be with us for a little while, at least," Janie said to ease Sibley's longing. "You can come over and spend time with her whenever you want." It was the best offer she could make for now.

"Thanks, Janie. I know from just the last hour that Lulu is a real handful."

Janie laughed as she absorbed a soulful stare from Lulu. "But she sure is cute, isn't she?"

Sibley nodded and then stood, reluctantly passing the now-calm Lulu back to Janie, who cuddled the warm puppy.

"Looks like you finally wore her out," Janie said.

They said goodnight, and Janie wondered what Ryan was thinking. He didn't exactly look her in the eye before they parted. That almost-kiss still hung between them and Janie couldn't help but feel disappointed that it hadn't happened.

Ryan sat outside in the pitch-black dark of night, under the stars on the back deck, obsessing over what had nearly happened between Janie and him. He wished Sibley was buzzing around to distract him, but she'd gone to her room early. Little Lulu had been a constant but adorable ball of energy, and either Sibley had felt the effects of it or the several hours they'd spent cleaning the garage and then kayaking had wiped her out.

His mind went back to Janie. Maybe he'd been compelled by the sunset and the ocean breeze, and Janie had clearly been caught up in the moment as much as he'd been. He'd stopped himself from kissing her.

But he was kidding himself if he believed his almost-action was brought on by the sunset. It was his attraction to Janie, and this feeling between them had been building in the weeks they'd known each other. She wasn't like anyone he'd ever met.

He'd been drawn to her this evening, enough to kiss her. And if that had happened, who knew how things might go? Sibley had become reliant on Janie's opinion and advice, which was a good thing... a great thing, actually. Leslie's recent absence in her daughter's life had left Sibley without enough motherly affection, and as much as Ryan tried to fill that hole, it wasn't the same, and he knew it.

But how would Sibley respond to his pursuing a relationship with Janie? Would it tilt the balance? He couldn't risk it. She was still so fragile, and just now getting her footing here, living on the island.

Sibley valued Janie's friendship and Ryan wouldn't get in the way of that. It was too important to her.

But what now? He couldn't just turn off his interest in Janie. And it appeared she was equally drawn to him. Maybe a little distance would be a good idea until his divorce was finalized and things moved back toward some kind of normal between Leslie and Sibley.

But Ryan couldn't stop remembering the look in Janie's eyes just before…

If they *had* kissed, things would have changed between them. Lately, her life's normal track *had* been thrown off its usually predictable path. Watching sunsets with a very attractive man was exciting and had her blushing like a teen. But a kiss? Well, that was something else entirely. That would be next-level stuff.

Janie thought back on meeting Ryan for the first time—how thrown for a loop she'd been at the mere introduction of someone new on the island. Someone who now lived only two doors down. Ryan and Sibley had kind of snuck up on her and added another dimension to her life. One that Janie was beginning to look forward to each day.

But were any of them ready for things to change between them? Maybe not. Sibley and Ryan had a lot going on in their lives and Janie didn't want to complicate matters further. Friendship was all that they could offer each other now and Janie knew she should be grateful for that.

Lulu whimpered from her makeshift pen in the kitchen, pulling Janie out of her muddled thoughts. Since she couldn't sleep anyway, she figured she might as well check on the puppy. Janie slipped out of bed and headed quietly into the kitchen. Lulu was tangled in a soft, pink blanket Momma had pulled out of storage. When she caught sight of Janie, her tail began wagging at high speed. She stood up on her short back legs, with her front paws resting against the side of the plastic gate. In addition to the blanket, Momma had found a stack of connectible plastic panels that must have been used as a playpen when Janie and her sisters were babies. It worked well to keep Lulu corralled at this size, since she wasn't yet housebroken.

"Hi, girl," Janie whispered as she approached the pen. Unable to resist Lulu's sweet brown eyes, she scooped her up for a cuddle. "Must be a little scary sleeping in a new place, huh?" Change for Lulu—and change for Janie. Janie quickly let Lulu out back to potty on the grass. "Good girl. Good potty." Janie praised the pup and then picked her up for another cuddle. "Who's a good girl?"

It had been such a long time since she'd had a dog in the house, and Janie had forgotten the happiness it brought—and the work, too. When she was a little girl, they'd rescued a hound named Barkley. Barkley spent his entire life chasing after Janie, Joy, and Jaclyn, cuddling, and suffering the indignity of being dressed up every chance the sisters got. She considered how nice it felt to have a faithful friend around again.

As she put Lulu back down and watched the little furball bouncing through the yard, Janie couldn't help but notice the puppy's joy. It was inspiring to have around. Was she ready for that kind of upheaval in her life?

Janie sighed and decided that three a.m. wasn't the time to ponder such an important decision. "C'mon, girl. Back to bed."

Chapter Nineteen

Lynn's waiting room was empty except for a woman with a very uneasy hound dog on a leash.

"Somebody's a little nervous, huh?" Janie spoke to the woman.

"Chester's a big ole' baby is what he is. Chases down anything he can, no matter how big or bad it might be. Been bitten by a snake and wrestled with a porcupine, but a little needle scares him."

"He's a beauty."

"Thanks." The woman pointed to Lulu. "That's a cute little one."

"Yes, we're here to adopt her from Lynn." The words made it real. Lulu really was going to be Janie's new companion. She couldn't help but experience a tiny thrill, and a rush of emotion that nearly swallowed her.

"Oh, hey, y'all." Lynn approached from the back and clapped her hands together. "Well, all right. Let me see to Chester here and Mary will get the paperwork for you to fill out, Janie."

Mary, the assistant, happily pulled out a form and began prepping it.

"Oh, by the way,' Lynn said, "your hatchling seems fine besides needing a little more nutrition. What will you do with him?"

"I would like to try and put him back in or near his nest, but I think the tree is too tall, and the nest is leaning, so I don't want to take the chance of tipping it. If you have any ideas, I'd love to hear them."

"Okay, see you in a sec." She opened the door between the reception area to let Chester and his momma go through.

Momma pointed at Chester's retreating back. "Reminds me a little of Barkley."

Janie smile. "Yes, he does."

Lulu squirmed in her bag.

"Shh. It's okay. Not much longer, girl."

Ten minutes or so later, the door opened, and Chester's mom led him through. Lynn motioned for Janie and Momma to come back.

"I wanted to let you have a quick look at Bert. I'd like to keep him the rest of the week to fatten him up with some live mealworms instead of the formula he's been getting. I want to be sure that he's thriving before we try to replace him near the nest."

Janie saw immediately that Bert appeared less stressed as well as cozier inside his box. Lynn had added some more torn newspaper to his bedding. Seeing Bert's big eyes squeezed Janie's heart.

"Hey there, little guy. We're going to somehow get you home soon." Talking to the little bird made Janie feel better.

Momma stepped closer to have a look. "He looks okay, doesn't he?"

Lynn stepped over. "He's perfectly healthy, from what I can tell. The issue now, I guess, is trying to get him back to his mother. She might take a couple days to reclaim him, and I need him to be fattened up in case it takes a little time before she feeds him again."

"I've been trying to figure out how to get him back near his nest. But he fell out of it because the tree is askew. There's no clear path on the property to transport the equipment needed to straighten the nest and get Bert back inside."

"Maybe you could place him nearby, just high enough to be out of reach from ground animals and let the mother do the rest," Lynne suggested.

"Yes, that might work. I was trying to figure out a way to get him higher and closer to his nest, but what you're suggesting sounds as good as anything I've come up with so far. Thanks, Lynn."

"So, let's have a look at this little pup. Lulu, was it?"

Momma suggested a trip to the pet store first. "Oh, my," she exclaimed once they arrived, "we *have* to get her this pink leash and collar."

They spent almost an hour outfitting Lulu with the latest gear: a new bed, toys, food, puppy pads, and, of course, the pink leash and collar. Lulu napped in her carrier bag like a little angel, which meant she turned into a little wild thing when they let her out to potty on the open grassy area beside the store.

"Glad we got that leash and collar," Momma said as she laughed at Lulu's chaotic rolling in the grass, dashing after a flying bug, and then grabbing onto the hem on a leg of Momma's jeans.

"We're really going to have to do something about that," Janie said, remembering Lulu had done the same thing to Ryan yesterday. She'd been avoiding thinking about him all day, still unsure what to take from last night. But spending time with Momma had distracted Janie from trying to figure it out, thankfully.

Janie and Momma hit another couple of clothing shops in Beaufort, then quickly stopped and picked up sandwiches, as Lulu had begun to squirm quite a bit. They took her to the nearby park to eat, while letting Lulu run around as much as the leash would allow.

The weather was overcast and humid, but it was cool enough to sit at one of the picnic tables sprinkled throughout the park. There were a few moms with young children having fun on the playground.

"I'm glad you suggested this outing. I've missed our time together lately," Janie said, taking a bite of her sub sandwich while Lulu hopped on blowing leaves and barked.

"I've missed it too, but I'm thrilled to see you rediscovering your enthusiasm for the things around you. We're navigating new waters, which is exciting."

But this day had been about spending quality time together and it had been wonderful. It seemed Momma agreed, for after they'd gotten Lulu settled and finished eating, Momma gave a contented sigh.

"This was a nearly perfect day, don't you think?"

"Yes, it has been," Janie said. She then turned to Momma, hedging her words. "Speaking of navigating new waters, you and Joe have been talking a lot lately, huh?"

Momma shrugged. "Yes, we have. He understands how I'm feeling."

"How are you feeling?"

"Darlin', since the neighbors moved in, I've been seeing you change. You've been pretty private about things lately, so I've taken up talking to Joe. Because, while it isn't a bad thing, changes in your life mean changes in mine, and you're not the only one who's changing. I've come to realize some things lately."

"What things?" Janie asked, completely flummoxed by whatever Momma had going on in her head.

"I see you moving toward a new life, one that doesn't include your mother in every single meal and decision that you make. You and Daniel had your private life aside from me, but since he's been gone, you and I have relied heavily on each other for support."

"I'm not going anywhere," Janie reassured her.

Momma gave Janie a tender smile. "I told myself when your father died that I was too busy to even consider my needs. I was raising three headstrong daughters and there never seemed to be enough time—for anything. Then, after Daniel died, you needed me so much, and I knew first-hand what that loss was like. I jumped right in to take his place for you. But what I didn't do for myself after losing your dad, or show you how to do, was to see that our lives don't end with theirs. Whatever this is with Ryan, or wherever it leads, it's helped you heal and become your own woman again. I think it's time for me to do the same."

As Lulu plopped down, finally tired, her little head resting on Janie's foot, Janie realized how much her mother had not only held their family together after their father's passing but also how much she had put her life on hold. Momma deserved a chance to build her life and to enjoy whatever that entailed and Janie was determined to support her every step of the way, just as Momma had done for Janie. As these thoughts filled Janie's mind, she experienced a lovely feeling of peace. Whatever happened, things were okay.

Excited about surprising Sibley, Ryan had rescheduled his afternoon patients in order to prepare for the boat's delivery. He'd still need to get the tags and stickers, but that was on his list.

The marine store where he'd bought the boat advertised a boating class, so he planned to stop by to check it out. Sibley was old enough to drive a boat, and Ryan figured they both could do with a refresh of the rules and regulations when out on the water. Maybe after her tennis season ended, they'd have more time.

He'd wanted to tell Janie about the boat, as she'd shared his earlier enthusiasm when he'd mentioned buying one, but he hadn't done so yet. He wondered what she thought about their almost-kiss last night on the beach. Part of him was terrified of jumping into a relationship this soon while he was still navigating the divorce from Leslie. The other part, admittedly, came alive whenever he was near Janie. He hated sending her mixed signals but, honestly, he was moving through uncharted waters here.

Hoping Janie was still willing to be his friend, Ryan decided to text her and tell her about the boat. Because as much as he was attracted to her, he also valued her friendship, and the thought of something affecting that cast a shadow on the day. In fact, when he'd been finalizing the boat selection, he'd asked himself, *What would Janie think?* Her opinion mattered to him because she had experience with boats and, well, because he somehow wanted her approval.

So, it was time to test the current temperature of things with Janie.

Hi there, I wanted to tell you that the new boat is being delivered this afternoon. It's a surprise for Sibley.

The three dots danced in a wave as she typed a response.

How exciting! I'd love to stop by and take a look later if that's okay.

Relief washed over him in that moment. She wanted to come over. So, he answered:

Feel free to head over anytime. Getting my licensing in town now.

Okay. See you later.

Now that he'd shed that worry, Ryan could enjoy the afternoon.

Chapter Twenty

Janie swerved the golf cart to avoid a box turtle in the middle of the road. She pulled over and reversed, then grabbed her work gloves from her backpack and approached the large turtle. She gently lifted the unexpectedly heavy creature by either side of his shell and then carried him over to a small creek within view that she knew led to a perfect habitat. She tried to maneuver the turtle as far down to the bank of the creek as possible before releasing him, hoping he wouldn't turn around and head back to the road.

"Take care, big guy," Janie whispered, more to herself.

As the turtle retreated into its habitat, Janie remembered how Daniel's passion for the creatures of the island had drawn her in. Now, she couldn't imagine driving past an animal in jeopardy. Some days, Janie felt as if she made large contributions. Other days, it was heartbreaking. But it was always worth it.

Once she'd parked the cart in its usual place near the habitat, Janie noticed the bright-yellow rezoning notice still stapled on the light pole. *How could she have forgotten about the notice?* She'd seen it the day Bert had fallen from the nest, but she'd been preoccupied with saving his life, and was only just now able to internalize the sign's impact.

She tilted her head and carefully reread the information on the page tacked to the wooden pole. There was just under two weeks until the hearing at the courthouse in Beaufort. It was time to deal with this.

She took a picture of the poster with her phone's camera, noting the nameless phone number. There was only one way to find out who it belonged to. She dialed the number right then and there.

A man's gruff voice came on the line. "Tax Assessor's Office. This is Hugh Duncan. What can I do for you?"

"Hi, this is Janie Brooks out on Fripp. This phone number was on a rezoning notice, and I wanted to get some more information about the property, if I could."

"Fripp, huh?" There was a shuffling of papers in the background. "Oh, here it is. Yeah, there are plans to subdivide the property into three buildable lots."

Janie tried to control her breathing. "Can I get any information about who is doing this?"

"Uh, not really. This is all the information I can share right now. I can't give out names. If you have any interest in the property, you should show up at the hearing."

Deep breaths. "Okay, thank you, Hugh."

"My pleasure."

After disconnecting the call, Janie moved to her golf cart and sat back down. Her worst fears were coming true. She'd worked so hard to protect this bird habitat for such a long time, and now the inevitable was happening. Years ago, Daniel had warned her that the protection from the Endangered Species Act would only do so much to prevent the sale and development of this property. Janie had been lulled into a false sense of security by the lack of any action toward its sale. Her eyes welled up with tears. She had to think clearly so she could save the nests and protect the hatchlings.

Once the hatchlings got to the fledgling stage and were better prepared for independence, she might not worry so much. The kites would migrate to South America once they were done with nesting for the season. There were at least four weeks to go until the nestlings became fledglings, and then they would learn to fly. Any activity on the land could put them at risk until then. If the nests weren't there on the birds' return next year, they would find another place to build them. It would break Janie's heart to see that happen, but, for now, she would pick her most immediate battle: delaying any kind of actions that would harm the vulnerable babies in the current nests.

She sighed and stood, grabbing her camera bag and supplies, and made her way to Bert's family nest to check on his siblings. Janie only hoped everything was as it had been with the nearly toppled nest.

The mother flew in circles overhead, squawking at Janie's arrival. Janie wanted nothing more than to reassure her that Bert was safe and cozy and getting fattened up for his return to the family.

Through her binoculars, Janie noticed that the nest remained in the same odd position it had been in since the storm hit. She was careful on her approach to check all around in case either of the other babies had fallen out. Thankfully, that hadn't happened as far as she could see.

She noticed the tree's branches were turning brown, which meant either the storm had zapped it, or it had been overcome by heart rot because of the damage done to it. If heart rot was the cause, it might only be a few months before it spread to the other trees. This was a huge blow for all involved. Besides the developers, of course. If heart rot was determined, the trees would need to be cleared anyway.

Janie took some bark samples from the base of the tree and picked up some of the needles that had been shed. She could send these to the forestry division at the university and find out for sure. As much as she wanted to fight for the nests, they couldn't thrive another season on dead or dying trees.

This was a hard realization, but if Daniel had taught her anything during their years together, it was that nature was sometimes cruel. Despite fighting against her panic and tears, Janie needed to put on a brave face. Figuring out how to navigate the next few weeks would be important—not only for her but for the nestlings, who'd recently graduated from being tiny hatchlings. Each stage had its challenges, but as they grew, they were infinitely less at risk from predators.

As Janie neared her house, Ryan and Sibley were outside in the driveway. It appeared the new boat was being delivered, and she was a beauty, looking to be around twenty-feet long with a full windshield. A combo sporting and fishing boat, if the rod holders told the tale. The sight was a welcome distraction from what she'd just witnessed.

Sibley waved, drawing Janie's attention to the smile on the girl's face, and giving her a flutter of happiness. She pulled in at the end of the driveway, attempting to stay out of the way as the large boat was maneuvered toward the garage. Janie figured they wouldn't actually put the boat inside the garage yet since the season was only starting.

"Hi, Janie, isn't it pretty?" Sibley approached her, pointing toward the Stingray deck boat. "I can't believe Daddy bought it and didn't tell me."

"What a fun surprise. It's gorgeous."

"Oh, hey there," Ryan said, walking up the drive to join Sibley. "What do you think?" He waved a hand toward the boat.

"I think you've got great taste in boats." Janie slid him a knowing grin. "Well done."

"How's your day been?" he asked, his gaze swallowing her fondly.

She almost told him about the birds, but she didn't want to dampen the excitement. "Good," she lied, her chest squeezing with the thought of what she faced.

"Can I go see Lulu?" Sibley asked Janie.

"Of course you can. You can play with her in the yard if you want. She's probably due for a good run by now. We'll need to figure out a good exercise schedule for her."

Sibley's eyes lit up. "Are you going to keep her?"

"Why, yes we are. Momma and I had a big talk about it this morning and decided we couldn't send her back. So, Miss Lulu has found her forever home here with us."

"Wow, that's a big deal. Congratulations." Ryan sounded almost as enthusiastic as Sibley regarding Lulu's new permanent status. "You've got puppy sitters two yards down, if you ever need us."

"Thanks so much."

"I'm heading to the marina to launch the boat in about a half an hour. Joe's meeting me there to gas up and go with us. Would you and Georgia like to come out with us for her maiden voyage?" Ryan asked.

"I'd love to. And I'm sure Momma would too." Janie thought being out on the water may help to distract he and take her mind off her worry about the kites. Certainly being around Ryan was enough to divert her attention.

"Can you bring Lulu?" Sibley asked with wide-eyed delight. "It's okay, right, Dad?"

"Of course," Ryan replied. "I'll text you when I'm ready," he said to Janie.

"You can help me with getting Lulu ready for her first boat ride," Janie suggested.

Bouncing over to the golf cart, Sibley jumped onto it, ready to go.

As Ryan pulled up at the marina, Joe was there to meet him and guide the trailer into the water to launch the boat.

Sibley, Janie, and Georgia arrived in the golf cart just as Ryan had parked the truck and empty trailer. Ryan had been thrilled by Sibley's reaction to the surprise when she'd seen the boat earlier and he was looking forward to their first trip out on the water. It was great to have Joe and Georgia there, too, but Ryan was especially pleased that Janie was joining them. He'd wondered if there'd be any awkwardness between them after the moment they'd shared watching the sunset together, but Janie was her usual friendly, warm self and he couldn't wait to share another evening with her.

They all climbed into the boat, and Ryan familiarized himself with the controls. "Everybody have life vests?"

From her stern seat behind Joe, Janie shot him a huge grin that hit him right in the heart. She looked absolutely adorable with her hair pulled back in a ball cap and a pair of silver, wire-framed sunglasses. He wasn't sure how he'd not just gone ahead and kissed her the night before; being friends was getting trickier by the day for Ryan, but he was adamant he wouldn't jeopardize the friendship, nor Sibley's with Janie.

With everyone aboard and suited up in their life vests, Ryan put the throttle in gear. The water slapped against the hull, and the sea breeze blew in his face. It was an almost magical combination. Right there and then, things felt right in his world.

Chapter Twenty-One

"Daddy, do you think I'm ready for my road test?" Sibley asked for the third time from the passenger seat, her nerves clear.

Now that the day had arrived, Ryan had an uneasy lump in his throat about this huge step in their lives. Once Sibley was driving, she would inevitably spend less time with him and more time with friends and away from their home, which he understood was important at her age, but it still tore at his heart.

"Relax, honey," he said, making the turn toward her school. "You're ready for this. You've put in the hours driving and I'm certain it will go great." He pulled to a stop sign and peered over at his daughter, giving her an encouraging smile.

Sibley nodded, turning her attention back to her phone as he hit the gas. She chuckled when she read a new text.

"Who's that?" he asked in a conversational tone as he tried to peek at the number while pretending to check his rearview mirror.

"Oh, nobody." She dismissed his question and pulled her phone lower where he couldn't see it.

Surprised by the gesture, Ryan glanced over at his daughter and got the impression she was attempting to keep the texts private. "Nobody, huh?"

Sibley's expression was guarded when their eyes met. "Yeah, it's nothing. Just one of my friends wishing me good luck with my driver's test today."

Ryan didn't respond, but he did wonder why she was suddenly hiding those texts. If he thought about it, she'd been going up to her room earlier lately. He'd heard her talking on the phone behind her closed door, and, while she'd done that before with her girlfriends every now and again, it made him curious about it, given this new, more secretive behavior.

"You know you can talk to me, right? About anything," Ryan said, pulling to a stop on the road behind a line of cars. Traffic filled the street. Admittedly, he could be overreacting. Sibley hadn't actually done anything wrong.

"Sure, I know that. If I need to talk, I'll tell you." She smiled briefly at him, grabbing her backpack from the floor of the truck as they neared the school. "Oh, is it okay if I spend the night with Mom this weekend?"

Her question took him by surprise.

"I want to hang out with my friends Saturday night and Mom said it was okay if I stayed with her. Plus, I think it'll be good for me to stay there and sleep in my old room sometimes."

"Oh, um, I guess that would be okay. Do I need to call your mom about it?" Ryan understood there was no way back for Leslie and him. But he didn't want to keep Sibley from her. His thoughts heavy, he crawled along behind the other cars as they began to move.

"No. I'll let her know it's okay."

Ryan had a sudden urge to call Leslie and have her pay attention to anything out of the ordinary next time she spoke with Sibley, but he'd wait a little longer, maybe. Until he was sure something was up with her.

"Have a good day, honey." He pulled into the circular drop-off area in front of the high school.

"You too. Bye, Daddy." She opened the car door, stepping out, and all of a sudden, as she adjusted her backpack, she looked more like a young woman than a little girl.

"I'll be here at three to get you," he said, feeling an immediate urge to scoop her up and take her home. Time was beginning to move too quickly for his liking. He tried to appreciate every day they had together with Sibley at home with him but his heart could hardly take that she was growing up so quickly.

"Okay, Daddy." She turned away, walking over to catch up with a few of her friends.

He sat in the line, watching her go. But then, she turned around and gave him a little wave, making his heart sing. With an emotional chuckle, he pulled away, wondering if there had been anything with those texts she'd gotten. He wanted to protect her so badly but he knew that he had to give her space as well.

After he'd dropped Sibley at school, Ryan headed into the office, still thinking about those texts and praying that he'd taught Sibley everything she needed to take care of herself. As he pulled into his parking space at work, his phone rang, causing him to snap out of his thoughts on Sibley's actions.

"Hello?" he answered, putting the car in park.

"Hey there, it's Michael," his realtor said on the other end of the line. "You know how I've been keeping an eye out for buildable lots on Fripp."

"Yes?" Ryan said, his curiosity piqued. They occasionally spoke to check in, but this was the first call he'd received out of the blue.

"I wanted to show you a piece of property on Sand Dollar Road that's coming on the market soon. It's tied up with a little red tape right now, but we feel certain we'll be able to move forward with purchase pretty quickly once it goes on sale. If you like the property, I don't want you to lose this opportunity, so I suggest we get cracking now."

Hearing this news lifted Ryan's spirits, as the house plans were nearly done. "Great. I've got to take my daughter to get her driver's license after school, but I could be free around five thirty."

"All right, I'll pick you up at your house then."

Ryan's day had just improved. Michael knew exactly the kind of lot he hoped to find. Building a new house gave Ryan something to look forward to in the long term—a place for just him and Sibley that they could put their stamp on. But he had to admit he was going to miss being neighbors with Janie when the time came.

As Janie sat in front of her computer at the kitchen table that morning, sipping her coffee and checking on supply orders for additional sea glass and new glue guns, she was restless, her mind elsewhere. She wouldn't be able to sit still until she knew the fate of the land at the south end of the island, which wouldn't happen until the public hearing. In the meantime, she was determined to learn as much as she possibly could about the condition of the trees, so she made a phone call to someone who might be able to help.

"Since I'm working on Lady's Island, I'm not far from Fripp and can stop by around noon to look at the trees, if that works for you," Kyle Parker, one of the best arborists in the state, and someone Daniel had known pretty well, told her.

"Thanks so much, Kyle. I owe you."

"Happy to take a look," he said. "It sounds like heart rot, but hopefully it isn't. We don't want it posing a threat to all the trees nearby."

She tipped her mug to view the cooled coffee, and decided to abandon it, instead spending the morning in the workshop with Momma, completing special orders for packing and shipping while Lulu played in her pen in the corner. While they boxed up everything, Janie told Momma about her call.

"Do you have a way of relocating the nests if you have to?" Momma asked after Janie had outlined the situation.

"If the trees can't be saved, we can put up nesting stands to encourage the kites to return if the new owners agree to it, but that's unlikely. Most people wouldn't want to have that right near their home. I need to make sure nothing happens on the property until the kites fly south. By the time they get back for the next nesting season, they could build new nests, maybe on Hunting Island where it's less populated."

"Sounds like that would be the best-case scenario," Momma said.

But there were several ifs involved: *if* she could get a temporary restraining order prohibiting any heavy equipment that might place the nestlings at risk until they became more independent fledglings and flew away, and *if* she was able to pull together a plan for the next nesting season and execute it. And that was *if* the trees didn't have raging heart rot. One *if* hinged on the other and all of them had to work in a timely manner to save the habitat. And if they didn't work in a timely manner—well, Janie didn't even want to think about that.

Lulu barked loudly, the sound excessively high-pitched in the workshop, pulling Janie out of her funk.

"Sounds like somebody wants attention," Momma said.

"I'll take her out for a little bit."

Janie took the puppy outside, allowing Lulu to run and play while she sat on the grass, throwing the tiny ball they'd gotten at the pet store. The salty air was cathartic for Janie, so she soaked up the sunshine and tried to focus on all the good things in her life.

Janie waited in her golf cart, reading emails on her phone, until Kyle arrived at the habitat just after noon. Relief spread over her when he pulled up, and she waved, glad that he could make time for her today.

"Thanks for coming so quickly," Janie greeted him, slipping her phone in her back pocket.

"No problem." He turned around and peered up at the trees. "Which ones have the issue?"

Janie led Kyle to the area, and he peered through his binoculars first to get a closer look at what might be happening at the top of the tree.

"There's obvious damage to this one from a lightning strike. Notice how the fungi is growing on the bark not far from the break? It's likely to have already started before the storm hit it. Let's have a look at the others nearby."

Janie ran her hand along the trees as Kyle inspected the bark and foliage, and then he identified her worst fear.

"These trees will need to go as soon as possible," he said, pointing to a group of the loblolly pines. "We can't take the chance of the fungus spreading."

Janie had tried to prepare herself for this terrible news, but she felt tears well. "The hatchlings have another four weeks until they can leave the nests. Can we wait that long?"

Kyle peered up again at the tall pines, deliberation on his face. "The sooner they can go, the better, you know? Six trees appear to be affected. It's only a matter of time before it spreads to the others." He pointed to the grouping. "Four weeks could do a lot of damage to the healthy trees. I know this isn't what you hoped to hear, but I have to be honest with you."

Janie used her pair of binoculars to try to catch a glimpse of what was happening with the nest. She could now see the tiny heads poking up—likely stretching their little necks, hoping for their momma to feed them.

"Looks like the other trees are good for now," Kyle said as he finished checking out the rest of the property.

"That's good, at least."

It wasn't her property, she realized, but this land was special. All of the land on Fripp was special. Any diseased vegetation could spread like wildfire and cause chaos among the island's flora and fauna. Janie knew Kyle was right and the diseased trees had to go, but it was a bitter pill to swallow with the nestlings still vulnerable.

Janie walked with Kyle to his truck. "Thanks again for coming," she said as he opened his door and climbed inside.

All of it was out of her control now, but until the trees were cut down, she would do everything she could to make certain the birds survived until they moved on after nesting season.

Chapter Twenty-Two

Once he'd picked up Sibley from school, Ryan headed toward the Department of Motor Vehicles. He glanced over at his daughter who had the driver's manual open on her lap. Her long, dark hair was pulled back into a ponytail and she was wearing heavier makeup on her eyes than usual, but he didn't comment on that. Right now, he knew she'd want to focus on the driving test. When he parked the truck, she hadn't even noticed, all her attention was on studying. Ryan knew she was anxious—he was nervous for her too—but he was confident she was prepared.

When they got inside, the driving examiner was ready as soon as they arrived at the desk for road testing. She was a middle-aged woman who wore a nametag with "Rhonda" printed on it. Rhonda explained to Sibley that she'd be her examiner for the test. The woman's calm demeanor seemed to help Sibley relax a little.

"Are you ready?" the woman asked.

When Sibley nodded, Ryan handed her his keys and then gave her a quick wink of encouragement. "You've got this."

Ryan stood on the sidewalk, fighting a surge of nerves as Sibley checked her mirrors, adjusted the driver's seat and put the truck in gear. As she began to pull away from the curb, his pride took over. She had this.

Twenty minutes later, Sibley pulled up like an old pro with a huge grin on her face. After she'd put the truck in park, she climbed out and waved a paper at him. "I scored a ninety-eight percent!"

"That's awesome, honey." He put an arm around her shoulder, trying to hide his relief that it had gone so well for her. She had been so set on getting her license that it would have crushed her if she hadn't passed.

"She did great. Now, you can take her score sheet inside and make it official," Rhonda said. "Congratulations, Sibley."

After a surprisingly easy process, they were out in a half an hour, and back in the truck.

"We should celebrate," Ryan suggested. "I've got to meet with the realtor to see a lot when we get home, but why don't we grab a bite after?"

"Can we get ice cream, too?" she asked, still shining.

"You got it, honey."

She immediately began posting her new success on social media and sending out several texts in rapid succession. Ryan was delighted to see Sibley so excited, although it all felt a bit surreal to him—his little girl sure was growing up fast.

While Sibley did homework upstairs in her room, Michael picked up Ryan and they drove a short distance to the waterfront property Michael had been telling him about. It sat on the south end of the island, where the population was a little thinner.

"They're planning to divide this property into three buildable lots," Michael said, waving his hand toward the stunning landscape that gave way to a pristine coastline. "*If* the interested developer has his way."

"That's a shame. This lot is perfect just the way it is." Ryan stood on the sandy strip of beach, staring out into the ocean inlet, its gentle waves lapping at the sand. It was so calm and tranquil out here; Ryan couldn't imagine why anyone would want to spoil that.

"Precisely, which is why I brought you here," Michael said as he tipped his head up, his interest moving to the trees. "Technically, it's still on the market, and if we move fast, we might be able to put in an offer."

"I'm certainly interested, and I'd like to find out how much it would cost to buy it outright and eliminate the developer."

"They're still waiting on the zoning and a couple other things to get resolved, but we can ask."

Ryan stepped over the thick brush to get a better look at the property. "This line of palms next to the water is perfect," he said.

"The hearing for zoning is in just over a week, so we should know more about it soon. But I'll contact the owner personally about your interest in buying the land as one parcel."

Ryan returned to the water's edge and stared out at the massive expanse of the dark blue of the Atlantic where it met the lighter blue sky in the distance. This was a view he could only imagine having the privilege of experiencing every single day.

"How was the lot?" Sibley asked as they parked the golf cart at the beach club and headed for the tables that sat out back, overlooking the bright-blue waters as they gurgled and splashed onto the shore.

"It was pretty great, actually. Right on the water with a western view, which means the sunsets there would be perfect. I should hear back from the realtor in a week or so." He pulled out a chair for Sibley under the breezy porch overlooking the ocean. "Right, I'll just go and order."

Ryan went over to the counter and ordered for them, grabbed the drinks, and returned to their table. Sibley was staring at her phone and smiling again.

"Something funny?" He fiddled with her arm, teasing her, and slid her drink across the table before he sat down.

She turned her phone over on the table, face down. "Just a text about Friday night. I'm planning to go out with my friends."

"Where are you going?" Ryan's gut clenched every time he thought about giving her the independence he knew she needed. It was tough, but he trusted her to make good choices.

"To the boys' varsity lacrosse match after school. Claire's boyfriend is on the team. After that, we're going to a bonfire on the marsh."

"Bonfire, huh? Will there be any adults there?" Ryan asked.

"No, Daddy, it's not a school-sponsored thing. Just a bunch of us sitting around a fire. We'll be careful."

"Promise me you'll leave if anyone's drinking. Fire and drunkenness aren't safe."

"I promise."

"Did your mom give you a time to be home?" he asked, tensing, the brokenness of his family still fresh enough to affect him as he asked the question.

"She said eleven."

"Eleven sounds fine to me. If you're running late for any reason, call your mom and let her know."

"I will, Dad," she said with a grin. "You don't have to worry."

He chuckled for her benefit but he'd always feel protective of his little girl, no matter how old she got.

When their pizzas came, they settled into easy conversation, and then headed home, just as the sun was beginning to show off as it set in the west, exploding in vibrant pinks and oranges across the sky.

When Ryan pulled into the drive, they could hear Lulu barking like crazy.

Sibley brightened. "Oh, they must be outside. Can I go and say hi? I want to tell Janie about my license. I promise not to be long."

Ryan's attention turned to Janie as she laughed at something the dog had done. His spirits lifted just catching sight of her, and he wanted nothing more than to rush over, but he hesitated. He was uncertain if allowing himself to spend a lot of time with Janie was a good idea and he didn't want Sibley to be affected by whatever happened with them. She'd made such progress and her friendship with Janie was crucial. One wrong move and he could tip the boat.

"It's been a long day and you've got homework. Maybe you can visit Lulu tomorrow."

The wind left Sibley's sails immediately and her shoulders slumped. "I really want to talk to Janie. Why don't you want me to go?"

"What do you want to tell her?"

"Just… girl talk."

He wasn't convinced, but instead of weighing Sibley down with his insecurities, he relented. "Okay, be back in fifteen minutes, though."

"Hey Janie, guess what?!" Sibley called as she approached Janie in the yard behind the house. She immediately squatted next to Lulu, who greeted her with happy whines and puppy kisses and then rolled over onto her back.

Janie moved closer to her to rub the puppy's belly. "What is it?"

"I got my license!"

"Oh, Sibley. Congratulations, that's fantastic." Janie was pleased for the girl and could see how proud she was feeling.

"Thank you," she said, grinning. "I'm excited. But I also came over to ask for your help."

Janie raised an eyebrow. 'Of course. What can I do for you?"

"My dad's fortieth birthday is coming up and I want to do something special for him. Can you help me plan it?"

Janie lifted her brows in excitement. "Of course I can. What kind of celebration are you thinking about?"

"Maybe a small birthday party with you, Miss Georgia, and Uncle Joe, and maybe my mom... maybe."

Janie kept her smile, even though the mention of Sibley's mom joining them for Ryan's birthday threw her for a tiny loop. "Do you have any plans in mind?"

Sibley lifted her shoulder in a quick shrug. "I haven't gotten that far, which is why I wanted to ask for your help. I've never thrown a party before. My mom always did the birthdays, but I feel like I should plan something with y'all. I'm not even sure if Mom would want to come. It just seems nice to ask her."

"Of course. Why don't I talk to Momma and Joe and see what we can come up with, okay?"

"Thank you so much. I knew I could count on you."

Sibley's words found their way to Janie's heart. Then Sibley hushed her quickly as she nodded across the yard toward their house. Ryan was striding toward them.

"Looks like Lulu is adjusting to her new home, huh?" he said when he'd reached them.

Lulu licked his hand. He pulled the pup into his arms for a little squeeze. His broad hands were as big as Lulu, and watching his gentle touch made Janie's heart flutter.

"I think Sibley's her favorite person," Janie said.

Ryan set Lulu down next to Sibley, and the two ran off toward Momma's backyard, next door, the golden hour just before evening settling on the grass as Sibley and Lulu danced across it—two lone shadows.

"So, the sunset is pretty crazy this evening, huh?" he pointed toward the west, the horizon alight like an orange flame.

Janie followed his glance. "Yes. It never gets old. Do you want to ride over to the beach?" she asked, understanding his excitement over every spectacular sunset on the island because she shared that passion.

Ryan glanced over to where Sibley and Lulu were playing. "I'd come over to tell Sibley it was time to let you get on with your evening, but I'll let her know we'll be gone for a bit." He jogged over to his daughter and Janie felt her heart skip at the thought of watching another sunset with Ryan.

When he returned, Janie took his hand, and a little tingle traveled through her fingers at his touch. His eyes were on their intertwined fingers, thoughts etched on his face. He returned her gaze, smiling at her when he'd realized her attention was on him.

They climbed into her golf cart together and Janie drove them in the same direction they'd gone a few days ago. *The day of the almost-kiss.* That's how she referred to it in her mind. Something had irrevocably changed between them then, whether either was ready to admit it or not.

When they arrived at the beach, Janie pulled out the quilt, just like before, and they found an excellent spot for viewing near the water's edge. It was an exact replica of that previous time. Same spot, same time of day. Same two people, who, in Janie's opinion, had something between them that they were both wrestling with.

Ryan let out a deep breath and stared for a moment toward the water, its surface a calm, dark blue.

"What are you thinking about?" she asked, digging her toes into the sand.

"I was remembering when we were here last time."

Janie faced him, their eyes meeting. A nervous knot settled in her stomach. He'd brought it up, so she would let him guide the discussion.

"I wanted to kiss you," he said, his voice soft. "And I'm sorry if how I behaved was confusing. My reaction at being that close to you surprised me, but I hesitated because I didn't want to do something neither of us was ready for."

"I understand," she said. His words had reassured her that there was something between them, that he felt it too, it wasn't just her, but he knew as well as she did that it was a big step for both of them.

"You do?" he asked, looking relieved.

"I was just as surprised. And if you hesitated getting closer to me, even for a minute, then it's too soon."

"I have Sibley to think about, you know?"

"Yes. Absolutely."

"I still want to kiss you," he said, his dark-blue eyes boring into her soul. "But it's probably better not to."

Janie's heart pinched at the idea of pulling away. Before, she'd believed it was for the best, but she wasn't sure anymore. She finally felt ready to take the next step with him, but he needed to be ready, too.

Chapter Twenty-Three

By the time Friday rolled around, it occurred to Ryan that he would have the night to himself, with Sibley going out with friends, before spending the night at Leslie's. As he sat on the sofa in his empty living room, his first instinct was to check if Janie was outside—maybe she'd want to do something—but then he reflected on their last conversation. And how that had ended.

Ryan needed to be sure that his wanting her company didn't have anything to do with his *not* wanting to spend the evening alone. He'd had a comfortable marriage and partnership for a good many years, and that's how he rolled best, so was he motivated to be near Janie because he was lonely?

Questioning himself at this point felt like a smart idea. The last thing he intended was to use Janie as a surrogate for a partner and to mother his child. But this didn't feel like that. It felt like he liked Janie and being with her lightened his spirit.

He hadn't run into her since that evening at the beach, which he had to admit hadn't really solved anything between them—although it had allowed for them to admit their mutual hesitation to explore their feelings for each other.

It had been a long and busy week. Ryan was tired and decided to watch a movie and enjoy a beer or two. He changed into his comfiest old T-shirt and shorts and was just about to settle down for the evening, when he realized he hadn't checked the mailbox. There probably wasn't anything important, but he was on the lookout for the divorce papers, which were due to arrive any day now.

When Ryan headed outside, Janie was standing at the end of her driveway, flipping through her mail, and his mood brightened at the coincidence.

"Hey there," he called over.

Lulu was tousling with a rope toy. Janie glanced up as he approached, and her smile made it hard to focus on anything else.

"Have you ever noticed there's never anything good in the mail anymore?" he asked to keep things from being awkward. He bent down and patted Lulu on the head when she galumphed through the grass to greet him.

Janie let out a little laugh that sounded like music to his ears after a long day. "True. Just junk mail." She waved the envelopes in the air before tucking them under her arm. "With the mail a disappointment, what will I read tonight?" she said.

Her teasing gave him a zinging feeling of electricity. It was just so easy and comfortable with her.

"I guess you'll have to settle for a movie or something."

"Hmm," she said, clearly considering it. "And some pizza rolls and popcorn."

"Yeah. Sounds like a great evening, if you ask me. I might do the same. Sibley's out with friends tonight and staying at her mom's house."

"Good for her," Janie said, and then bit her lip in a nervous gesture. "If you want some company, you're welcome to join me for pizza rolls and popcorn."

"That sounds nice. I don't have much to offer, but I can bring some beer over. I'll bet I can round up a six pack." Ryan's earlier concerns had evaporated the second he'd gotten near Janie again and he couldn't think of a better way to spend his evening.

Ryan arrived at Janie's at exactly seven o'clock, bearing a full six-pack variety of craft beers. "Can I put these in the fridge?" He held them up just before commenting on the spread of dips, chips, and pizza rolls. "Good thing I didn't eat a big dinner before I came over," he teased.

"Well, dig in." Janie swept a hand over her offerings. She hadn't expected to spend time with Ryan tonight, but when she ran into him outside and he'd mentioned that Sibley was away for the evening, she'd found herself wanting to invite him over and she'd just sort of blurted it out. She still felt a little conflicted over how the evening a couple of days ago had ended and wasn't entirely sure how to navigate it, so she'd decided to show her feelings by preparing food. She valued Ryan's friendship and watching a movie was always more fun with someone else. "And I'll just grab a pale ale. What kind do you want?" she asked.

"Something dark. Surprise me."

She picked out two beers for them from the fridge and then turned back to where he was piling snacks onto a small paper plate, setting them down.

"Do you have a movie in mind for us?" Ryan asked, removing the first beer cap in one swift motion and then popping off the second.

"I'm not sure. There are several I've been wanting to watch again." Janie made herself a plate and grabbed the large bowl of popcorn to carry into the living room.

Lulu settled between them, lifting her small nose, and sniffing the scent of their snacks.

"You've already been fed, my girl." Janie stroked the puppy's soft fur.

They scrolled through the top ten movies for the week, while they discussed their favorites of all time.

"*Shawshank Redemption* is the perfect movie, though I know it's a little dated," Ryan said firmly.

"I liked it, too, but I'd rather watch *Almost Famous* any day."

"My tastes are pretty eclectic, though I haven't done a lot of movie watching through the past few years. When you raise a daughter, there's a lot of Disney and princesses, you know, which requires tremendous flexibility."

Janie laughed, imagining Ryan sitting with his little girl watching *Frozen*. "I've probably watched every Disney movie ever made—twice."

He held up his beer for a toast. "That's something else we have in common."

They clanked bottles and agreed on *Hamilton* for their evening's entertainment. There was an easiness between them tonight that helped Janie relax and not ponder so much about naming their relationship. Right now, it didn't matter. As the movie got going, Janie immersed herself in the enjoyment of just being with Ryan.

By the time they'd finished the remarkable *Hamilton*, it had grown dark.

Janie checked the time. "It's only ten o'clock," she said, not wanting Ryan to go. "Want to watch another?" When she offered, she swore she recognized a sparkle in his eyes.

"I've got nowhere to be."

They sat together on the sectional, Lulu having climbed onto Ryan's end of the couch, which left him room to scoot toward the middle and closer to Janie. She could smell the clean scent of him and feel the warmth of his body heat. He moved slightly, his hand brushing her leg, causing her breath to catch. She swallowed, the movie running along without her attention. His eyes fluttered to the side and caught hers, both of them turning back to the movie. She wondered what was going through his mind, but she didn't want to question it. She sat back and kept her eyes glued to the screen, even as her body registered Ryan's next to her.

Ryan's phone rang around midnight, which had him immediately pulling away from her and taking out his cell from his pocket. "Can you give me a sec? I need to take this." He settled Lulu on the couch and stood. "Slow down, Leslie. Okay, I'll be right there," he was saying into his phone before Janie could answer.

There was clearly a problem, and Ryan went from relaxed and calm to being a certified basket case in about ten seconds. Janie felt herself grow anxious as to what had happened.

Even with the call ended, Ryan still had the phone in one hand as he ran his fingers through his hair with the other. "Leslie says she hasn't heard from Sibley and she's not home yet." Ryan checked the time on his phone. "That makes her almost an hour late. That's not like her."

"Do you know where she was planning to go?" Janie asked, suddenly on high alert.

"Yes," he said, clenching his jaw. "The game and then the bonfire. Leslie's out looking for her now."

"You've had at least two beers; I've only had one. We can take my Jeep," Janie said, turning off the TV and grabbing her purse from the hook by the kitchen door.

"I can't imagine why she hasn't called or returned any of Leslie's texts," Ryan worried aloud as he tried Sibley's number. "No answer. The call went to voice mail."

"Could her phone be dead?"

Ryan frowned. "Not likely; she charges it every night. I'm hoping she's just lost track of time at the bonfire."

Janie hoped that was all there was to it.

Janie drove over the bridge that connected the island to the mainland as fast as she could while still being safe. "Where's the bonfire?"

"On the marsh at the edge of town."

She focused on the road, her pulse pumping in her ears.

"This isn't like Sibley," Ryan repeated, shaking his head. "She knows how I worry."

"Almost there."

They arrived at the deserted open field. Janie had made record time.

Ryan's nerves were clearly on high alert, scanning for any sign of a bonfire or his daughter. "Nobody's here. Where could she be?"

Janie peered down at her phone. "There's no service, which explains why Sibley didn't call or text."

"Maybe they went mudding. I heard they do that around here."

Janie could almost hear Ryan's thoughts as he calculated the odds of the situation, clearly attempting to stay calm.

"Yep, I know where to go." Janie put the Jeep in gear. "This thing should be able to get us in and out."

They headed down two separate dead-end lanes that were indeed muddy and rough. The third one was the worst, but Janie shifted gears to all-terrain, allowing them to move through it easily.

"Wait, what's that?" Ryan pointed to lights in the distance.

"It might be kids parking. Or maybe…" She squinted, trying to make it out. "Somebody is stuck in this mud."

They moved forward slowly, but not so slowly as to get bogged down. Sure enough, there was a vehicle that had spun out and was completely stuck in the marsh mud.

"Do you recognize the vehicle?" Janie asked, parking where they weren't in danger of getting stuck.

Ryan shook his head. "Whoever they are, they look like they're in trouble." He climbed out and headed toward the truck, then turned and called through the open window, "Keep the headlights on."

Ryan approached the vehicle, while Janie stayed put with her eyes focused on him. He spoke with the driver and then he began pointing and gesturing. He went around to the passenger's side, which was sunk so deeply in the mud that the truck was lopsided from its weight and spinning its wheels to get free.

Janie watched, helpless, as Ryan assisted someone out of the truck through the window. As they moved closer to the Jeep, she recognized that it was Sibley. Janie had never seen the girl this upset. As they passed through the headlights, Sibley's shoulders heaved with sobs.

She was also a dirty mess from trudging through the thick mud, as was Ryan. Janie jumped out and grabbed a couple of old towels she kept in the back. She gently wrapped one of them around Sibley and handed the other two to Ryan.

Their eyes met just over Sibley's head. Janie could read relief at finding her safe in Ryan's gaze.

"Thanks, Janie," Sibley mumbled in a pitiful voice.

Janie gave her a little squeeze as she handed her off to Ryan, who opened the door for her. Ryan's eyes were unstill, as if processing the moment.

"Do you have a winch and cable that works on this thing?" Ryan asked after he'd helped Sibley into the back seat. "Kid needs a rescue." He pointed toward the stranded vehicle.

"Yes. The winch works. Let me get a little closer."

They worked together and attached the hook to a thick strap looped around the frame of the young man's truck. Janie placed a line dampener to keep the cable from snapping back toward the Jeep. She plugged in the winch control and got back in the Jeep. The driver slid to the passenger's side and Ryan climbed into the stuck truck and gave Janie the hand signal to start pulling. It only took a few seconds to rescue the lighter truck from the mud.

Ryan honked the horn as a signal to stop pulling, then drove the truck slowly forward until there was enough slack in the cable to easily disengage the line. Ryan and the young man approached the Jeep. Janie climbed out and met Ryan in front.

"Thanks so much, sir. I didn't think we would get stuck. I'm Conner O'Reilly." Conner stuck out his hand toward Ryan, who eyed the tall, wiry young man for a second before shaking his hand.

"It's nice to meet you, Conner. Are you okay to get home?"

"Yes, sir."

The boy was incredibly polite, but it was clear he was shaken from the ordeal. Janie was pretty sure he wouldn't be going mudding again any time soon.

"Hi, Conner. I'm Janie, Sibley's neighbor."

"Oh, hi. She told me all about you." The kid looked up at Janie, relief etched across his face.

"Well, if you're okay here, we're going to head home now. Nice to meet you." Janie lifted her hand in a wave.

"Thanks for pulling me out," Conner said just before he turned to walk over to his truck.

"Don't mention it," Janie called back.

Janie could sense Ryan's restless mood as soon as she climbed into the Jeep after placing the winch controller back inside its case.

"Let's wait a second to be sure he gets out okay." She turned the Jeep around, careful not to get it stuck in the bog. "Looks like he's clear."

Conner waved as he passed, and Janie waved in reply. She then followed behind him back to the marsh road. Sibley hadn't spoken a word and Ryan, too, was silent.

Ryan blew out a heavy breath. "Sibley, who is that, and why were you out here alone with him?"

Sibley sniffed. "Conner is my boyfriend." She said it in a soft voice, as if she were afraid of Ryan's reaction.

Ryan turned to look at her. "Your boyfriend? The one you didn't tell me about?" His voice was serious.

"I was going to tell you. It just never seemed like the right time," Sibley admitted. "I told Janie about him."

Those words fell like a lead weight and guilt swarmed Janie as strongly as it had the moment Sibley had asked her to keep the secret initially.

Ryan turned to Janie with a hurt and confused expression. "And you didn't think I should know she had a boyfriend? It might have helped if you'd mentioned it tonight."

"Sibley promised she would tell you." Janie stiffened. "I had no idea she hadn't."

Sibley then flew to Janie's defense. "I asked her not to tell you. I told her I would when I was ready. She said you should know."

His jaw clenched. "What happened? Where are your friends?"

"When it was time to go, Tina left me. I guess she assumed I was riding home with Conner because we were talking at the bonfire. So, when I didn't have a ride, Conner said he would take me home. I was going to call Mom and tell her, but there wasn't any service. And then we got stuck."

"Why were you off the main road in the first place?"

"Conner wanted to show me the mudhole he and his friends had gone through when they were out here before."

"Show you a mudhole, huh?" Ryan scoffed at the flimsy explanation.

Janie knew she shouldn't be here for this conversation. It was too private, and she vowed to remain silent. There was already enough tension between them.

"Daddy, we weren't doing anything wrong. I promise. It was just a dumb thing that happened, you know?" Sibley beseeched.

"Maybe you didn't do anything wrong, Sibley, but we're building trust here, honey. You got in a boy's truck without our knowledge or permission."

Janie saw Sibley hang her head through the rearview mirror. Janie wanted to put her arms around the girl in support, despite her situation and poor judgment. She could relate, having been in similar situations as a teen girl, recalling her desperation to make Momma understand.

"Daddy, I really didn't mean to do anything wrong. Tina left me and I needed a ride. And the thing with Conner, well, I told Janie because I thought she would understand, and I wasn't sure how you would react. I've never had a boyfriend before."

"Have I ever given you a reason not to tell me something?" he asked.

"I'm so sorry, Daddy." Sibley hiccupped a sob, then she added, "Conner is a responsible boy, I promise."

"A responsible boy wouldn't take you out to the middle of nowhere alone with no service and get stuck in the mud," he retorted.

"I'm really sorry for not telling you about him. Please don't hate him," Sibley sobbed.

"I don't *hate* Conner. I don't *know* Conner. That's the problem." Ryan sighed. "You're old enough to start dating, Sibley. The fact that you didn't feel like you could introduce me to Conner and then went to meet up with him at a bonfire concerns me. It feels sneaky."

"I know," Sibley said, "but this all looks so much worse than it is. Conner is on the lacrosse team, and the bonfire was an after-game thing. He would've been there anyway, even if I wasn't."

Ryan turned and gave Janie directions to Leslie's house.

"How about we communicate better in the future?" he said.

"I can still stay with Mom tonight, right? We're supposed to go out to breakfast together in the morning."

"I'm going to speak with your mother, and we'll decide what to do."

The two of them got out of the Jeep, leaving Janie there alone, the snacks from earlier sitting heavily in her gut.

Ryan came back outside. He climbed in, his expression less tense now.

"Everything okay?" Janie asked for lack of anything better to say.

"It's tough being a dad," he said, the thought giving Janie a little punch of insecurity, having not experienced being a parent. "I hate that Sibley felt she needed to keep a secret from me."

"I wasn't comfortable with not telling you, and I let her know that." Janie hoped her explanation was enough to reassure him.

"Well, Sibley and I are going to have a long conversation when she gets home tomorrow."

As Janie drove Ryan home, the wind in her ears through the open window was the only sound between them, the realization of what she'd be taking on if she went any further with Ryan setting in.

Chapter Twenty-Four

By the time she'd dropped off Ryan and arrived home, pulling into her driveway, Janie was wrung out. She could only imagine how both Ryan and Sibley felt. She tipped her head back onto the headrest, rolling her shoulders.

Her attention was immediately drawn to the sight of Joe's old truck in her mother's driveway. The lights were on and she spotted Momma and Joe talking at his driver's window. Instead of going straight inside her house, Momma waved goodbye to Joe and made her way across the yard to the porch, meeting Janie.

"You're out late. Everything okay?"

"Wanna come in and have a cup of tea?" Janie needed to shake off what had happened.

"Sure, darlin'."

Momma settled at Janie's kitchen table while Janie put on the kettle. Lulu whined softly at being disturbed from her sleep, but she wasn't disturbed enough to get up. Janie joined Momma at the table while they waited for the water to boil.

"So, what's got you so bugged, honey?" Momma's eyes were soft with concern.

Without warning, Janie burst into tears. "Momma, it was awful—"

The kettle whistled. Momma put a hand on Janie's arm. "I'll get it."

Once they were sipping hot, fragrant tea with honey and lemon, Janie did her best to retell the events of the evening. Janie wondered at her investment in Ryan and Sibley. When had she gotten so attached that tonight's events would have this kind of emotional impact?

Momma said, "It's a lot to take in."

Janie nodded, feeling a bit of calm wash over her at Momma's words. As usual, Momma knew how to smooth her frayed nerves.

"Did you have a nice time with Joe?" Janie asked.

Momma actually blushed. "We had a fine time. Sarah and Dean—you know Sarah from when we used to play cards together—well, they made excellent dry martinis and a steak dinner, and then we played Pictionary. I'd forgotten how much fun it was."

"Going out with friends or playing games?"

"All of it. It makes me feel lively and young again." Momma's cheeks were rosy and she breathed a contented sigh.

"Sounds nice," Janie said, delighted that her mother was moving along with her life. She made it look so effortless.

Janie had dreamed all night. She couldn't shake the evening's upset. She woke up groggy, her head pounding and her eyes burning from lack of deep sleep, and the misting weather and dark skies matched her mood. She decided to drive into Beaufort to check on baby Bert to clear her mind.

When Janie arrived at Lynn's office, Lynn met her at the front door. "How's Lulu doing?" Lynn asked as she unlocked the front door for Janie and led her toward the back.

Janie couldn't help the grin that spread across her face at the mention of the pup. "She's great. Momma and I love her so much."

"I'm so glad to hear it," Lynn said as they approached Bert's small box. "Your little guy is doing much better. He's put on enough weight that I think it's time to try and reintroduce him to the nest and his mother."

"Really?" Janie's mood brightened then. "Can I take him home today?"

The baby bird was moving around quite a bit and making little flapping motions with his wings. His feathers were beginning to fill in and Janie could tell he was emerging from a hatchling to a nestling, based on his appearance and movements.

"Yes. I think he's good to go," Lynn said. "Have you made any progress in figuring out where to place him?"

Janie filled her in about the dying trees and the zoning issue. "I'm just hoping the nestlings mature enough by the time the trees need to come down that they're independent."

Lynn gave her a worried nod as she tucked the fresh bedding in Bert's box. "Maybe place a nesting box in a nearby tree for protection. An old straw hat with leaves and yarn works well."

"That's an idea."

"But do keep in mind that the mother bird might still reject him. He's been gone for quite a while, so that's a possibility."

"Yes, I do realize that can happen." But the thought of it broke her heart. "I'm hoping for the best."

"Do the temporary nest and see what happens." Lynn lifted Bert's box and handed it to Janie. "Oh, and if you use a hat, make sure he's in a place where there's some protection from the sun and rain."

"Yes, it's supposed to clear up this afternoon, so I might give it a shot then."

Lynn handed her a small round cardboard container. "Worms."

"Ah, he'll appreciate these. Thanks."

Lynn gave her feeding instructions for Bert as they moved toward the entrance. "Good luck to you."

"Thanks, Lynn."

As Janie carried Bert outside, a plan formed in her mind for a temporary nest. She remembered that Momma had a straw hat packed away with some other items in the garage. It was old and should've probably been thrown out years ago. But Janie was glad now that it hadn't been.

She settled Bert's box on the passenger seat and pulled out of the parking lot, turning the car toward home. The dispersing clouds had lessened the falling rain to a fine mist. It was a perfect day to get Bert settled in his new home since the rain was tapering off. It would also serve to distract her. She hoped Ryan and Sibley would both be feeling better, having had some time to get over the ordeal of the previous night, but Janie was still worried that she'd betrayed Ryan's trust, even if she'd only been keeping a promise to Sibley. Gosh, it was all so complicated.

When she got home, she let Lulu out, and then began to gather the materials for Bert's temporary nest from items in the garage; filling the hat with yarn and such only took a few minutes. She fed Bert several live worms, which he scarfed down in about a second, and then she carefully transferred him from his box to the newly crafted nest, and carried it out to the golf cart.

When they arrived at Bert's habitat, the mother kite flew low, screeching at Janie. She must have caught Bert's scent.

"I've got your baby boy," Janie said to the concerned momma, delighting in the hopeful reunion and feeling a real sense of purpose.

Janie sat the hat on a log nearby just long enough to try to find a good spot to place the nest. She hoped she could place Bert high enough so that he was safe from ground predators. As she was looking up, there was a kerfuffle nearby. Screeches and motion in the corner of her eye caused her to turn around lightning fast. It took a second for her to realize that Bert's mother had swooped down and plucked him from the makeshift nest on the log. Janie grabbed the binoculars hanging from her neck and peered upward to see the mother kite fly around the nest and deposit Bert into his old home.

Her heart hammered in response. The nest didn't move or fall, which was one of Janie's biggest worries. As she watched the mother bird tending to her young, tears of relief swelled without warning.

"Great job, Momma," she whispered to the large female raptor.

The moment took her back to the previous night's rescue of Sibley. In a way, this was a full circle.

Ryan sat at the kitchen table, his attention on the dark phone beside him rather than the half-eaten turkey sandwich he'd made himself for lunch. Trying to allow his daughter her independence, he'd decided to wait until the afternoon to check on Sibley. When the clock clicked over to noon, he grabbed his phone off the table and dialed her number. He'd had a restless night thinking over what had happened, but felt calmer with the light of day, although he still missed her like crazy. He put the pulsing phone to his ear.

"Hello?" Sibley answered.

"Hey," he said, trying to sound like he hadn't been watching the second hand on the clock for the last hour. "Have fun with Mom?"

"Yeah," Sibley replied. "We went to breakfast at The Pancake House this morning, and I got blueberry pancakes, but they weren't as good as the ones you make. The blueberries were tiny."

His affection for her bubbled up. "Let me know when you want them and I'll make my famous ones."

"Okay," Sibley said, her voice notably guarded.

"So, do you all have any other plans?"

"No, Mom's got a hair appointment in a few hours. Wanna come get me?"

"Yep, I'll come right now."

"Okay, Daddy. See you soon."

Ryan didn't delay in going to get her.

As he arrived at Leslie's house, Sibley was sitting outside on her front step with her mom. When he got out, he noticed Sibley's eyes were puffy.

"Have you been crying?" he asked her.

"No. I just didn't sleep very well. I was worried about what happened last night."

"I tried to tell her that things like that happen," Leslie said.

"Am I grounded?" Sibley asked.

"Do you think you should be?" Ryan asked, interested in her perspective.

"Probably." She hung her head then.

Sibley had always been a good kid and Ryan knew the last few months had been tough. Teenagers made mistakes and he could see that Sibley was remorseful even as he knew she wasn't entirely to blame. Perhaps he'd been a bit heavy-handed, too. It was hard, though, trying to give Sibley her independence but also protect her, and he knew he wouldn't always get things right.

"I'm not going to ground you for this, partly because a lot of it wasn't your fault directly, but I would like to know what kind of person you're dating."

She lit up at the mention of Connor. "He's a really nice boy. He plays lacrosse and is going to USC on a scholarship in the fall."

Ryan lifted his brows in surprise. "He's a senior?"

"Yes. He's seventeen."

As much as the thought unsettled him, he knew he wasn't in the best position to challenge Sibley's choices and doing so probably wouldn't be the wisest move anyway. "Your mom was three grades below me when we started dating in college, so I get it. She was a freshman, and I was a junior... We haven't exactly had a real discussion about dating, have we?"

She shook her head. "Mom and I had a long talk ages ago, and then again last night."

Ryan breathed a sigh of relief; he would happily talk to Sibley about anything, but he was glad that Leslie seemed to be stepping back up, even if she still had a long way to go to make amends in his eyes. "Would you like to go out in the boat this afternoon?" he asked. "It looks like the weather is clearing."

Sibley suddenly cheered up. "I'd like that."

Chapter Twenty-Five

Janie gripped her steering wheel tightly as she drove to the courthouse, prepared to battle for the kites' habitat. Just that morning on her way out, she'd yanked off the note from the utility pole where she'd first noticed it and taken it with her, glancing every now and then at the date on the page. The weight she'd carried in her chest as this rezoning hearing had neared had grown each day and had reached the size of a boulder. During the wait, so many things had occurred. The trees had rotted, the land was put up for sale, and Baby Bert had fallen from his nest, taking years off her life.

Successfully handling this to preserve the habitat for the birds meant everything to her. She understood that the diseased trees would need to be cut, but it would be nothing if the habitat itself could be kept safe. The nests could be moved to other trees, although it wasn't easy.

As she parked the car, she mentally rehearsed her protest, running through each of her arguments and possible rebuttals. She wished she had Daniel's calm demeanor and resolve. He'd have breezed in with an air of complete control, and changed everyone's mind in a matter of minutes. But while there was more of an emotional edge to Janie's plea, she knew she had the strength to do it. Armed with her defense, she walked into the courthouse, squared her shoulders, and made her way to the courtroom.

With her hand on the large solid door, she took in one last steadying breath. *You can do this*, she told herself. She was the advocate for these birds and it was up to her to save them. Feeling calmer now, she pushed open the door.

Her breath caught when she found that the room was completely empty. Maybe they'd changed locations? Somebody definitely should have been there already. She'd recited the date from the poster over and over in her head; there was no way she could've gotten it wrong. She pulled the folded poster from her handbag and smoothed it out, double-checking. Yes, it was today. A nagging sensation in her gut told her something wasn't right, but she wouldn't let it rattle her.

Janie walked in, pacing down the center aisle and taking a seat in the front row, clasping her hands in her lap. She'd give it a few minutes. Surely the room would fill up. An analog clock on the wall to her right ticked loudly in the silence that followed. Perhaps something had delayed the meeting. She'd just use the time to run through her speech once more. When she'd gone over her points again, Janie turned to look at the door, just waiting for someone—anyone—to walk through it. But no one did. So she left the room to check in with the clerk of the court's office.

She walked up to a woman at the admin desk. "Excuse me, do you know where I could find the rezoning meeting for the vacant lots on the west side of Fripp Island on Sand Dollar Road?"

"That meeting was yesterday, I'm afraid," the woman replied.

Janie's eyes widened in panic, the blood draining from her skin, sending a cold shiver slithering through her veins. "No, I've got the notice right here." She pulled out the stained and torn piece of yellow paper.

The woman took the weathered note and pursed her lips as she studied it. "It was rescheduled recently due to a conflict in the judge's schedule." She handed the page back to Janie.

"But there wasn't a new notice posted about the change in time." She put her hands on the desk to get the woman's full attention, trying to keep her emotions in check, fearing she'd failed the birds and trying to keep calm like Daniel would have, but she was struggling miserably. "I *need* to speak with someone about this. There are endangered birds on that property." There was a shrill thread running through Janie's voice, but she didn't care anymore, this was important.

"I'm sorry. It does happen with these public land hearings from time to time. It's out of my hands."

This *couldn't* be happening. It was bad enough that there were plans to rezone the habitat, and now the hearing had taken place without an opportunity for Janie to explain the significance of the land. She needed Daniel. He'd know what to do next. Janie sucked in her breath, fighting tears, her stomach in knots, scrambling for some way to fix this all by herself. What could she do...

"Wait. What about the endangered species protection?" she asked.

The woman offered an empathetic sigh. "I'll check to see if someone can get you up to speed with the ruling." She picked up her desk phone's receiver and punched in a series of numbers.

When the woman finally reached someone, she began to explain the situation. Janie hung on every word of the call, but she wasn't able to make out what was going on with only hearing one side of the conversation.

"Good news," the woman said, hanging up the receiver. "One of the members who was present at the hearing yesterday is available to meet with you in his office now. His name is Leon Green."

At least that was something.

"You'll take a left out of this office and go down the hall until you see A-5 on a sign. Mr. Green's name is on his door," the woman instructed.

"Thanks for your help."

"Best of luck to you."

When Janie got to the office, she paused outside the door and closed her eyes, channeling Daniel's calm. This was her battle now. Time to show Daniel he'd left his work in good hands. She sent up a quick prayer for strength. She opened the outer door and went inside, encountering a well-dressed man on the other side of a wide desk set up as reception in the entryway, full of neatly stacked paperwork.

"How may I help you?" he asked, fiddling with his bowtie before he stood to greet her.

"My name is Janie Brooks. I'm here to see Mr. Green."

"Follow me, please." The man led her down a hallway, past rows of closed doors with beveled glass windows, stopping at the very end. He knocked and turned the knob. "Mr. Green, you have a visitor: Ms. Janie Brooks, sir."

"Let her in."

The man opened the door and ushered her in before leaving them to return to his desk.

When she entered the room, Mr. Green looked over the top of his readers at her from behind his computer.

"Come on in and have a seat there." He pointed to one of the wingback chairs across from his desk.

"Thanks for seeing me this morning," Janie said, sitting down, her shoulders tense. She quickly stated the purpose of her visit.

"I see that there was a ruling in the original notes," Mr. Green said, trailing off as he flipped through the paperwork. "The protection for the birds has to be renewed every four years. It ended last year and wasn't renewed by the conservation agency."

The blood ran out of Janie's face and she sat there, unable to speak. Daniel had handled the initial paperwork for the courts, and Janie hadn't had that renewal date on her calendar. It had slipped right by her with everything else that had happened since then.

"Can I get an emergency injunction to stop this, at least until the hatchlings can survive on their own out of the nest?" she asked, grasping for anything to undo this.

"If you'd been here yesterday, it might have helped to hear your claims. But if we stopped progress every time we ran across a protest, nothing would ever be developed."

Janie swallowed her grief. She swiped away a tear as it fell. "But all I need is a month."

Mr. Green shook his head and flipped through his paperwork once more. "You could try to appeal to the developer, since the sale hasn't yet closed. They plan to sell the lots and can't officially put them on the market until the zoning clears, which will be in about a week."

Janie tried not to let her desperation rule her rational thought. "Do you know how I can get the owner's number?"

"It's all public information, but I've got it right here." He scratched out a number and a name on a small notepad, ripped off the sheet and passed it to Janie.

"Thank you." Janie pulled out her business card with her cell number on it. "If you learn anything that might be helpful, please contact me."

Janie trudged back to her Jeep, defeat permeating every corner of her heart. As she started the engine, the sun shone brightly, in opposition to her thoughts. But even the salty breeze didn't improve her mood.

The ramifications of missing the zoning adjustments meeting were truly sinking in now. She'd lost. The birds had lost. And if she were completely honest, losing access to the habitat area broke her heart almost as much as losing it as protection for the kites. *That property felt like hers.* But not anymore. And it never would again.

"We're free and clear," Michael said through the speaker in Ryan's phone that was wedged in the center console as he drove to pick up Sibley. "The zoning variance is approved."

"That's great news," Ryan told the agent, relieved it had all been settled.

"I know you wanted to buy the entire property outright and unparcelled but the developer is sticking to his guns. He knows he can get a better price if he sells the lots individually."

"All right," Ryan said as he drove parallel to the ocean, the warm breeze coming in through his open window. "Let's go ahead and put in an offer on two adjacent lots."

"Yes sir," Michael said. "I'll get working on the contract."

"Great. Thanks, Michael," he said as he pulled into the school parking lot.

Sibley was standing outside. She waved goodbye to her friends and ran over to him.

"Hey, pumpkin," he said as she climbed in, tossing her backpack into the backseat. "I've got some good news."

She twisted in her seat to face him.

"Looks like we might be close to building a house," he said, waggling his eyebrows excitedly.

Sibley clapped a hand over her mouth. "Really?"

"Yep!"

By the time he'd filled in Sibley on the news and they'd gotten home, the agent's email had come through with the paperwork to get the ball rolling.

"I'll be in my room," Sibley said, dropping her backpack by the door and running off.

"All right," Ryan said as he took his laptop into the living room and settled on the sofa, a wave of excitement rushing through him as he pulled up the contract. Feeling as if things were finally getting on track, he signed and initialed all the designated spaces and sent it back.

Now he would have to wait.

He grabbed a beer from the fridge, then headed to the back deck to relax. His gaze traveled across the grassy area between his and Janie's backyard, wondering what she was up to. He hadn't seen her since the night they'd rescued Sibley. There had been a lot going on since then, but he hoped she wasn't avoiding him. He knew he shouldn't have blamed Janie or taken his frustration out on her that night. She'd been in an impossible situation, and he was grateful that Sibley had Janie in her corner. With the distance between Sibley and Leslie of late and the difficulty Ryan and Sibley had of finding their way around each other in their new life, it was no surprise, really, that Sibley had taken Janie into her confidence. Ryan appreciated that Janie had simply not wanted to betray Sibley's trust and had even encouraged Sibley to tell Ryan about Conner.

No, he'd overreacted and, if he were honest, he knew part of that had come from his guilt and regret at not being the one Sibley felt she could speak to. He was determined for that to change, and he was also determined to make things right with Janie. It had only been a matter of days since he'd seen her, but he'd missed her company.

He went up to Sibley's room and knocked on the door.

"Come in," she called, her phone to her ear.

"I'm gonna pop over to Janie's. Want to come with me?" he asked.

"Maybe in a little bit. I need to do my homework and I'm talking to Breanna."

He smiled, happy to see her content. "All right. Be back soon."

"Okay, Daddy," Sibley said before returning to her conversation, her giggles like music to his ears.

As he crossed the yard, he found Janie sitting on the steps throwing a ball for Lulu to chase. When she caught sight of him, she waved, and a rush of happiness washed over him at the sight of her smile.

"Want some reinforcements?" he asked when he'd reached her, picking up Lulu's ball and throwing it a short distance, from where it landed at Janie's feet.

"Always. She's got a ton of energy and wants to be outside constantly."

He took a seat beside her on the steps. "So, how are you?"

"I'm okay. Momma and I have some things we've been finishing up in the shop. Lulu was restless, so I popped out to let the wild puppy run free for a few minutes."

"Listen, I wanted to make sure we're good. You know, from Friday night? I didn't want you to think I was upset with you about Sibley's boyfriend."

"Thanks. And I'm sorry I didn't tell you. I made Sibley promise me that she'd tell you and if I'd thought that wasn't the case, I would have had a quiet word with you."

"You don't need to explain, Janie. I overreacted, when I should have thanked you for being there for Sibley and also being there for me when she was missing. Friends?" he asked.

She smiled at him. "Friends." She met his eyes then, her blush creeping up.

Relief flooded him. There was nothing better than knowing they were okay.

The setting sun cast diamonds on the surface of the water as Janie and Ryan made small talk on the deck. Janie pulled her hair back in her fingers, the humidity settling upon her skin. Ryan's eyes went to her neck, causing her heart to patter. Even the short time they'd been apart had been too long since she'd seen him and she was glad the awkwardness was behind them. Janie understood that his reactions on Friday night came out of love and fear for his daughter, but that he was able and willing to admit his mistakes and see her side of things spoke volumes of the man.

"Would you and Sibley be up for a sunset cruise with me and Momma this weekend?" she ventured, seizing the moment to squeeze in an opportunity for the birthday surprise Sibley had mentioned the other day.

"That sounds really nice," he replied, stroking Lulu's back. He cleared his throat and sat up straight. "But we don't have to wait for the weekend, do we? How about I take you out on Friday night?"

A thrill swam through her. Janie hadn't expected that. "What did you have in mind?"

"We could go to that new craft brewery on the way to Charleston I told you about, do a tasting, and maybe grab a bite to eat."

"I'd love to." She immediately began to envision what it would be like to be with Ryan without the restrictions they'd be negotiating up until now.

He took her hand and held it for a second, then he lifted it to his lips and gently kissed it, sending a shot of electricity up her arm. He stared at her, deliberation in his eyes, as if he were testing the waters. She scooted a little closer and put her head on his shoulder.

He stiffened and let go of her hand suddenly, giving Janie a jolt. Then she noticed Sibley running their way, her feet bare and hair flying.

"I'm all done with my homework, so can I play with Lulu?"

Janie knew that a relationship with Ryan wouldn't be as easy as just letting herself fall for him—she had to consider Sibley and her feelings in all of this; she'd been through so much already in recent times—and it was clear by his response that he'd had the same thought. Janie adored Ryan's daughter and they had an easy and mutual friendship, but taking things to the next level with Ryan was an entirely different prospect, and Janie didn't know how Sibley would react to that.

Janie put a little distance between her and Ryan, mentally shaking off the moment, and answered, "Of course. I'll bet she was wondering where you were."

"C'mon, girl." Sibley grabbed the ball and ran over by the big oak tree on the far side of the yard.

Ryan and Janie shared a look.

"That was close," he said.

"Are *we* keeping a secret?" she asked, trying to find their boundaries.

He pursed his lips, his gaze unstill. "I don't want to confuse her with *this* yet." He waggled a finger between them.

"It might be good to figure out what *this* is," she said, repeating his gesture.

"Yes, it would. Maybe we can work on that Friday night."

While she didn't have an answer, she definitely didn't mind spending more time with him to figure it out.

Chapter Twenty-Six

Two days later, Ryan got the call he'd been waiting for.

"Great news! They've accepted your offer," Michael said.

"Wow. That is good news. So, what's the plan now?" Ryan sat in his truck along the edge of the school drive, waiting for Sibley to finish up after her match. He was excited he could give her the news when she came out.

"I'm sending over some additional forms for signature now. When do you want to close?"

"As soon as possible."

"Okay, let's see if we can get this done in a couple weeks."

Sibley climbed in the car just as Ryan finished the call. She fastened her seatbelt, her adorably curious stare warming him.

"What are you so excited about?"

"The developer accepted our offer on the lots and it's a done deal."

Sibley's face lit up and then fell in a second. "Oh, wow, I *guess* that's good news?"

Her reaction surprised Ryan. "I thought you were happy about the new house."

"I am. But it means I'll have two houses now—forever. I guess I sort of felt that maybe one day you and Mom might get back together.

That maybe we could go back to being all in the same house—a family—again. So, you're really getting a divorce?"

Ryan sobered. "Honey, some broken things can't be fixed. And it will be *our* house, yours and mine. Mom and I had you together and you're our greatest joy, which means I'll always care about her. I know things have been turned upside down, but we're making peace with it."

Sibley sighed. "I guess this isn't about me, huh? I don't want to try and force you two back together if that's not what you really want."

He put his palm to her cheek. "It's not. Not anymore. I'm sorry if that hurts you."

Sibley nodded and then worked up a little smile for his sake, he was sure. "Did you say *lots* with an s?"

"Yes, well, we'll want a view, won't we?"

Sibley seemed to rouse then. "It sounds awesome. I'm looking forward to planning my room like you said I could."

"I'm looking forward to that, too." He put an arm around her shoulders and gave a squeeze.

Once they were almost home, Sibley said, "I made plans with Conner Friday night, if that's okay."

"As long as I know where you'll be," he said lightheartedly to keep the thrill of the moment alive.

"Okay. He's planning to come to our house and get me." Sibley grinned from ear to ear at Ryan. "We're going to a movie in Beaufort and then out to eat."

Ryan would always be protective of Sibley, that was just his job as her father, but he knew he had to give her some leeway. "Sounds like a nice evening."

"Will you be okay alone?" she asked, teasing him.

"Don't worry about me," he said, wrinkling his nose at her. "I'm taking Janie out." He'd parked in the driveway but they hadn't gotten out of the truck yet.

"Like on a real date?"

Ryan nodded. "Yes. Are you okay with that?"

"I really like Janie, so yeah, I guess so. I mean, I kind of noticed the two of you flirting."

Ryan breathed an internal sigh of relief, before he realized that it had been so very long since he'd been on an actual date.

Janie stood in front of her full-length mirror, smoothing her cheery yellow sundress and turning to see how it went with the sandals she'd chosen. Approving of her reflection, she reached into her closet and pulled out a lightweight sweater, draping it over her arm to take with her in case it was cold in the brewery. Janie had never thought after Daniel died that she would get to the point where she would consider starting a new relationship, but her feelings for Ryan had crept up on her. She also knew Daniel wouldn't have wanted her to miss out on living. With another quick glance in the mirror, she considered how much she'd changed this summer. She couldn't have imagined it in her wildest dreams.

Ready earlier than she'd expected, she headed over to Momma's house while she waited for Ryan to arrive, feeling a mixture of excitement and nerves. The last couple of years had been a struggle and Janie had retreated into herself, but these past few months with Ryan and Sibley—the laughter and fun they'd shared—had shown Janie that wasn't any way to live and that she had to keep moving forward. She would always love Daniel, but Janie realized now that she still had a lot of love to give. Maybe she and Ryan would just turn out to be friends, but she deserved to give this a chance—even if the thought still terrified her a bit.

She let herself into her mother's house and met Momma in the kitchen.

"Oh, hey there, honey. Don't you look pretty!"

"So, do you," she said.

She took in Momma's navy top, white slacks, and comfortable-looking white sandals. She'd pinned her silver hair up in a lovely braided bun.

"Well, thank you very much." Momma twirled in a dramatic turn, happiness shining through her eyes.

Janie broke out into a grin. "What time is Joe picking you up?" she asked.

Momma looked at her watch. "Any minute now."

"Same. Look at us!"

Momma pressed her fingers to her lips to stifle a giddy laugh. "Give Ryan my best. Our surprise should be fun tomorrow."

"Yes. I texted Sibley to fill her in on the food and balloons we found at the store. And about the cake. She was so excited."

"It's a sweet thing for her to plan something special for her daddy's birthday," Momma said.

"Oh! There's Ryan. Gotta go." Janie's heart raced as she saw him through the window.

"Have a wonderful time," Momma called after her.

"You too!"

Ryan pulled into her driveway just as Janie was walking out of her house. When he climbed out of the truck, Janie's breath caught at the sight of him. He was clean shaven and wore a button-down shirt tucked in dark jeans, and a nice pair of boots. He held a bouquet of springtime flowers as she reached him in the drive.

"These are for you." He handed Janie the blooms.

"Thank you. They're gorgeous." Janie put a hand on his arm, and he bent down and pressed his deliciously warm lips to her cheek in a kiss.

"Mm. You smell nice," he said, sending a current of nerves through her.

"Thank you." She held up the bouquet. "I'll go put these in water. Come on up." She led him through the front door and into the kitchen.

He pulled up a barstool while she grabbed a vase from under the sink and added water.

"There." She slid the vase to the center of the island.

He gave her a warm smile. "Are you ready?" he asked.

"Yep." She grabbed her purse and sweater and the two of them walked out to his truck.

Their small talk on the way set her at ease a bit. She took in the strength in his hands on the steering wheel, the way he moved with the truck as he took a turn, the square of his shoulders... He pulled into the brewery's parking lot and then came over to open her door.

The brewery was a converted barn. Upon entering, they passed the large fermentation tanks and barrels in the old horse stalls until they reached the tables on the far side. Ryan pulled out her chair, and she slid onto her seat, taking in the down-home atmosphere.

This place was new to Janie and sat just outside of the bubble in which she traveled. "This is cool," she said.

Ryan ordered them each an ale first, and Janie didn't have to have much before a tipsy buzz settled over her. When the waitress took their orders, Janie's tummy was already growling. She chose the butter-and-herb garlic-roasted chicken. Ryan's darker beer called for a blackened pork tenderloin with vegetables, which looked delicious when it arrived.

"Would you like to try a bite?" He offered her a forkful.

When she reached over to grab the bite, it wobbled from his fork. Thankfully the vegetables fell onto her plate. She scooped them up with her own fork, feeling like a fish out of water with this dating thing.

"Well, that didn't go like I'd planned," she said, looking into those dark-blue eyes, his stare making Janie wonder if her clumsiness was more her inexperience dating or her nerves over her growing feelings. "Would you like to try mine?" She slid her plate next to his so he could have a taste. "I don't want to run the risk of dropping roasted chicken on the table," she said with a laugh.

With a chuckle and an understanding look that instantly calmed her, Ryan took a bite and the rest of the meal passed by comfortably, with plenty of laughter.

After dinner, they shared a chocolate-brownie sundae. Janie laughed at Ryan's closed eyes and moan of pleasure upon taking the first bite. Her focus was less on food now than him. There was no doubt that she had enjoyed their date—if that's what this was—and the more she got to know Ryan, the more her feelings toward him grew. She was looking forward to the surprise they had in store for him tomorrow.

"I hear you've got a big birthday in the next couple of days, huh?"

"Yes, it's a big one," he replied, rounding his eyes in mock horror and making her laugh as he paid the bill.

"I'm glad you're getting there before I am. You'll have to let me know how forty feels. I've still got a few years to go yet." She kidded with him.

"Rub it in, will you?" He laughed again, offering her his arm as they got up to leave.

They strolled hand-in-hand through the parking lot, Ryan's large warm grip covering Janie's and causing her such a fizzy happiness that she almost wanted to pinch herself to make sure it was real.

"So, it's early yet. Do you want to go someplace else?" he asked her.

The look in his eyes, the warm temperatures, and the fragrance of night-blooming jasmines hanging in the air made it impossible to say no. "I'd love to. Surprise me." Janie happily put herself into his capable hands.

"I've got just the place." He helped her into the truck and drove them back toward the island. Soon after they crossed the bridge, he took a left turn. Janie wasn't exactly sure what his plan was, but she was definitely curious. She wasn't aware of much out this way.

Ryan had turned onto an almost indiscernible gravel drive and stopped. "Hang on a minute." He got out of the truck, crossing in front of the headlights to unhook a chain that blocked entry. The sign read: *No trespassing.*

As Ryan continued down the unpaved, rutted lane, careful to avoid the largest potholes, Janie's curiosity ran amok.

"I've never gone down this road. In fact, I had no idea it was here."

"I haven't been out here in years, either. It was a secret fishing hole for me and Uncle Joe when I was a kid."

The road ended at a small pier about ten yards directly in front of them. It jutted out into the night. Ryan killed the truck's engine and turned off his headlights, sending them into darkness save for the light of the almost full moon and stars.

Janie got a tiny quiver of anticipation over this secret place. "Whose pier is this?" she whispered.

Ryan shrugged. "Joe says it was built years ago when the island was starting to populate, and then it was abandoned."

"A mystery," Janie murmured, energized by the idea. They were surrounded by woods and the chirping of crickets, cicadas, and croaking frogs—the night sounds that Janie loved.

Ryan went around to the passenger's door to help her out of the truck. She welcomed the touch of his fingers. He illuminated their way with his phone's flashlight, revealing the thick brush between them and the end of the little dock. Janie took care not to run into anything too scratchy in her sandals.

Once they reached the weathered wood, Ryan stepped in front of her, stomping the boards to make sure the pier wasn't rotted. When nothing moved or splintered, he held his hand out to Janie.

"We'll take it slow."

Intrigued, Janie followed his lead. The walkway was narrow, so that Janie paced behind Ryan single file. At the end of the structure, there was a small, postage-stamp-sized platform, maybe ten feet by ten feet. They settled at the edge of the dock and leaned back against an old rowboat tilted on its side, as their eyes adjusted to the light of the moon casting its glow over the water's surface.

"This is gorgeous," Janie exclaimed. It was amazing to discover this part of the island she had never known about and for Ryan to share it with her. "I don't think I've ever seen the stars so bright. There are so many. Thanks for showing it to me."

Ryan settled in beside her, his hip and shoulder resting against hers. He reached over and clasped his hand in hers. She turned her head toward him, but Ryan was already staring at her when their gazes collided in the moonlight, a question in his eyes. Janie caught her breath.

He leaned forward, dropping her hand, his fingers barely touching her skin to guide her face toward his. He didn't let her down this time. His lips were warm on hers and she responded with pent-up yearning…

She inhaled his spicy scent and felt his arms tighten around her as he deepened the kiss. The feeling was like fireworks, it felt as if a piece of her that had been missing for so long had been found. Any awkwardness that she'd experienced before had melted away in the perfection of this moment. It was as if everything had led to this.

When they finally slowed to a more respectable level, Ryan pulled away gently, his affectionate gaze upon her. Janie shivered.

"Are you cold?" he asked softly.

She shook her head. "No, I'm just perfect."

They sat there together under the stars, and neither said a word. The water lapped against the old structure and the salty and sweet breeze wrapped them like a cozy blanket.

After two long years of grieving for Daniel, Janie felt she'd been given the gift of moving on, as if the mantle of grief had been miraculously lifted. She'd been happy with Daniel, but Ryan made her a different kind of happy, so it felt like one didn't compete with the other.

Janie bloomed with happiness and hope.

Chapter Twenty-Seven

"That looks great!" Janie commented on the colorful birthday banner they'd hung across the top of the dock. "Maybe two balloons on each side?" She pointed as Sibley and Momma affixed the shiny silver balloons with birthday messages on them. They'd spent the day preparing for the party, and the backyard looked fantastic.

They'd decorated the boat as well, wrapping colorful streamers tightly across the windshield and affixing a couple of clusters of balloons across the front, making sure they weren't in danger of blowing away when they hit cruising speed.

Janie had asked Sibley about inviting more people, but Sibley said she preferred that it was just the five of them so they could go out on the boat to celebrate.

"Dad's gonna be so excited," Sibley said, clapping her hands. Having given Ryan the excuse that she wanted to play with Lulu, she'd been there working on the decorations with Janie and Momma all afternoon.

"Where is your dad right now?" Momma asked, fastening the last streamer to the top of the boat.

"Uncle Joe called him to help with something so we could make sure he doesn't see any of this before it's time."

Sibley's enthusiasm was infectious and, after last night, Janie was excited about the surprise, too. Everything had felt so right with Ryan as they'd ended the previous evening and Janie hoped they could continue to take baby steps together. However, one thing plagued her mind.

"Is your mother coming?" Janie finally asked Sibley. She'd been wondering about that ever since Sibley had mentioned the possibility. They'd not discussed it again and now Janie was anxious about how the day would pan out.

Sibley shook her head. "I decided not to ask her since you and Daddy are dating. I don't think she would feel comfortable, anyway. And this is his celebration, so I didn't want to take a chance on things not going well."

Janie was surprised by Sibley's admission about her parents, and also the fact that she knew Janie and Ryan were dating. Last night had been their first real date, and it warmed her to think that Ryan had told Sibley about it, but she was cautious, too. Although Sibley seemed completely levelheaded about it all, it had to be a big deal for her, and Janie wanted to make sure that Sibley was comfortable with everything that was happening. She needed Sibley to know that her mother was welcome, no matter what, and not feel split in her allegiances.

"If you'd wanted her to come, it would've been okay, honey," Janie said.

"At first, I thought about inviting her because I still hoped we might be a family again someday, but Daddy and I had a long conversation about it and I understand that too many things have gone on between them for it to happen." Sibley appeared resigned to that fact.

"I'm sorry you've had to go through this. It must be a lot. I hope our dating hasn't upset you." Janie had to know if Sibley was bothered by it.

"No. Daddy really likes you. You make him smile. I wondered if I'd ever see him happy again."

Such a big worry for a young girl.

"Well, he's a great guy with a fantastic daughter."

"Thanks."

Sibley smiled at her and Janie felt reassured that whatever happened, her and Sibley could work it out together.

"Oh!" Sibley's nose was in her phone. "I just got a text from Uncle Joe saying they're on the way."

Janie hadn't spoken to Ryan since he'd dropped her off last night after their date. After the kiss. That kiss had told her a lot about the two of them moving forward as a couple. Their chemistry was off the charts. They hadn't taken it any further last night, but Janie couldn't stop thinking about him and was looking forward to seeing him again.

The trio gathered up the remaining things, lumping them into the compartment under the seat of the boat, and stood together under the birthday banner flanked by balloons.

The minute Ryan rounded the back of the house and caught sight of them they yelled, "Surprise!"

A huge grin lit up his face. "Wow," he exclaimed, coming aboard. "Youuu," he said, pointing at Sibley and wrinkling his nose at her. "What have you been up to?" He eyed the streamers and Janie could see the love and pride on his face.

"It wasn't just me, Daddy," Sibley said.

"Thanks, y'all. Turning forty isn't so bad with such great friends to celebrate with." He gently pulled Janie to him and held her an extra second, and then kissed her temple. She nearly melted at his touch.

"You're so welcome," she whispered in his ear.

There was food, a birthday song sung badly, and fresh air and sunshine. For Janie, it was a near-perfect day on the water and Ryan seemed to have a grand time, hardly letting go of her hand. For the moment, Janie could envision all the things to come between her and

Ryan and, for the first time in a long time, she was excited with what
lay ahead.

A few hours later, after Ryan had helped Janie winch the boat out of
the water, they sat together on the back steps. She leaned in.

"I've got something to show you if you're up for it," she said, feeling
as if she could tell him all her secrets at this moment.

"Sure, I'm game," he said, a sparkle in his eyes. As they climbed
into Janie's golf cart he asked, "Where are we going?"

"It's a surprise. You showed me your special place last night, and
now I'm going to show you mine. Somewhere that means the world
to me." Until now, she hadn't felt comfortable sharing the habitat with
anyone, Ryan included. Part of the reason was that she was honoring
Daniel's memory, and because it had been their special place. Nor had
Janie wanted to burden Ryan with her troubles. Now, she felt secure
about her decision… it was time. Past time.

Janie had held this part of her world back from Ryan, being that
it was such a private thing, and she'd guarded it so jealously. Now it
was too late to invite Ryan into her world beyond the sale of the land.
She'd failed to protect her tiny paradise. She'd called the owner and
left messages but hadn't heard back.

"I can't wait," he said, a grin spreading across his face.

"It has the best view of the sunset next to the beach on the point."

They drove down the road in her golf cart and took a left at the creek,
trundling over the tiny bridge that spanned it. As they approached,
they were met by a large front loader and a dozer parked at the edge
of the property, their sheer size and presence overwhelming her. She

turned to Ryan as if he would be able to explain. But just when she told herself there was no way he'd know anything, the pale white on his face stopped her in her tracks.

"Let's not panic yet," she said out loud more for herself than for him as they stepped out of the cart. "They aren't supposed to move forward with building until the kites can fly, and they aren't ready yet. I've been filling out paperwork and making calls for the last week just to be sure of it."

Ryan didn't say a word. He just stood there, looking as mortified as she was, but not especially surprised.

She trudged through the brush, leaving Ryan to follow.

"Nooo… oh, no."

Her eyes darted all around and then focused on the six freshly cut stumps. Janie's heartbeat double-timed in her chest as she worked to control the deep, desperate anxiety taking hold.

"Where are the trees? The nests?" she croaked, her throat going dry, her body beginning to tremble. *They had to still be here.* "The trees had nests with babies in them. Swallow-tailed kite nestlings too young to fend for themselves." She blinked away tears as she tried to focus on Ryan. And she realized that he wasn't surprised at all. "Did you know about this?" she asked.

"I bought this lot and the one beside it. The trees with the nests in them were diseased, so they had to cut them down and move the nests."

She whirled on him as the pain and shock hit her like a wrecking ball, tears spilling from her eyes. "But not yet. They were supposed to wait. Where *are* the nests?" she pleaded desperately through clenched teeth to keep the sobs from rising up her throat.

Ryan shrugged. "I really don't know. I was told the developer was handling it."

Janie worked to digest his words. She'd trusted him enough to bring him here to the one spot that was hers and hers alone—except it wasn't. Ryan had known about this place all along and he'd gone ahead and bought it without a care for the wildlife.

"How could you not care about the plight of four nests with babies inside? What if their mothers don't follow the nests or continue feeding them? They will die." Suddenly, her legs weren't steady, and she sat down right in the middle of the cleared area, head in her hands, weak and helpless.

"I wish I'd known…."

Ryan's concerned tone barely pierced Janie's shock. He sat down beside her and tried to take her hand, but she yanked it back with force, her past and present worlds colliding as if they were two speeding freight trains.

She nailed him with an anguished glare and stood back up as abruptly as she'd sat. "I can't stay here."

Ryan's decision clawed at her stomach. Daniel would never have done such a callous thing.

She ran to the golf cart, climbed in, and took off, not caring one bit about how Ryan would get home. He could walk for all she cared. She couldn't even look at him right now.

It had taken Ryan a half hour to walk home, which had given him a little time to process what had just happened. As close as he and Janie had gotten in the past weeks, Ryan hadn't discussed the lots with Janie because he hadn't known if the deal would work out. Maybe, too, because initially she'd not reacted with excitement or enthusiasm when he'd told her he was looking to build a new home. But he hadn't expected this.

He hadn't known that Janie had any particular connection to the site, but it was clear that it was special to her, and he'd gone and ruined that. Not on purpose of course—gosh, if he knew what the place meant to her and how important the nests were, he would have had the developers hold off. But it was too late now, and the look on her face as she'd run away made Ryan wonder if she would ever forgive him. He had to try to make this right somehow.

Ryan went straight inside as soon as he arrived home and pulled out his phone, calling Michael the second he cleared his front door.

"Is everything okay, Daddy?" Sibley asked, startling him.

"Oh, hi, honey," he said, much of his focus still on making the call.

"What's going on?" she whispered.

As the phone continued to ring, his stomach turned with what to say to his daughter. The very thing he'd tried to protect her from by not pursuing Janie had just happened. He should've known better than to move past friendship. Still, he'd let his feelings for Janie get in the way of his rational thought and now he'd not only ruined their relationship but potentially the relationship between Janie and Sibley. He forced a smile and held up a finger to keep Sibley at bay.

Michael answered.

"It's Ryan Kennedy. Do you know where they moved the birds' nests from the property?" he asked, skipping the pleasantries.

It took a second for Michael to catch up. "I don't. I was told it was handled, so I didn't ask."

"Well, I need you to find out right away." He didn't bother with niceties.

"All right. I'll look into it. Everything okay?"

"Call me as soon as you get some information."

When Ryan ended the call, Sibley's worried stare met his. "You look upset," she said. "What happened?"

"It'll all be okay," he told her, forcing a smile to hide the fact that he wasn't as sure of that answer as he was letting on. The last thing he wanted was to throw Sibley into a tailspin of worry due to his bungling of the situation.

Ryan could only hope that this was fixable. Surely there was a way to bring the nests back to their home *and* build a house.

The heavy, sick feeling hadn't diminished since Janie had been home. She couldn't even speak to Momma about it yet. It was too fresh. The trees were gone, and the land was sold. The place would never be the same again, and Janie already felt the loss keenly. It had been her special spot on the island, somewhere that held poignant memories for her, but not anymore. She'd cared for the habitat for so long; it was like bearing another death in her immediate family.

Her shoulders ached and her head pounded, so she decided to try a hot bath. It wouldn't bring back the birds, but it might ease the throbbing that was taking over her body. Janie dragged her feet as she headed toward the bathroom.

The worst thing about it all was that Ryan could've stopped the trees being removed or he could have questioned it or delayed it with minimal effort. Why hadn't he told her he'd bought the land? Had he known deep down that she would object to what he had planned? Well, he would have been right—she did object—but he'd gone ahead and done it behind her back anyway.

As Janie sank down in the fragrant tub, she didn't see a path forward with Ryan. And the reality of that shook her to the core and broke her heart.

Chapter Twenty-Eight

Ryan hadn't been able to get Janie and the birds off his mind all night. He'd tossed and turned, restless. He'd really screwed things up where both were concerned. Fortunately it was Sunday, which allowed him a little time to figure out a resolution for the birds. Hopefully.

After playing phone tag with Michael last night, the realtor finally texted around nine a.m. to give Ryan the name and contact information of the wildlife specialists who'd moved the nests. He called the number right away. As he sat at the breakfast table in the kitchen, the morning sun streaming through, he got their voice mail, so he left a message.

"Hey, Daddy, can I go to Janie's to see Lulu after we clean up?" Sibley asked as she was finishing her breakfast.

Ryan had been afraid she would ask him that. The only thing he could do was tell her the truth. "Honey, we might not see Janie for a while, I'm afraid."

Sibley's head snapped up. "What happened?"

"I made a terrible misjudgment." He told her about the kites.

"Oh, that's not good." Sibley bit her lip.

"No, it's not good. Someone called me about moving the nests, and I assumed it wasn't anything out of the ordinary here on the island, so I didn't ask any questions about where they might move them or what kind of harm could befall them."

"And Janie found out?" she asked. "Because I know she does conservation work here on the island."

Ryan had learned this in passing after they'd met, but he hadn't ever taken the time to ask Janie about what was involved. The fact Sibley seemed to know intrinsically that Janie would be affected by something like moving the birds only made him feel worse. It was clear from Janie's reaction that conservation was so much more than just a hobby for her, it was a purpose, a way of life, and his actions had ridden roughshod over that. He couldn't escape the rotten feeling he felt deep in his core.

"Well, it was more than that, too," Ryan said to Sibley. "The land we're buying has been a special place for Janie. She's cared for and protected the same bird habitat there for many years. But I didn't know that. I should've asked more questions, but I didn't."

"So, she hates you now?" Sibley's lip trembled, and what Ryan had dreaded since the moment he'd started falling for Janie shone on her face: disappointment and pain.

Not only had he hurt Janie, but he'd hurt Sibley, too.

"It might be a while before she wants to talk to me," he said carefully. The idea of Janie being permanently out of his life nearly swamped him with sadness.

Tears welled up in Sibley's eyes. "You've ruined everything, huh?"

Her words were like a spear through his heart.

"Right now, I'm trying to figure out where they moved the nests with the baby birds," he said.

Sibley shook her head, closing up right in front of him. "I can't believe I won't be able to see Janie or Lulu." Then, without warning, she scraped her chair back and left the room, shoulders sagging.

"So, are you gonna tell me what happened?" Momma asked Janie as she threaded a piece of driftwood into a new centerpiece project they'd been working on in the shop.

Janie sighed. "It's a long story."

"Well, let's have it. You can't solve problems by staying quiet about them."

Janie took a deep breath and launched into the situation, telling Momma about Ryan's part in losing the kites. She tried to keep her voice steady, but she wobbled, unable to keep her emotions at bay.

"Oh, honey. I'm so sorry. That's a big one to overcome."

"I'm not sure I want to. He chose his comfort and needs over what makes this island what it is. He could've stopped it, but he didn't even pause to ask a few questions."

"Have you put yourself in his position?" Momma asked.

"I've tried, but it's difficult to understand someone who hasn't spent most of their life living on the island and protecting it." This was always her fear about someone developing the land, that they wouldn't understand or care about the island's role in conservation, but she never thought that person would be Ryan.

"Is he really to blame? Was it his idea to move the nests?" Momma asked as she set down the shells she was sorting to look at her daughter.

"He knew about it, which makes me think he could've stopped it."

Momma sighed and smiled at Janie. "Honey, it's been so heartwarming watching you bloom. You've changed in so many wonderful ways. Isn't it worth at least trying to see Ryan's side?"

But Janie shook her head. "I can't. I don't see a way past this right now." Janie would miss Ryan and Sibley's popping over, and Sibley telling Janie about the things happening in her life. But it was Janie's fault for letting Ryan get too close. Her creativity depleted, she stood from the workbench. "I'm going to take Lulu for a walk," she said, hoping to clear her head, although something told her all the fresh air in the world couldn't help her with this one.

"Did you find out about the birds yet?" Sibley asked Ryan when she entered the living room after coming downstairs from her room for lunch.

He peered over the edge of the fishing magazine he was reading to take his mind off of everything. At least Sibley was speaking to him. That was a good sign after she'd stormed off at breakfast.

"Not yet. It's difficult to reach anyone on a Sunday."

It surprised Ryan when she asked, "Could we go out in the boat today?"

Ryan had been so distracted by his worry over finding Janie's birds that he hadn't even thought about his plans for the day, but until he heard back from the wildlife specialists, there was nothing he could do, and sitting there moping wasn't going to help comfort Sibley. Perhaps being out on the water would do them both some good and, after his admission, Ryan was grateful that his daughter wanted to spend some time with him. He had a lot of making up to do.

"Sure. Let's get out for a little while. Get ready and we'll head off in a few minutes."

The water's surface was like glass and a few wispy clouds dotted the sky. Ryan took a deep breath of the salty air, the act of it calming his frayed nerves, as they maneuvered out of the channel and into the one leading to open water.

Sibley appeared to be doing the same. The island and its waters had a way of improving a person's outlook, and Ryan looked at it all with fresh eyes. He took note of the variety of birds along the shore, recognizing osprey, a brown pelican diving toward the surface for his dinner, along with a couple of blue herons. There was life everywhere, but he'd taken the security of these wild birds for granted.

Once they were out on the open water, Ryan's phone went off with a text in response to his earlier voice mail. He opened the message, which confirmed that the birds were on the east side of Hunting Island.

Ryan remembered spending time with Uncle Joe on Hunting Island when he was a kid. It was only a couple miles from Fripp.

"I've found out where the birds were moved," Ryan told Sibley. "Do you want to head over there now and see if we can find them?"

Sibley's eyes lit up at his suggestion. "Can we get there in the boat?"

It was nearing three o'clock, so the sun still shone high, which would allow them to navigate their way easily. It was only two miles by water, so it wouldn't take long to get there.

"Yes. Let me pull it up on the GPS. There's a dock on the south side of the island."

When they approached the buoys that marked their arrival, Ryan slowed to an idle. The tide had gone down enough that it would be challenging to maneuver beside the small pier. Instead, he docked the boat in the sand, dropped an anchor in back, and placed another off the bow.

"Wow. Look at all the birds," Sibley said as they stepped out of the boat and onto the beach.

Birds of every size and color squawked and competed for fish at the shoreline. Some sat on dead logs or flew just above the water. Ryan realized then just how much he'd underestimated the importance of the island's wildlife. He'd never really thought about who protected it or even that it needed protecting, but the sight that greeted him was a reminder of just how precious this wildlife was. It wasn't every day or everywhere that you got to see wood storks and painted buntings, not to mention the loggerhead turtles and dolphins that called Fripp home. This was a special place. It was something that Janie understood, but he'd overlooked it, and that had been a massive mistake.

Sibley broke into his thoughts. "How will we find the birds we're looking for?"

"I looked up swallow-tailed kites and they like to live in the tallest pines, so I'm assuming they placed them in some of those." Ryan frowned at the massive number of trees on the island. He had to admit, locating the birds might be tricky.

For nearly half an hour, they scoured the high treetops, walking for ages, but there were no birds that matched the description of the kites.

"We might not find them on our own," Ryan said, disappointed, "and we'd better head back in case the tide goes low."

As Ryan launched the boat and guided it slowly away from where he'd docked, it was clear they'd spent more time on the island than Ryan had realized, and the tide was so low there was barely enough water to get off the sand. Ryan had to carefully idle out through the low spots, staying in the center of the inlet where the water was deep enough to navigate home.

"I'm not sure about this." Sibley was biting her lip with worry.

"We don't have a choice at this point but to move forward. Hang on in case we hit mud."

Ryan had been so eager to find the kites' nests that he'd forgotten the number-one rule around here: *always check the tide.* Marsh mud was black and thick and unkind to a boat's propeller. Ryan had hit a few low spots with Joe growing up and had almost gotten stuck a few times.

With a couple more calculated movements, they made it to deeper water. Ryan relaxed in a stretch of open water until it was time to enter the canal to get home. It was impossible to see under the surface in the channel and they hit mud, the propeller stalling out. Ryan cut the engine.

"Oh, no," Sibley said, worry on her face.

"We'll be okay. Let's call Uncle Joe and see what he suggests." If there was a way to rescue them, Joe would find it. He dialed Joe's number and explained their predicament.

"Son, send me a location pin so I can find you," Joe said. "The tide's getting lower by the minute, but we've still got a slip of time."

Ryan did what he was told, sending over his location.

"Sit tight," Joe said. "I'm on my way."

They waited for about twenty minutes before a boat materialized in the distance. As it got closer, he could see Joe, but he wasn't driving the boat. Janie was. She was meandering, careful to avoid low spots.

Ryan waved, thankful and relieved. He was grateful for her coming out to help, but he couldn't help but feel awkward about the situation. And stupid. He knew better than to leave by boat without checking the tide chart.

Janie pulled in just close enough, lining up the two boats from stern to bow.

"Toss me your towline," Uncle Joe called out.

Ryan disconnected the sand anchor from the towline at the bow so he could send it their way.

"Once the tension is out of the rope, use your trolling motor to give us some extra help." Janie was all business as she called out instructions to Ryan. "When we get you free, follow behind me to keep out of the mud. I know where the low spots are."

It took a couple of tries, but they were able to get Ryan's boat out of the marsh mud.

"Thanks for coming, Janie. I really appreciate it," Ryan called over to her.

She nodded but didn't say anything else, her expression contemplative as she turned her attention to helping them get home.

She pulled them out of the mud into deeper water so he could start his motor. Breathing a sigh of relief that the motor cranked, he slowly followed Janie's boat until they got to their docks.

After they'd both winched up the vessels, Ryan crossed the grass to where Janie was spraying off her hull. "I didn't check the tide chart, and I'm sorry you had to come out to get us."

"It's fine," she said quietly.

"I went to Hunting Island to see if I could find the kites," he ventured, trying to make this mess a little better.

"Did you find them?" she asked, sounding slightly hopeful.

Ryan shook his head. "No, I'm afraid not, but I know they're on the island."

"But of course moving them may have caused their mother to abandon the nests," she worried aloud before turning back to the boat in silence.

"Maybe—"

"Look, I don't want to talk about this right now," she said, cutting him off, her gaze on the stream of water as it hit the boat.

Ryan took in the lines between her eyes and the frown at her lips, his heart heavy.

Chapter Twenty-Nine

Had the risk to open herself up again—to love again—been worth the thrill ride she'd been on since Ryan had come into her life? Janie had thought so, but she was no longer so sure, she realized as she sat in the rocker out on her porch in the afternoon sunshine, with Lulu snuggled tightly next to her, the coastal breeze tickling her skin.

But even if she and Ryan *were* over, she'd still changed. She couldn't go back to the less-evolved day-to-day life she'd had before meeting him, and she could thank him for that, at least. Waking up every day to new possibilities these past weeks had infused her with life and purpose again. She reached down and nuzzled Lulu, allowing the puppy's soft breathing to comfort her.

As she stroked the dog's fur, she made a firm decision to manage her expectations for both her relationships and her work. Not everyone would understand her or try as hard as she did to protect and nourish the island or even care to.

She hadn't intentionally planned to see Ryan again, but when Joe had called her to say that Ryan and Sibley were stuck in the marsh mud at low tide, Janie had launched her boat in record time to get out there to them. When Ryan had tried to speak with her afterward, it had rattled her because she was so vulnerable where he was concerned. A swarm of emotions had passed between them in a short period, causing

Janie's head to swim. But the reality that she wouldn't be able to avoid him forever was creeping in.

And then there was Sibley. She and Janie had developed a bond of trust, and Janie hated the idea of not being there for the teenager. But could Janie expect to have any kind of friendship with Sibley without seeing Ryan?

Janie had fallen hard for Ryan… harder than she'd first realized. Grieving the loss of a possible future together rated right up there with losing her kites. Right now, it was a pretty even race, despite having come to her shiny new self-realization that life could be different for her. The sadness was still a real thing.

Ryan finally got a break at lunchtime to make a phone call to Shane Mathis at Shoreline Conservation. He settled in at his desk in the office. Even though he'd spent a lot of time on the island, he realized he was still essentially an outsider with a lot to learn. Now he was determined to make it right.

A man's gruff voice answered the call. "This is Shane."

"Hi, Shane, this is Ryan Kennedy. I'd hoped to get some information about the swallow-tailed kites your company moved from the property I'm purchasing on Fripp. I understand they're on Hunting Island, but can you give me some more specific information?"

Shane proved to be a great help, detailing the location of the nests to Ryan. "If you need anything else, let me know."

As Ryan hung up, a huge weight lifted. The birds were okay, according to Shane. Now, he'd let Janie know what was happening so she could see them for herself.

Janie answered on the first ring. "Hello?"

The sound of her voice hit him right in the heart.

"Hi, it's Ryan. I just spoke with Shane Mathis at Shoreline Conservation, and he said the birds were in good shape when they moved them."

He agonized for the few silent seconds she took.

When Janie answered, her voice was gruff with emotion as she said, "I'm so relieved. Thank you for letting me know. Do you have an exact location for them?"

Ryan repeated the information he'd written down. "Does that tell you enough?"

"Yes. They used a good company at least." He could hear a tiny amount of relief in her tone. "I'll head over there later today and see for myself."

"Could I go with you?" Ryan asked, not wanting to intrude but also wanting to show Janie he cared.

"I need to do this alone. It's a very personal issue."

Her rejection hit him like a physical blow, but he didn't let her know how much it hurt that he'd lost her trust. "I understand. But please let me know if there's anything I can do to help."

"Okay."

"Janie, I can't tell you how much I appreciate you coming to our rescue yesterday. It was irresponsible not to check on the tide before heading out."

"It all ended well, so I guess that's the main thing. Thanks again for this info." She said her goodbyes and ended the call, the absence of her laughter like a hole in his heart.

Ryan stared down at his cell phone, absorbing the depth of the silence that stretched between them. And the blame.

He did his best to focus on patient treatment plans and checkups the rest of the day and he breathed a huge sigh of relief when the last patient cleared the front door. A seed of something had taken root in the back of his mind. But he needed to get home and take some time researching it.

Despite Janie wanting to go alone, Momma was worried that she would be venturing beyond their usual haunts, so she'd insisted on accompanying Janie in the boat to Hunting Island. Hunting Island was situated to the north of Fripp across the Fripp Inlet. It was a state park, and although Janie didn't visit it often, she knew it was a thriving habitat for all kinds of wildlife, including tanagers and skimmers. She fervently hoped the kites would settle there easily enough, but she needed to see the area with her own eyes.

When they arrived on the island, Janie followed the coordinates Ryan had given her with her GPS to find the exact location for the new kite habitat. As they moved through the brush, Momma carried a walking stick for navigating palmetto bushes—and to poke at unfriendly critters, like snakes and spiders.

"Looks like this is it." Janie pointed up at a grouping of trees. She peered through her binoculars to see if she could get a sighting of the kite nestlings.

"Do you see them?" Momma asked.

Janie spotted a nest about halfway up a loblolly pine. "I've found one." She pointed it out to Momma and handed her the binoculars. "Right there."

"It's fuzzy, so I can't make out any birds." Momma put her hand over her eyes to shield them from the sun, squinting up at the nest.

"When I heard Ryan had spoken to Shoreline Conservation, I called Shane, and he filled me in on the situation. He said they hadn't been able to place the nests as high as they'd wanted to because their trucks' ladders wouldn't reach, but he felt they'd gotten them high enough for safety. I'm not so sure, though," Janie said uneasily. It wasn't a best-case scenario for the birds, but there also wasn't much to be done until the birds matured and began migrating south. "Oh, look, I can see their little heads in that one." Janie pointed to several active hatchlings stretching their necks, calling for food, and she prayed the momma bird found them and fed them.

Unable to do anything more, Janie and Momma headed home. At least for now, she could adjust her emotional red-alert status down a notch or two. The damage had been done, though, which caused a ball of regret in Janie's gut for how they'd gotten themselves in this mess.

Chapter Thirty

"You were quiet on the way home," Ryan said to Sibley as he pulled a few chocolate chip cookies out of the box and set them on a plate, sliding them toward his daughter.

Sibley shrugged, appearing tired. She hadn't had much to say, even when he'd asked her about her day at school and tennis practice, which was unusual for her.

"Is there anything you want to talk to me about?" Ryan asked.

She lifted her eyes to meet his, sadness lurking in her gaze. "I miss Janie and Lulu."

"You saw them yesterday," he countered gently.

"But I feel like I won't be able to spend time with them anymore. You know, since y'all had your falling out."

Ryan wanted to tell her that all would be well, but he couldn't guarantee it and he refused to appease her. "I understand, honey. But Janie needs her space, and I don't know if she's able to get past this."

"That doesn't sound like Janie. She's one of the nicest people I've ever met."

"She is. It's just that right now, she feels strongly that I let her down—I *did* let her down—and in a way that matters to her a lot."

"I get that the birds are a big deal to her, but if the birds are safe now, won't she be able to understand that you didn't think about asking more about the nests because birds aren't your thing? Can't she see that you wouldn't have known the choices to make and that you would have done it differently if you'd realized?"

Ryan had to give it to Sibley. She got it.

"Yes, that's all true. But sometimes, when you care about someone enough, it's important to try to see things from their side, even if it's not your usual thing."

"So, this means I can't go over and see Lulu... or Janie?"

Ryan could hear the sadness in her voice, and he wished he could give her a positive answer. "For now, that's what it means. Not that Janie doesn't want to see you, it's that she's in the middle of figuring out something right now and I don't want to bother her."

"Are you going to keep trying to get her back? Because I think she's worth it," Sibley said.

It struck Ryan that she hadn't said the same thing about Leslie. He knew she loved her mother, but she'd seemed to take him at his word that they were done. And they still had a long way to go in repairing their relationship long term, which made Janie's absence all the more difficult for Sibley, Ryan knew.

"I think the best thing to do is not pressure her. She has to figure out what she feels."

Sibley cocked her head to the side. "Yeah, I get that. Sometimes you've got to make things right inside yourself so you can move on."

Sibley amazed him every day. She was wise beyond any sixteen-year-old he'd ever met.

"You're such a sensitive soul, and I'm so proud of you."

"Thanks, Daddy. But I still wish I could see Lulu—and Janie."

He knew the feeling, but he was determined to give Janie space. The loss of the kites was tremendous for her and one that she would need to process on her own.

"Let's just see how this goes, okay?"

"Okay." She took her plate to the sink. "I've got a paper to work on, so I'll be in my room."

"All right."

After she'd gone upstairs, Ryan pulled out his laptop, taking it outside with him on the deck, and he began his search.

Ryan rubbed his tired eyes and let out a loud, wide yawn. He'd stayed up far too late researching shorebird conservation and, specifically, swallow-tailed kites. He now realized how important this area was for their preservation as a species. And how protective Janie must have felt having them nesting here on their tiny island home. He rubbed his face as if he could remove the exhaustion with the pressure of his fingers, wishing he'd been able to find this out before letting the developers go ahead at the site. Hopefully, it was better late than never.

The following day, Sibley had appeared more cheerful than the night before after having slept well, unlike Ryan, and her mind was on the last tennis match of the season, which was that afternoon. It was a home match, so they wouldn't have to travel after school, which Ryan was grateful for. But his day passed slowly at work, and he was glad to get away that afternoon.

His mind still on Janie, he arrived at the match and settled in on the bleachers.

Leslie appeared, approaching him. "Mind if I sit here?" she asked Ryan.

He motioned to the spot next to him. "Sure."

She looked a lot calmer and more like the old Leslie than the last time he'd seen her. Their communications had been sporadic since then, and she'd texted to let him know the plumber had fixed the leak and sent him a message to wish him a happy birthday. Thankfully, she'd said no more about wanting to get back together or the end of her relationship with Coach Todd, and Ryan hoped they could begin to move forward amicably for Sibley's sake.

"I thought I'd come see Sibley play," Leslie said with a tentative smile.

She sounded sincere, so he bit back a comment about how it was past time she showed up. Ryan was glad they were seated far enough from any other parents, so nobody would overhear their conversation.

"My life's getting back on track now, and I wanted you two to know it." She hung her head. "Listen, Ryan, I know the damage I've caused, and I'm truly sorry. There's no excuse for it."

"Yeah…" As he looked at her, he realized how much he'd moved on. "It's time for us *all* to move forward."

She nodded. And they watched Sibley win her singles match together. Ryan was relieved that Leslie was in a better place, for Sibley's sake. He didn't wish her ill, and his emotions weren't involved anymore. There was only a hollowed-out shell of what they'd once been to each other, but they could both still be there for Sibley, and that's all that mattered to him.

When Sibley approached afterward, she appeared taken aback at seeing her mother sitting next to Ryan. "Hi, guys."

"I got off a little early to come and watch your last match," Leslie said, her words careful. "You played great."

"Thanks, Mom," Sibley said.

"Well, we've got an errand to run," Ryan told Leslie.

"Okay, see you soon?" Leslie asked them both.

"Of course," Ryan replied.

The look between mother and daughter gave Ryan hope that they might all be able to heal at some point. Sibley gathered up her things, and they made their way up the hill toward the parking lot.

"Where are we going?" Sibley asked.

"I'm checking into something for the house."

"Can I roll down the windows and wait in the truck?" Sibley asked.

"Sure, honey. I won't be long."

Chapter Thirty-One

Sibley arrived in the golf cart as Ryan finished up with the contractors. "Wow, a lot is happening, huh?" she remarked as she pointed to the fresh slab of concrete.

The new homesite had been a flurry of activity the past couple of weeks, since Ryan had closed on the lots. The concrete guys had poured the slab a few days ago, and he had explicitly asked the contractor to remove as few trees as possible during the building process. Most of the heavy equipment for the work was positioned where they would pour the driveway later.

"Yes, let's pray for good weather so there aren't delays." He put his arm around his daughter's shoulders, and they moved together around the side where the extra lot remained pretty much intact.

Between the electricians, plumbers, and other subcontractors, there was constant progress. His general contractor, Hank, seemed to have everything on schedule with his subs. But despite the excitement of breaking ground on the new house, the situation with Janie these past two weeks still loomed. As difficult as it was for him, he'd given her space and hadn't tried to barge his way back into her life.

Ryan couldn't imagine how it must feel to her watching the clearing of the land for his house or that he'd done all of this without mentioning it before. He'd shared that he was looking for land to build on and that he'd hired an architect, but he'd wanted to keep any further details under wraps until things were official. And then it had all happened so fast.

"I like that it's still natural here," Sibley said, peering up at the trees.

Ryan agreed, having only had some of the underbrush cleaned out to prevent the danger of snakes and such to the workers.

"I've been making some notes about my room. Can you show me where it's going to be?" she asked.

Ryan led Sibley over to the finished slab, where the stubs for the electrical and plumbing components stuck up from the concrete. "Your room will be upstairs, in the back of the house so you can see the water, and there will be two other guest bedrooms. The master will be here." He pointed to the back corner on the left-hand side.

"So, we'll have to go up some stairs to reach the main floor?"

"Yes, and there will be a wide covered front porch across the front, and the back will have a covered deck and some exposed deck." Ryan motioned left to right.

"Can I have a big closet and a built-in desk?" she asked, getting into the flow of envisioning things.

"A walk-in closet and whatever kind of desk you want. If you want it built in, we can check with the architect to make sure it works with the house plans."

Janie sat on her back porch, staring out at the creek as the tide receded, trying to keep her focus on the novel she'd brought home from the bookstore in an attempt to settle her busy mind. But as hard as she'd tried, it couldn't keep her attention. Finally, she shut the book with a smack and stood up, unable to stand it anymore. Her curiosity about what was happening over at the former habitat got the best of her.

Janie went through the house, locking up, and then climbed in her golf cart. She stared at her steering wheel, chewing her lip, deliberating. *Would it solve anything to see it?* she wondered. Until now, she'd avoided driving by there. Why did she want to torture herself like this? She knew that seeing the habitat decimated would only serve to wreck her emotionally. Maybe it was morbid curiosity or the fact that seeing it might give her some kind of closure, but she started the cart and hit the gas.

She wasn't entirely sure what to expect, but what she was certainly *not* expecting was the punch in her gut that she received when she arrived and saw Ryan and Sibley there. She parked the cart and viewed the lot from afar. Not only had Ryan already begun building, but Janie had to admit to a feeling of loss—the loss of not being a part of their little family, the loss of Ryan's smile when it was directed at her, and loss of her bond with Sibley. This seemed to Janie to make no sense, seeing as it was her choice to separate herself from Ryan, but she felt it nonetheless.

The bulldozer smacked against a tree with a *crack*, clearing it to make more space for Ryan's house. Janie winced, looking away, the sight ripping at her heart as everything she loved in her tiny paradise was destroyed.

If she were being honest with herself, she knew she had no official right to complain about the owner selling his land. It would've happened eventually, but knowing the new owner was Ryan made it a lot harder to take. Barely able to control the urge to take her anger out on the gas pedal, Janie headed home as fast as her cart would take her.

Janie was certain she didn't ever want to move backward to the days after Daniel had died—when she couldn't find the motivation to drag herself out of bed and move through her normal routine without feeling sluggish and hopeless. Ending things before they'd truly begun with Ryan had been devastating. And, sometimes, the same end-of-her-world emotions swarmed her. But she was a stronger person now, and her experience with grief had taught her how to keep going, even when the pain of loss overwhelmed her. With a steadying exhale, she allowed her tense shoulders to fall, and she quietly made her way back home.

Janie still wished the best for Ryan and Sibley, if only from a distance. She silently celebrated that. She didn't hate him, but she couldn't reconcile his actions.

Ryan stood on Janie's porch that evening, making fists and releasing his fingers to expel his nervous energy as he rehearsed one more time what he wanted to say. With a deep breath, he rang the bell on her door. His heart pounded as he stood, waiting for her to answer. With the click of the latch, every nerve was on high alert.

Janie opened the door.

"I hoped we could talk," he started, deliberately keeping his voice calm when what he really wanted to do was throw his arms around her and comfort her, telling her everything would be okay.

She wasn't smiling, but she didn't say no either. "Okay." She motioned for him to come inside, shutting the door behind them, and led him into the sunroom, where the windows glowed with late-afternoon sunlight. Lulu jumped up from lazing in a patch of warmth on the wood floor, her tail wagging furiously.

Ryan reached down to pet her. "Hey, girl." He scratched her between the ears, giving him a chance to compose himself. He'd never felt this nervous in Janie's presence before.

"So, what did you want to tell me?" Janie asked.

He shifted his attention from Lulu to Janie, staring into her green eyes, noticing immediately that they'd lost the hope he'd seen in them before, and knowing it was his fault. "I've bungled this up so badly. Us, I mean."

She stared at him, her face unreadable, and his heart ached to see her light up with that smile of hers.

He shook his head, frustrated with himself. "I didn't see you coming," he said. "You were the greatest surprise of my life. You came in and turned the lights back on in my bruised heart—you revived me."

Her lips parted just so, letting him know that his admission surprised her, and her gaze softened, giving him courage. He swallowed, trying to get the words just right so that she'd know without a shadow of a doubt how he felt.

"I don't want to lose you," he told her.

Janie's eyes filled with tears, but she remained silent, tentative, puzzling him as to what she might be thinking.

Ryan took her hand and placed in it the folder he'd brought with him, opening it to show her the diagrams and sketches he'd worked on. "I've done the research and spoken with experts, and I'm buying the third lot next to mine so I can recreate the kite sanctuary without any interference.

She peered up at him, a small line of confusion forming between her beautiful eyes.

"I plan to put up nesting poles for the kites so that we can move the nests back to their original spot." He tapped the spot on the map where he planned to put the birds. "I need to make it up to you."

She stared at him, her lips moving slightly as if she wanted to say something, but she remained silent, more tears in her eyes.

He took the folder, set it on the coffee table, and pulled both of her hands into his. "Let me make this right. Please. Just let me try. The habitat will always be accessible to you. You have my word."

Her mouth opened and then closed as if she were trying to process the abrupt change and find her words, and then she said, "You said I was a surprise to you, but you knocked me off my feet that first day at the marina. Nothing in my life has been the same since."

"But that's good, right?" he asked, his heart hammering in his chest. "We can work together to fix the habitat for the kites, and I can try and prove to you how invested I am in learning about your passion."

She looked up at him. And then he saw it… the first glimmer of hope in her eyes since this had all gone down. It was time to put his heart entirely on the line—now or never. He was absolutely certain of his feelings.

"I love you, Janie," he said, holding his breath and staring into her eyes.

Janie's trembling hands covered her mouth in surprise. "I… I don't know what to say, Ryan."

"Say you'll give me another chance."

Her eyes shimmered with tears. "I love you too, Ryan. I've been so miserable without you." More tears rolled from her lashes to her cheeks.

A tidal wave of relief and joy washed over him. He pulled her gently into his arms. "I'm going to show you that we will absolutely work." He reached down, cradling her chin, and tipped it up to face him, looking deeply into her eyes. Then, he did what he'd wanted to for a very long time: softly, he pressed his lips to hers and showed her exactly how he felt about her.

Epilogue

"You ready?" Ryan asked.

Janie nodded, still unable to believe she'd found this incredible man. Ryan took her hand and led her to the golf cart for the short drive to their new home, now that the final landscaping was finished. It was the last step of the building process, and tomorrow they would take vows to begin their new journey.

The kite's nests had been successfully moved with the help of student volunteers from the University of South Carolina. Ryan's plan would allow the existing nests to sit atop tall poles, among the grouping of healthy trees, at roughly the same height and location as they'd sat originally to ensure that the kites would return and lay eggs in them again and again.

All of that would be a perfect backdrop for the wedding that Janie had been immersed in planning. A few months prior, after a nice dinner out at a fancy restaurant, Ryan had surprised her with a new bike, complete with a basket of wildflowers on the front, and they'd ridden to their land at sunset. They'd kicked off their shoes, splashing in the undertow, her dress wadded in her hand, delighting in their little island, when Ryan had suddenly turned her around, dropped to one knee, and produced a stunning emerald-cut diamond ring just as the sky erupted into the most stunning summer sunset. Janie couldn't have imagined a more perfect proposal.

The house was decorated for their wedding tomorrow because Janie hadn't been able to think of a better place to marry Ryan. Sibley would be her maid of honor alongside her two sisters as bridesmaids. Joy and Jaclyn were driving in later that day. The florist had arranged bundles of magnolias and white roses along the exterior railings and porches of the house, with fragrant rose petals covering the back steps that led to the beach. Enormous white bows had been tied around the nesting poles that now graced the lot next door—a nod to the nests, which had new occupants currently.

Sibley was thrilled that Janie was marrying Ryan. She'd helped with the wedding planning and volunteered to move the nests so that the birds were secure before the ceremony. Sibley was considering a major in veterinary medicine in college, with an emphasis on conservation. She spent plenty of her spare time with Janie. When they weren't picking out flower arrangements together or taste-testing cake options, Sibley was getting to know the island and all of its wildlife, and the shared passion had brought the two women even closer together.

After a short ride to the property, Ryan parked in the new driveway. The house was everything Janie could have dreamed of. It had plenty of rear windows facing the inlet to the Atlantic Ocean, a sunroom, and it even had a baby's room, which made her heart sing with joy. But the very best thing about it was that she would move into it with Ryan and Sibley tomorrow. This view and this land would be hers and Ryan's. Without fear of anyone taking it away.

This had always been her special spot on the island, and now it was hers for real. Ryan had given her that and so much more. When they'd first met, she could never have imagined how much her life would change. Daniel's death had seemed to break her, but Ryan and Sibley had put her back together again, and although her future would look very different than she'd imagined, the one that now lay ahead was absolutely the one she wanted.

Moving to a new home and leaving Momma behind, until recently, would have been impossible. But just as Ryan had breathed new life into Janie's world, Joe was making Momma happier than Janie had seen her in a long time, and though she would miss having her just next door, she was comforted by the fact that Momma now had Joe. And, of course, there would always be an open door at the house for Momma and Joe to pop by whenever they liked.

It was nearing sunset, her favorite time of the day, so she and Ryan naturally moved toward the beach, as sunset-watching was something they did together almost daily now. They sat together on the log that still lay crosswise on the beach amidst the swaying palms and packed sand. Staring at the bright-blue water, Janie's head on Ryan's shoulder, on the eve of their wedding, they contentedly waited for the golden and magical burst of orange and red to cover the sky in all directions, the last moments before the sun disappeared for the evening.

The evening was warm and humid, as it most often was in the middle of summer. The tourists were currently renting every available house and cottage on the island, so there were far more people around town, but this spot was still their special place to share magical moments, now and in the future.

Ryan took Janie's hands. He stared into her eyes and said simply, "I'm the luckiest man, and I can't wait to be your husband."

Tears sprang to Janie's eyes at the perfection of the moment. "And I'm the luckiest woman on earth."

A Letter from Susan

Hi there,

Thank you so much for reading *The Island of Summer Sunsets*. I really hope it whisked you away to a wonderful island escape.

If you'd like me to drop you an email when my next Harpeth Road Press book is out or whenever this one goes on sale, you can sign up here:

www.harpethroad.com/susan-sands-newsletter-signup

I won't share your information with anyone else.

If you did enjoy *The Island of Summer Sunsets*, I'd be very grateful if you'd write a review online. Getting feedback from readers is so exciting, and it also helps to persuade others to pick up one of my books for the first time. It's one of the biggest gifts you could give me.

Until next time,
Susan

Acknowledgments

Many thanks to Jenny Hale for the hours she's invested in *The Island of Summer Sunsets* and to the many hands at Harpeth Road Press who helped edit and shape Janie and Ryan's story. This book has been a labor of love for me, and I'm thrilled to share it with all of you.

A special thanks to Jessica Klepchick for inspiring this novel set on the gorgeous Fripp Island. You opened your home to me so I could immerse myself in all things Fripp as I wrote this story. I hope I've done your beloved island justice.

Thanks to my mom, Linda Noel, for always being my first reader and my biggest cheerleader. Much appreciation to my writer buddies Christy Hayes, Laura Alford, and George Weinstein. Your friendship and encouragement mean the world to me.

Hugs to my kids, Kevin, Cameron, and Reagan, for inspiring me. Y'all are the best!

To my husband, Doug: Thanks for making a living so I can write full time. Oh, and thanks for being flexible when I don't stop writing in time to make dinner.

Made in the USA
Coppell, TX
28 June 2022

79362523R00152